John Barth was born in Cambridge on the Eastern shore of Maryland in 1931, and by the age of 25 he had published his first novel and was married with three children. A teacher of literature since he left graduate school roughly 25 years ago, he is presently the Alumni Centennial Professor of English and Creative Writing at Johns Hopkins University. His first novels, *The Floating Opera* and *The End of the Road* received fine critical acclaim. There followed two mammoth picaresque novels, *Giles Goat-Boy* and the revised version of *The Sot-Weed Factor*, in 1966 and 1967 respectively. Both novels became instant bestsellers and have achieved lasting critical and popular success. His newest book is *LETTERS*, a gigantic comic masterpiece which revives an old form – the epistolary novel – and took all of seven years to write. In between came the National Book Award-winning *Chimera*, in 1973, and a series of short fictions for print, tape, and live voice, *Lost in the Funhouse*. In 1974 he was elected to both the National Institute of Arts and Letters and the American Academy of Arts and Sciences. John Barth lives in Baltimore, Maryland.

Also by John Barth

John Barth

The End of the Road

A PANTHER BOOK

GRANADA
London Toronto Sydney New York

Published by Granada Publishing Limited in 1981

ISBN 0 586 05282 8

First published in Great Britain by
Secker & Warburg 1962
Copyright © John Barth 1958

Granada Publishing Limited
Frogmore, St Albans, Herts AL2 2NF
and
3 Upper James Street, London W1R 4BP
866 United Nations Plaza, New York, NY 10017, USA
117 York Street, Sydney, NSW 2000, Australia
100 Skyway Avenue, Rexdale, Ontario, M9W 3A6, Canada
PO Box 84165, Greenside, 2034 Johannesburg, South Africa
61 Beach Road, Auckland, New Zealand

Set, printed and bound in Great Britain by
Cox & Wyman Ltd, Reading
Set in Monotype Baskerville

Granada ®
Granada Publishing ®

Chapter One
In a sense, I am Jacob Horner

In a sense, I am Jacob Horner

It was on the advice of the Doctor that I entered the teaching profession; for a time I was a teacher of grammar at the Wicomico State Teachers College, in Maryland.

The Doctor had brought me to a certain point in my original schedule of therapies (this was in June 1953), and then, once when I drove down from Baltimore for my quarterly checkup at the Remobilization Farm, which at that time was near Wicomico, he said to me, 'Jacob Horner, you mustn't sit idle any longer. You will have to begin work.'

' I'm not idle all the time,' said I. ' I take different jobs.'

We were seated in the Progress and Advice Room of the farmhouse: there is one exactly like it in the present establishment, in Pennsylvania. It is a medium-size room, about as large as an apartment living room, only high-ceilinged. The walls are flat white, the windows are covered by white venetian blinds, usually closed, and a globed ceiling fixture provides the light. In this room there are two straight-backed white wooden chairs, exactly alike, facing each other in the center of the floor, and no other furniture. The chairs are very close together – so close that the advisee almost touches knees with the adviser.

It is impossible to be at ease in the Progress and Advice Room. The Doctor sits facing you, his legs slightly spread, his hands on his knees, and leans a little toward you. You would not slouch down, because to do so would thrust your knees virtually against his. Neither would you be inclined to cross your legs in either the masculine or the feminine manner: the masculine manner, with your left ankle resting on your right knee, would cause your left shoe to rub against the Doctor's left trouser leg, up by his knees, and possibly dirty his white trousers; the feminine manner, with your left knee crooked

5

over your right knee, would thrust the toe of your shoe against the same trouser leg, lower down on his shin. To sit sideways, of course, would be unthinkable, and spreading your knees in the manner of the Doctor makes you acutely conscious of aping his position, as if you hadn't a personality of your own. Your position, then (which has the appearance of choice, because you are not ordered to sit thus, but which is chosen only in a very limited sense, since there are no alternatives), is as follows: you sit rather rigidly in your white chair, your back and thighs describing the same right angle described by the structure of the chair, and keep your legs together, your thighs and lower legs describing another right angle.

The placing of your arms is a separate problem, interesting in its own right and, in a way, even more complicated, but of lesser importance, since no matter where you put them they will not normally come into physical contact with the Doctor. You may do anything you like with them (you wouldn't, clearly, put them on your knees in imitation of him). As a rule I move mine about a good bit, leaving them in one position for a while and then moving them to another. Arms folded, akimbo, or dangling; hands grasping the seat edges or thighs, or clasped behind the head or resting in the lap – these (and their numerous degrees and variations) are all in their own ways satisfactory positions for the arms and hands, and if I shift from one to another, this shifting is really not so much a manifestation of embarrassment, or hasn't been since the first half-dozen interviews, as a recognition of the fact that when one is faced with such a multitude of desirable choices, no one choice seems satisfactory for very long by comparison with the aggregate desirability of all the rest, though compared to any *one* of the others it would not be found inferior.

It seems to me at just this moment (I am writing this at 7.55 in the evening of Tuesday, October 4, 1955, upstairs in the dormitory) that, should you choose to consider that final observation as a metaphor, it is the story of my life in a sentence – to be precise, in the latter member of a double predicate nominative expression in the second independent clause of a rather intricate compound sentence. You see that I was in truth a grammar teacher.

6

It is not fit that you should be at your ease in the Progress and Advice Room, for after all it is not for relaxation that you come there, but for advice. Were you totally at your ease, you would only be inclined to consider the Doctor's words in a leisurely manner, as one might regard the breakfast brought to one's bed by a liveried servant, hypercritically, selecting this, rejecting that, eating only as much as one chooses. And clearly such a frame of mind would be out of place in the Progress and Advice Room, for there it is you who have placed yourself in the Doctor's hands; your wishes are subservient to his, not vice versa; and his advice is given you not to be questioned or even examined (to question is impertinent; to examine, pointless), but to be followed.

'That isn't satisfactory,' the Doctor said, referring to my current practice of working only when I needed cash, and then at any job that presented itself. 'Not any longer.'

He paused and studied me, as is his habit, rolling his cigar from one side of his mouth to the other and back again, under his pink tongue.

'You'll have to begin work at a more meaningful job now. A career, you know. A calling. A lifework.'

'Yes, sir.'

'You are thirty.'

'Yes, sir.'

'And you have taken an undergraduate degree somewhere. In history? Literature? Economics?'

'Arts and sciences.'

'That's everything!'

'No major, sir.'

'Arts and sciences! What under heaven that's interesting isn't either an art or a science? Did you study philosophy?'

'Yes.'

'Psychology?'

'Yes.'

'Political science?'

'Yes.'

'Wait a minute. Zoology?'

'Yes.'

'Ah, and philology? Romance philology? And cultural anthropology?'

'Later, sir, in the graduate school. You remember, I –'

'*Argh!*' the Doctor said, as if hawking to spit upon the graduate school. 'Did you study lock-picking in the graduate school? Fornication? Sailmaking? Cross-examination?'

'No, sir.'

'Aren't these arts and sciences?'

'My master's degree was to be in English, sir.'

'Damn you! English *what*? Navigation? Colonial policy? Common law?'

'English literature, sir. But I didn't finish. I passed the oral examinations, but I never got my thesis done.'

'Jacob Horner, you are a fool.'

My legs remained directly in front of me, as before, but I moved my hands from behind my head (which position suggests a rather too casual attitude for many sorts of situations anyway) to a combination position, my left hand grasping my left coat lapel, my right lying palm up, fingers loosely curled, near the mid-point of my right thigh.

After a while the Doctor said, 'What reason do you think you have for not applying for a job at the little teachers college here in Wicomico?'

Instantly a host of arguments against applying for a job at the Wicomico State Teachers College presented themselves for my use, and as instantly a corresponding number of refutations lined up opposite them, one for one, so that the question of my application was held static like the rope marker in a tug-o'-war where the opposing teams are perfectly matched. This again is in a sense the story of my life, nor does it really matter if it is not just the same story as that of a few paragraphs ago: as I began to learn not long after this interview, when the schedule of therapies reached Mythotherapy, the same life lends itself to any number of stories – parallel, concentric, mutually habitant, or what you will.

Well.

'No reason, sir,' I said.

'Then it's settled. Apply at once for the fall term. And what will you teach? Iconography? Automotive mechanics?'

'English literature, I guess.'

'No. There must be a rigid discipline, or else it will be merely an occupation, not an occupational therapy. There must be a body of laws. You mean you can't teach plane geometry?'

'Oh, I suppose – ' I made a suppositive gesture, which consisted of a slight outward motion of my lapel-grasping left hand, extending simultaneously the fore and index fingers but not releasing my lapel – the hand motion accompanied by quickly arched (and as quickly released) eyebrows, momentarily pursed lips, and an on-the-one-hand/on-the-other-hand rocking of the head.

'Nonsense. Of course you can't. Tell them you will teach grammar. English grammar.'

'But you know, Doctor,' I ventured, 'there is descriptive as well as prescriptive grammar. I mean, you mentioned a fixed body of rules.'

'You will teach prescriptive grammar.'

'Yes, sir.'

'No description at all. No optional situations. Teach the rules. Teach the truth about grammar.'

The advising was at an end. The Doctor stood up quickly (I jerked my legs out of his way) and left the room, and after I had paid Mrs Dockey, the receptionist-nurse, I returned to Baltimore. That night I composed a letter to the president of the Wicomico State Teachers College, requesting an interview and indicating my desire to join the staff as an instructor in the prescriptive grammar of the English language. There is an art that my diffuse education had schooled me in, perforce: the art of composing a telling letter of application. I was asked to appear for an interview in July.

Chapter Two
The Wicomico State Teachers College
sits in a great flat open field

The Wicomico State Teachers College sits in a great flat open field
ringed with loblolly pine trees, at the southeastern edge of the
town of Wicomico, on the Eastern Shore of Maryland. Its
physical plant consists of a single graceless brick building with
two ells, a building too large for the pseudo-Georgian style in
which it is constructed. A deep semicircular drive runs in
from College Avenue to the main entrance.

In July, when the day of my interview approached, I
loaded my belongings into my Chevrolet and relinquished
the key to my room on East Chase Street, in Baltimore, for I
meant to take lodgings in Wicomico at once, whether I were
hired or not. This was on a Sunday. The date of the interview
had originally been set for Tuesday in the letter I received in
answer to my application, but on the Saturday afternoon
before I left Baltimore the president of the college had telephoned me and asked that I come on Monday instead. The
connexion was poor, but there is no doubt in my mind that
he changed the date to Monday.

'I can make it either day,' I recall saying.

'Well, as a matter of fact I suppose we could too,' the president said. 'Monday or Tuesday. But maybe Monday would
be better than Tuesday for some of the Committee. Unless
Monday is out of the question for you, of course. Would
Tuesday be better for you?'

'Monday or Tuesday, either one,' I said. I was thinking
that actually Tuesday (which remember was the original
date) *would* be better for me, because there might be last-
minute errands or some such for me to make before I moved
out of Baltimore, and on Sunday the stores would be closed.
But I certainly wasn't going to make an issue out of it, and for
that matter an equally good case could be made for Monday.
'If Monday is better for you all, then it's all right with me.'

'I know we'd planned on Tuesday before,' admitted the president, 'but I guess Monday would be best.'

'Either day, sir,' I said.

So on Sunday I piled my clothes, my few books, my phonograph and phonograph records, whiskey, piece of sculpture, and odds and ends into the car and set out for the Eastern Shore. Three hours later I checked in at the Peninsula Hotel in Wicomico, where I meant to live until I found suitable permanent quarters, and after lunch I began looking for a room.

The first thing that went wrong was that I found an entirely satisfactory room at once. As a rule I was extremely hard to please in the matter of renting a room. I required that no one live above me; that my room be high-ceilinged and large-windowed; that my bed be high off the floor, wide, and very soft; that the bathroom be equipped with a good shower; that the landlord not live in the same building (and that he be not very particular about his property or his tenants); that the other tenants be of an uncomplaining nature; and that maid service be available. Because I was so fussy, it usually took me a good while to find even a barely acceptable place. But as ill luck would have it, the first room I saw advertised for rent on my way out College Avenue from the hotel met all these qualifications. The landlady, an imposing widow of fifty whom I just chanced to meet on her way out of the old two-story brick house, showed me to a second-floor room in the front.

'You're teaching at the college?' she asked.

'Yes, ma'am. Grammar teacher.'

'Well, pleased to meet you. I'm Mrs Alder. Let's shake hands and all now, because you won't see me very much around here.'

'You don't live in the house?'

'Live *here*? God, no! Can't stand tenants around me. Always pestering for this or that. I live in Ocean City all year round. Any time you need anything, don't call me; you call Mr Prake, the janitor. He lives in town.'

She showed me the room. Six-foot windows, three of them. Twelve-foot ceiling. Dark gray plaster walls, white woodwork. An incredible bed three feet high, seven feet long, at least seven feet wide; a black, towering, canopied monster with four posts as thick as masts, fluted and ringed, and an elaborately carved headboard extending three feet above the bolster. A most adequate bed! The other furniture was a potpourri of styles and periods – one felt as if one had wandered into the odd-pieces room of Winterthur Museum – but every piece was immensely competent. The adjective *competent* came at once to mind, rather than, say, *efficient*. This furniture had an air of almost contemptuous competence, as though it were so absurdly well able to handle its job that it would scarcely notice *your* puny use of it. It would require a man indeed, a man's man, to make his presence felt by this furniture. I was impressed.

In short, the whole place left nothing to be desired. Shower, maid service – everything was there.

'What about the other tenants?' I asked uneasily.

'Oh, they come and they go. Bachelors, mostly, a few young couples now and then, traveling men, a nurse or two from the hospital.'

'Any students?' In Baltimore it was desirable to have students for neighbours, for they are singularly uncritical, but I suspected that in Wicomico all the students would know all the teachers rather too well.

'No students. The students generally live in the dorms or get rooms farther out College Avenue.'

It was too perfect, and I was skeptical.

'I guess I should tell you that I practice on the clarinet,' I said. This was untrue: I was not musical.

'Well, isn't that nice! I used to sing, myself, but my voice seemed to go after Mr Alder died. I had the most marvelous voice teacher at the Peabody Conservatory when I was younger! Farrari. Farrari used to tell me, "Alder," he'd say, "you've learned all I can teach you. You have precision, style, *éclat*. You are *una macchina cantanda*," he'd say – that's Italian. "Life will have to do the rest. Go out and live!" he'd say. But I never got to live until poor Mr Alder died five years ago, and by that time my voice was gone.'

'Do you object to pets?'

'What kind?' Mrs Alder asked sharply. I thought I'd found an out.

'Oh, I don't know. I'm fond of dogs. Might pick up a boxer sometime, or a Doberman.'

My landlady sighed. 'I forgot you were a grammar teacher. I had a biology teacher once,' she explained.

I snatched at a last hope: 'I couldn't go over twelve a week.'

'The rent's eight,' Mrs Alder said. 'The maid gets three dollars a week extra, or four-fifty, depending.'

'Depending on what, for heaven's sake?'

'She does laundry, too,' Mrs Alder said evenly.

There was nothing to do but take the room. I paid my landlady a month's rent in advance, though she required only a week's and ushered her out to her car, a five-year-old Buick convertible.

I call this windfall a stroke of ill luck because it gave me the whole of the afternoon and evening, and the next morning, with nothing to do. Even checking out of the Peninsula Hotel, moving to my new quarters, and arranging my belongings took but an hour and a half, after which time there was simply nothing to be done. I had no interest in touring Wicomico: it was the sort of small city that one knows adequately at the first glance – entirely without character. A humdrum business district and a commonplace park, surrounded by middle-class residential neighborhoods varying only in age and upkeep. As for the Wicomico State Teachers College, one look was enough to lay any but the most inordinately pricked-up curiosity. It was a state teachers' college.

I drove about aimlessly for twenty minutes and then returned to my room. The one dusty maple outside my window exhausted its scenic potential in a half minute. My phonograph records – nearly all Mozart – sounded irritating in a room with which I was still too unfamiliar to be at ease. My sculpture on the mantel, a heroic plaster head of Laocoön, so annoyed me with his blank-eyed grimace that, had I been the sort of person who did such things, I'd have turned his ugly face to the wall. I got the wholesale fidgets. Finally, at only nine o'clock (but I'd been fidgeting since three-thirty, not counting supper hour), I went to my great bed and was somewhat calmed by its imposing grotesqueness, which, however, kept me from sleep for a long time.

Next morning was worse. I slept fitfully until ten and then went to breakfast logy and puffy-eyed, nursing a headache. The interview was set for two in the afternoon, and so I had more than enough time to become entirely demoralized. Reading was impossible, music exasperating. I nicked myself twice while shaving and ran out of polish before the heel of my left shoe was covered. Since I'd put off shining my shoes until the last minute, hoping thus to occupy those most uncomfortable moments before I left the room, there was no time to go downtown for more polish. In a rage I went down to the car. But I'd forgotten my pen and my brief case, which, though empty, I thought it fitting to carry. I stormed back upstairs and fetched them, glaring so fiercely at a nurse who happened to look from her doorway that she sniffed and closed her door with some heat. Tossing the brief case on to the seat, I left with an uncalled-for spinning of tyres and drove out to the college.

My exasperation would have carried me safely into the interview had there not been a cluster of young people lounging on the front steps. I took them for students, although, it being vacation time, it is unlikely that they were. At any rate they stared at my approaching car with a curiosity no less unabashed for its being mild. My courage failed me; as I passed them I glanced indifferently at my wrist watch, to suggest that it was only to check the time that I'd slowed down. I was assisted in my ruse by the college clock, which at that instant chimed two: I nodded my head shortly, as though satisfied with the accuracy of my timepiece, and drove purposefully down the other arc of the semicircular drive, back to College Avenue. There my anger returned at once, this time directed at myself for being so easily cowed. I went again to the entrance drive and headed up the semi-circle for another try. But if it took determination to approach those impassive gatekeepers the first time, with their adolescent eyes as empty as Laocoön directing a stupid enfilade along the driveway, it took raw courage to run their fire again. I shoved the accelerator to the floor and rocked the Chevrolet around the bend, not even deigning to glance at them. Let the ninnies think what they would! The third time I did not hesitate for a moment, but drove heedlessly around to the parking lot behind the building and entered through a doorway near at hand. I was six minutes late.

I found the president's office without difficulty and introduced myself to the receptionist.

'Mr Horner?' she repeated, vaguely troubled.

'That's right,' I said shortly.

'Just a minute.'

She disappeared into an inner office, from which I heard then a low-voiced conversation between her and, I presumed, Dr Schott, the president. My heart sank.

A gray, fatherly gentleman came smiling from the inner office, the receptionist in his wake.

'Mr Horner!' he exclaimed, grasping my hand. 'I'm John Schott! Glad to meet you!'

Dr Schott was of an exclamatory nature.

'Glad to meet *you*, sir. Sorry I'm a little late . . . .'

I was going to explain: my unfamiliarity with the little city, uncertainty as to where I should park, natural difficulty finding the office, *etc.*

'Late!' cried Dr Schott. 'My boy, you're twenty-four hours early! This is only Monday!'

'But isn't that what we decided on the phone, sir?'

'No, son!' Dr Schott laughed loudly and placed his arm around my shoulders. '*Tuesday!* Isn't that so, Shirley?' Shirley nodded happily, her troubled look vindicated. 'Monday in the letter, Tuesday on the phone! Don't you remember now?'

I laughed and scratched my head (with my left hand, my right being pinioned by Dr Schott).

'Well, I swear, I thought sure we'd changed it from Tuesday to Monday. I'm awfully sorry. That was stupid of me.'

'Not a bit! Don't you worry!' Dr Schott chuckled again and released me. 'Didn't we tell Mr Horner Tuesday?' he demanded again of Shirley.

'I'm afraid so,' Shirley affirmed. 'On account of Mr Morgan's Boy Scouts. Monday in the letter and Tuesday on the phone.'

'One of the Committee members is a scoutmaster!' Dr

Schott explained. 'He's had his boys up to Camp Rodney for two weeks and is bringing them home today. Joe Morgan, fine fellow, teaches history! That's why we changed the interview to Tuesday!'

'Well, I'm awfully sorry.' I smiled ruefully.

'No! Not a bit! I could've gotten mixed up myself!'

He was.

'Well, I'll come back tomorrow.'

'Wait! Wait a minute! Shirley, give Joe Morgan a call, see if he's in yet. He might be in. I know Miss Banning and Harry Carter are home.'

'Oh no,' I protested; 'I'll come back.'

'Hold on, now! Hold on!'

Shirley called Joe Morgan.

'Hello? Mrs Morgan. Is Mr Morgan there? I see. No, I know he's not. Yes, indeed. No, no, it's nothing. Mr Horner came in for his interview today unexpectedly; he got the date mixed up and came in today instead of tomorrow. Dr Schott thought maybe Mr Morgan just might happen to have come back early. No, don't bother. Sorry to bother *you*. Okay. 'By.'

I wanted to spit on Shirley.

'Well, I'll come back,' I said.

'Sure, you come back!' Dr Schott said. He ushered me toward the front door, where, to my chagrin, I saw the sentries still on duty. But I threw up my hands at the idea of attempting to explain to him that my car was in the rear of the building.

'Well, well, we'll be seeing you!' Dr Schott said, pumping my hand. 'You be back tomorrow, now, hear?'

'I will, sir.'

We were outside the main door, and the watch regarded me blankly.

'Where's your car? You need a lift anywhere?'

'Oh, no, thanks; my car's in the back.'

'In the back! Well, say, you don't want to go out the front here! I'll show you the back door! Ha!'

'Never mind, sir,' I said. 'I'll just walk around.'

'Well! Ha! Well, all right, then!' But he looked at me. 'See you tomorrow!'

'Good-by, sir.'

I walked very positively past the loungers on the steps.

'You dig up that letter!' Dr Schott called from the doorway. 'See if it doesn't say Monday!'

I turned and waved acknowledgement and acquiescence, but when, back in my room at last (which already seemed immensely familiar and comforting), I searched for it, I found that I'd thrown it out before leaving Baltimore. Since I would not in a hundred years have been at home enough in Dr Schott's office to ask Shirley to investigate her letter files, the question of my appointment date could not be verified by appeal to objective facts.

One might suppose that after such an inauspicious start I would have been less prepared than ever to face my interview, but this supposition, though entirely reasonable, does not correspond to the fact. On the contrary, I was disgusted enough not to care a damn about the interview. I didn't even bother to polish the rest of my left shoe the next morning; in fact, after breakfast I sat in the park for several hours watching the children romp in the small artificial lake and didn't even think about the interview more than two or three times. When it occurred to me at all, I merely ticked my right cheek muscle. At ten minutes before two I drove out to the college, parked unhesitatingly in the front driveway, and walked through the main entrance. The steps happened to be uninhabited, but no reception committee could have daunted me that day. My mood had changed.

'Oh, hello,' Shirley said brightly.

'How do you do. Tell Dr Schott I'm here, will you please?'

'*Everybody's* here today. Just a minute, please, Mr Horner.'

I turned my smile on, and then I turned it off, so, as a gentleman might tip his hat politely, but impassively, at absolutely any lady of his acquaintance, whether she merited the courtesy or not. Shirley stepped into and out of Dr Schott's office.

'Go right on in, Mr Horner.'

'Thank you.'

Inside I was introduced by Dr Schott to Miss Banning, teacher of Spanish and French, a dear-elderly-lady type whom one accepted on her own terms because there was absolutely nothing else to be done about her; Dr Harry Carter, teacher of psychology, a thin scholarly old man about whom one wondered at once what he was doing in Wicomico, but not so strongly that one didn't decide rather easily that he doubtless had his reasons; and Mr Joseph Morgan, scoutmaster and teacher of ancient, European, and American history, a tall, bespectacled, athletic young man, terribly energetic, with whom one was so clearly expected to be charmed, he was so bright, busy, and obviously on his way up, that one had one's hands full simply trying to be civil to him, and realized at once that the invidious comparisons to oneself that he could not for the life of him help inviting would prevent one's ever being really tranquil about the fact of his existence, to say nothing of becoming his friend.

Pleasantries were made about my being so eager to join the faculty that I came a day early to my interview. The Committee took a lively interest in one another's summer activities. There was joshing. Applicants for jobs at the Wicomico State Teachers College were obviously not so numerous that such meetings of the Appointments Committee were but a dull addition to the members' regular duties.

'You can count on Miss Banning's support for your application, Mr Horner,' Dr Carter chortled. 'She needs new victims to show off her mustache-cup collection to.'

'Oh?' said I. This remark of Dr Carter's was addressed not *to* me, but through me, as a grandmother teases her daughter by speaking to her grandchild.

'I have a simply marvelous collection, Mr Horner,' Miss Banning declared good-naturedly. 'You'll surely have to see it. Oh dear, but you don't have a mustache, do you?'

All laughed. I observed that Joe Morgan *did* have a mustache.

'Ethel's been after me for fourteen years to grow one!' Dr Schott guffawed at me. 'Not a trim little affair like Joe's, mind you, but a great bushy one, so I can try out her collector's items! Now don't you start on Mr Horner, Ethel!'

Ethel was poised to make a retort, in all good humor, but Joe Morgan pleasantly interjected a question about my academic experience.

'Do I understand you're from Johns Hopkins, Mr Horner?'

'Yes, sir.'

The others nodded approval at Joe's getting so tactfully down to business. He was a find, was Mr Morgan. He'd not stay in their little circle long. Serious attention was focused on me.

'Oh, please, not *sir*!' Dr Carter protested. 'We don't stand on ceremony out here in the provinces.'

'No indeed!' Dr Schott agreed benignly.

There ensued some twenty minutes of unsystematic interrogation about my graduate study and my teaching experience – the latter, except for occasional tutoring jobs in Baltimore and a brief night-school class at Johns Hopkins, being nil.

'What made you decide to get back into teaching, Mr Horner?' Dr Carter asked. 'You've been away from it for some time, I presume.'

I shrugged. 'You know how it is. You don't feel just *right* doing other things.'

All acknowledged the truth of my observation.

'Then too,' I added casually, 'my doctor recommended that I go back to teaching. He seems to think it's the thing I'm best at, and the thing that's best for me.'

This was well said. My examiners were with me, and so I expatiated.

'I seem never to be content with ordinary jobs. There's something so – so *stultifying* about working only for pay. It's – well, I hate to use a cliché, but the fact is that other jobs are simply unrewarding. You know what I mean?'

They did know what I meant.

'You take a boy – bright kid, alert kid, you see it at once, but never been exposed to *thinking*, never been in an environment where intellectual activity was as common as eating or sleeping. You see a fresh young mind that's never had a chance to flex its muscles, so to speak. Maybe he can't speak good English. Never *heard* good English spoken. Not his fault. Not wholly his parents' fault. But there he is.'

My audience was most receptive, all except Joe Morgan, who regarded me coolly.

'So you start him off. Parts of speech! Subjects and verbs! Modifiers! *Complements!* And after a while, rhetoric. Subordination! Coherence! Euphony! You drill and drill, and talk yourself blue in the face, and all the time you see that boy's mind groping, stumbling, stretching, making false steps. And then, just when you're ready to chuck the whole thing –'

'I know!' Miss Banning breathed. 'One day, just like all the rest, you say the same thing for the tenth time – and *click!*' She snapped her fingers jubilantly at Dr Schott. 'He's got it! *Why, there's nothing to it!* he says. *It's plain as day!*'

'That's what we're here for!' Dr Schott said quietly, with some pride. 'That's what we all live for. A little thing, isn't it?'

'Little,' Dr Carter agreed, 'but it's the greatest miracle on God's green earth! And the most mysterious, too.'

Joe Morgan would not have committed himself on the matter, I believe, but that Dr Carter addressed this last reflection to him directly. Cornered, Morgan made a sucking noise in the left side of his mouth, to express sympathetic awe before the mystery.

'I sometimes compare it to a man making fire with flint and steel,' I said calmly to Joe Morgan, knowing I was hitting him where he lived. 'He strikes and strikes and strikes, but the tinder lies dead under his hands. Then another strike, not a bit different from the rest, and there's your fire!'

'Very apt,' Dr Carter said. 'And what a rewarding moment it is, when a student suddenly becomes *ignited!* There's no other word for it: positively *ignited!*'

'And then you can't hold him back!' Dr Schott laughed, but as one would laugh at a sudden beneficence of God. 'He's like a horse that smells the stable up the lane!'

There were reminiscent sighs. Certainly I had scored a triumph. Joe Morgan brought the conversation back to my qualifications for a minute or two, but it was plainly in the nature of an anti-climax. The other members of the Committee showed very little interest in the interrogation, and Dr Schott began to describe very frankly the salary scale in Maryland state colleges, the hours I'd be expected to work, non-teaching duties, and the like.

'Well, you'll hear from us soon,' he concluded, rising and shaking my hand. 'Maybe tomorrow.' I shook hands all around. 'Shall I show you the back door this time?' He explained jovially my departure of the day before.

'No, thanks. My car's out front this time.'

'Good, good!' Dr Carter said heartily, for no reason whatever.

'I'm going out that way,' Joe Morgan said, falling in beside me. 'I live just down the block.' He accompanied me across the driveway to my car, and even stood beside the front fender while I got inside and closed the door. I started the engine, but delayed putting the car in gear: apparently my colleague-to-be had something on his mind.

'Well, be seeing you around, Horner,' he grinned, shaking hands with me again through the open window.

'Sure.'

We released hands, but Joe Morgan still leaned against the car door, his face radiating cheerful candor. He was well tanned from his stay at camp, and had a look about him that suggested early rising, a nutritious diet, and other sorts of virtue. His eyes were clear.

'Say, were you making fun of me in there?' he asked cheerfully. 'With that flint-and-steel nonsense?'

I smiled and shrugged, very much embarrassed at being thus confronted. 'It seemed a good thing to say at the time.'

My colleague laughed briskly. 'I was afraid you'd gone out on a limb with that line of horseshit, but it looks like you know what you're doing.'

Clearly he was unhappy about it nonetheless, but wasn't going to voice his criticisms.

'We'll see about that pretty soon, I guess.'

'Well, hope you get the job,' he said, 'if it's what you want.'

I put the car in reverse and eased out the clutch. 'Be seeing you.'

But there was a point still unsettled in Joe Morgan's mind. His face mirrored faithfully whatever was in progress behind it, and even as the car began to move backwards out of the parking space I saw a question settle itself on his pellucid brow.

'Say, we'd like to have you over to dinner – Rennie and I – before you go back to Baltimore, whether you get the job or not. I understand you've taken a room in town.'

'Oh, I'll be around for a while, I guess, either way. Nothing special on the agenda.'

'Swell. How about tonight?'

'Well – better not.' It seemed the thing to say.

'Tomorrow night?'

'Sure, I guess so.'

There was another thing, dinner invitations aside: 'You know, if you weren't just being funny about that flint-and-steel, then you might as well lay off it, don't you think? There's nothing silly about working with the Scouts that I can see. You can tease me about them, or you can argue with me about them, but there's no sense just poking fun to be malicious. That's too easy.'

This speech surprised me; I immediately labelled it bad taste, but I must admit that I felt ashamed, and at the same time I appreciated the subtlety with which Morgan had precluded any protest on my part by prefacing his reproof with a dinner invitation. He was still smiling most cordially.

'Excuse me if I offended you,' I said.

'Oh hell, no offense! I'm not really touchy, but what the hell, we'll probably be working together; might as well understand each other a little. See you tomorrow for dinner, then. So long!'

'So long.'

He turned and strode cleanly across the lawn, grown tall in the students' absence. Apparently Joe Morgan was the sort who heads directly for his destination, implying by his example that paths should be laid where people walk, instead of walking where the paths happen to be laid. All very well for a history man, perhaps, but I could see that Mr Morgan would be a fish out of water in the prescriptive grammar racket.

Chapter Three
A turning down of dinner damped, in ways subtle past knowing

A turning down of dinner damped, in ways subtle past knowing, manic keys on the thin flute of me, least pressed of all, which for a moment had shrilled me rarely.

It began with Laocoön on the mantelpiece, his voiceless groan. The set of that mouth was often my barometer, told me the weight of day; on Wednesday after my interview, when I woke and consulted him with a happening glance, his pain was simply Bacchic! That was something, now! Out of bed I sprang, unclothed, to put a dance on the phonograph while the spell should last. Against all of Mozart I owned a single Russian dance, a piece of *Ilya Mourometz*, measured and sprightly, lively and tight – there, now, Laocoön!

The dusty maple incandesced; sunshine fired the speckled windows and filled my room with a sparkle of light, and I danced like an unfurred Cossack, spinning and jumping. Once in a blue moon I felt that light – sweet manic! – and it lasted a scant three minutes, till a ring from the phone dispersed it.

I shut off the music, furious. A man with so short time to prance deserved a history of unanswered phones.

'Hello?'

'Hello, Jacob Horner?' It was a woman, and I felt naked as I was.

'Yes.'

'This is Rennie Morgan, Joe Morgan's wife. Say, I think Joe already asked you over for dinner tonight, didn't he? I just called to make it official.'

I allowed a pause to lie along the line.

'I mean, after your interview, you know, we wanted to make sure you'd come on the right day!'

'Jacob? Are we still connected?'

'Yes. Excuse me.' I was checking my barometer, who now looked dolorous enough. Batygh the Tartar had breathed on us.

'Well, it's all set, then? Any time after six-thirty: that's when we put the kids to bed.'

'Well, say, Mrs Morgan, I guess –'

'*Rennie*. Okay? My name's Renée, but nobody calls me that.'

' – I guess I won't be able to make it tonight after all.'

'What?'

'No, I'm pretty sure I can't. Thanks a lot for inviting me.'

'But why not? Are you sure you can't make it?'

Why not? Bitch of an Eagle Scout's *Hausfrau*, you spoiled my first real manic in a month of Sundays! I spit on your dinner!

'I'd kind of planned on riding up to Baltimore this afternoon, have a look around. Something came up.'

'Oh, now, aren't you just getting out of it? Come on and say so; we're not committed to each other.' This from a wife? 'Don't be a chicken – it doesn't make a damn to us if you don't like us.'

So caught, *flagrante delicto*, I flushed and sweated. What was this beast *honesty* ridden by a woman? An answer was awaited: I heard Joe Morgan's wife breathing in my naked ear.

Very discreetly I hung up the phone. Not only that: I walked the first three steps away on tiptoe before I realized what I was doing, and blushed again to notice it.

Ah, well, the spell was broken, and I knew better than to try Glière and his *Ilya Mourometz* again. He's the fizz that makes the collins bright, is Glière, but he's not the vodka; these manics can't be teased or dickered with. Now I was not only unmanic, I was uncomfortable.

And resentful! There's something to be said for the manic-depressive if his manics are really manic; but me, I was a placid-depressive: a woofer without a tweeter was Jake Horner. My lows were low, but my highs were middle-register. So when I'd a real manic on I nursed it like a baby, and boils plague the man who spoiled it! That was one thing. More's the damage to have it suggested, and by a woman, that my honesty was flagging. That it was in fact was beside the point. Great heavens, Morgans, the world's not *that* easy!

Even as I was dressing, the telephone rang again, with a doggedness that bespoke Mrs Morgan. In a moment of lewdness (for I was pulling up my trousers at the time) I considered allowing that beskirted Diogenes to address her quest to my bare backside – but I let the moment go. Rennie, girl, said I to myself, I am out; be content that I don't commit a lewdness with your voice, since you've aborted my infant manic. Ring away, girl scout: your quarry's not in his hole.

Later that morning I drove the thirty miles from Wicomico to Ocean City, there to fry my melancholy in the sun and pickle it in the ocean. But light and water only made it blossom. The beach was crowded with human beings whose reality I found myself loath to acknowledge; another day they might have been as soothingly grotesque as was my furniture, but this day they were merely irritating. Furthermore, perhaps because it was a weekday, there was not a girl on the beach worth the necessary nonsense involved in a pickup. Only a forest of legs ruined by childbirth; fallen breasts, potbellies, haggard faces, and strident voices; a rat's nest of horrid children, as unlovely as they were obnoxious. When one is not in the spirit of it, there are few things less diverting than a public beach.

When I reached the saturation point, about three o'clock, I washed the sand off me and headed back to the car. But one who felt as gloomily competent as I that day wouldn't leave Ocean City without at least going through the motions of picking up a girl, any more than one would leave Pikes Peak without spitting – the trip were pointless otherwise. Along the boardwalk a few girls prowled in twos and threes, most wearing T-shirts with the name of either a college or a sorority printed on them. They met my glowering haughtily, each of us considering the other unworthy. I walked the three blocks to my car without seeing a target worth the ammunition, and so, like many a hunter nearing home, had finally to settle for even less satisfactory game or take none at all.

A woman of forty – well preserved but definitely forty –

whose car was parked in front of mine, was wrenching the handle of her door in vain when I approached. She was slender, not very full-breasted, well tanned, and in no way extraordinary. I lost my taste for the hunt and walked past.

'Pardon me, sir: I wonder if you could help me?'

I turned and glared. The woman had been all brightness with her classic request, but my stare made her falter.

'You'll think I'm stupid, I guess – I locked my keys inside the car.'

'I can't pick locks.'

'Oh, I didn't mean that! My motel is just across the bridge. I was wondering if you'd run me over there, if you're going that way. I have another key in my suitcase.'

It is small sport shooting the bird who perches on the muzzle of your gun, but what hunter could keep from doing it?

'All right.'

The whole situation was without appeal, and as I drove Miss Peggy Rankin (her name) over the bridge from Ocean City to the mainland, I was made more desultory by the fact that I guessed she didn't deserve to be so severely judged. She appeared to be fairly intelligent, and indeed, had I been her husband I should doubtless have been proud that my wife still retained such trimness and spirit at age forty. But I was not her husband, and so I made no such allowances: she was a forty-year-old pickup, and only the most extraordinary charm could survive that classification.

All the way to the motel Miss Rankin chattered, and I honestly didn't hear a word of it. For me this was unusual, because, although I admired the ability to lose oneself in oneself, I was far too conscious of my surroundings, as a rule, ever to manage it. A real point against Miss Rankin, that.

'This is the place,' she said presently, indicating the Surf-side, or Seaside, or some such motel along the highway. I pulled into the driveway and parked. 'Gee, I sure appreciate your doing this. Thanks a lot.' She moved lightly out of the car.

'I'll take you back,' I said, without any particular inflection.

'Oh, would you?' She was very pleased, but not over-whelmed with either surprise or gratitude. 'Just a minute, while I run get my keys.'

'Have you got anything cold to drink in there, Peggy? I'm pretty dry.' This was as far as I was willing to go in the non-sense line just then: I decided that if she didn't ask me in, I'd take off at once for Wicomico.

'Sure, come on in,' she invited, again not entirely stunned by my request. 'There's no refrigerator in the room, but there's a soda fountain right next door here, and I've got whiskey. Why don't you get two large ginger ales, with lots of ice, and we'll make highballs.'

I did, and we drank in her little room, she curled on the bed and I slouched in the single chair. The gloom was still on me, but it grew somewhat easier to endure; especially when we found that we could talk or not talk with a reasonable degree of ease. At one point, as might be expected, Miss Rankin asked me what I did for a living. Now, I didn't necessarily subscribe at all to honesty as a policy in adven-tures of this sort, and I can't imagine myself answering such stock questions truthfully as a rule; but 'I'm a potential instructor of prescriptive grammar at the Wicomico State Teachers College' is so nearly the type of answer one usually dreams up at such moments that without really thinking about it I told her the truth.

'Is that so!' Peggy was genuinely surprised and pleased this time. 'I graduated from WTC myself – so long ago it embarrasses me to remember! I teach English at the high school in Wicomico. Isn't that a funny coincidence? Two English teachers!'

I agreed that it was, but in fact I felt like turning in my highball and calling it quits. It was necessary to move rapidly to keep the situation from disintegrating. There was only a half inch of highball left in my paper cup: I tossed it down, dropped the cup into the wastebasket, immediately went to the bed, where my colleague lay propped on one elbow, and embraced her with some *élan*. She opened her mouth at once under my kiss and thrust her tongue between my teeth. Both of us had our eyes quite open, and I was pleased to accept that fact symbolically. *Let there be no horse manure between teachers of English*, I declared to myself, and without more ado gave the zipper of her bathing suit a meaning yank.

Miss Rankin froze: her eyes closed tightly and she clutched my shoulders, but my ungentle attack was not repulsed. The zipper undid her down to the small of her back and so gave me access to a certain amount of innocuous skin, but I could go no farther without her assistance.

'Let's take your bathing suit off, Peggy,' I suggested.

This injured her. 'You're in a great hurry, aren't you, Jake?'

'Well, Peg, we're old enough not to be any sillier than we have to be.'

She made a noise in her mouth, and, still holding my shoulders, pressed her forehead against my chest.

'By that you mean I'm too old for you to bother being silly with, don't you?' she observed. 'You're thinking that a woman my age can't afford to be coy.'

Tears. Everybody was digging truth out of me.

'Why hurt yourself?' I asked over her hair to the whiskey bottle on the night stand.

'You're the one that's doing the hurting,' Miss Rankin wept, looking me square in the eye. 'You go out of your way to let me know you're doing me a favor by picking me up, but your generosity doesn't include wasting a little time being gentle!' She flung herself, not violently, upon her pillow, burying her face in it. 'It doesn't make the least bit of difference to you whether I'm bright or stupid or what, does it? I might even be more interesting than you are, since I'm a little older!' This last piece of self-castigation, while it choked her completely for a moment, made her mad enough to sit up and glare at me.

'I'm sorry,' I offered politely. I was thinking that even if she were talented as, say, Beatrice Lillie is talented, one would not pick her up in order to witness a theatrical performance: one would purchase a theater ticket.

'Sorry you wasted your time on me, you mean!' Peggy cried. 'Just making me defend myself is awful enough!'

Back to the pillow. Up again at once.

'Don't you understand how you make me feel? Today is

my last day at Ocean City. For two whole weeks not a soul has spoken to me or even looked at me, except some horrible old men. Not a *soul*! Most women look awful at my age, but I don't look awful: I just don't look like a child. There's a lot *more* to me, damn it! And then on the last day you come along and pick me up, bored as you can be with the whole thing, and treat me like a whore!'

Well, she was correct, of course.

'I'm a cad,' I agreed readily, and rose to leave. There was a little more to this matter than Miss Rankin was willing to see, but in the main she had a pretty clear view of things. Her mistake, in the long run, was articulating her protest. The game was spoiled now, of course: I had assigned to Miss Rankin the role of Forty-Year-Old Pickup, a delicate enough character for her to bring off successfully in my current mood; I had no interest whatever in the quite complex (and no doubt interesting, from another point of view) human being she might be apart from that role. What she should have done, it seems to me, assuming she was after the same thing I was after, was assign me a role gratifying to her own vanity – say, The Fresh But Unintelligent Young Man Whose Body One Uses For One's Pleasure Without Otherwise Taking Him Seriously – and then we could have pursued our business with no wounds inflicted on either side. As it was, my present feeling, though a good deal stronger, was essentially the same feeling one has when a filling-station attendant or a cabdriver launches into his life-story: as a rule, and especially when one is in a hurry or is grouchy, one wishes the man to be nothing more difficult than The Obliging Filling-Station Attendant or The Adroit Cabdriver. These are the essences you have assigned them, at least temporarily, for your own purposes, as a taleteller makes a man The Handsome Young Poet or The Jealous Old Husband; and while you know very well that no historical human being was ever *just* an Obliging Filling-Station Attendant or a Handsome Young Poet, you are nevertheless prepared to ignore your man's charming complexities – *must* ignore them, in fact, if you are to get on with the plot, or get things done according to schedule. Of this, more later, for it is related to Mythotherapy. Enough now to say that we are all casting directors a great deal of the time, if not always, and he is wise who realizes that his role-assigning is at best an arbitrary distortion of the actors' personalities; but he is even wiser who sees in addition that this arbitrariness is probably inevitable, and at any rate is apparently necessary if one would reach the ends he desires.

'Get your keys,' I said. 'I'll wait for you out in the car.'

'No! *Jake!*' Miss Peggy Rankin jumped off the bed. I was caught at the door and embraced from behind, under my arms. 'Oh, God, don't go away yet!' Hysteria. 'I'm sorry I made you angry!' She was pulling me as hard as she could, back into the room.

'Come on, now; cut it out. Get hold of yourself.'

A forty-year-old pickup's beauty, when it is preserved at all, is fragile, and Peggy's hysteria, added to her previous weeping, left little of loveliness in her face, which normally was long, tan, unwrinkled, and not unattractive.

'Will you stay? Don't pay attention to anything I said a while ago!'

'I don't know what to do,' I said truthfully, trying to assimilate this outburst. 'This whole thing means more to you than it does to me. That's no criticism of anybody. I'm really afraid I might spoil it for you, if I haven't already.'

I was squeezed tightly. 'You're humiliating me! Don't make me beg you, for God's sake!'

By this time she stood to lose either way. We went back to the bed: what ensued was, for me at least, pure discomfort, and it was of a nature to become an unpleasant memory for her, too, whether she enjoyed it at the time or not. It was embarrassing because she abandoned herself to an elaborate gratitude that implied her own humiliation – and because my own mood was not complementary to hers. Her condition remained semi-hysterical and masochistic: she did her best to make grand opera out of nature's little *cantus firmus*, and if she didn't succeed it was more my fault than hers, for she strove elaborately. Another time I might have enjoyed it – that sort of voluptuous groveling can be as pleasant to indulge as it is on occasion to indulge in – but that day was not my day. That day had begun badly, had developed tediously, and was climaxing uncomfortably, if not distastefully: I was always uneasy with women who took their sexual transports too seriously, and Miss Rankin was not the sort whom one could leave shuddering and moaning on the bed knowing it was all just good clean fun.

That is how I left her, at five o'clock. At four forty-five she had begun, as I'd rather expected, to express hatred for me, whether feigned (this kind of thing can be sensuous sport) or sincere I couldn't say, since her eyes were closed and her face averted. What she said, throatily, was 'God damn your eyes, God damn your eyes, God damn your eyes . . .' in rhythm with what happened to be in progress at the time, and I was not so committed to my mood that it didn't strike me as funny. But I was weary of dramatics, genuine or not, amusing or not, and when things reached their natural *dénouement* I was glad enough to make my exit, forgetting entirely about Miss Rankin's keys. The lady had talent, but no discipline. I'm sure we neither wished to see the other again.

I ate at a roadstand outside Wicomico and finally got back to my room at six-thirty, feeling terrible. I was a man of considerable integrity within the limits of a given mood, but I was short on endurance. I felt bad already about this Peggy Rankin – irritated that at her age she hadn't yet learned how to handle her position, how to turn its regrettable aspects as much as possible to her own advantage – and at the same time very much sympathetic with her weakness. I had, abstractly at least, a tremendous sympathy for that sort of weakness – a person's inability either to control his behavior by his own standards or to discipline his standards, down to the last shred of conscience, to fit his behavior – even though in particular situations it sometimes annoyed me. Everything that had happened with Miss Rankin could have been high sport – the groveling, the hysterics, and numerous other things that I've not felt like sharing by recording them – had she kept hard control of her integrity; but her error, I feared, was that she would recriminate herself for some time afterwards for having humbled herself in fact, and not in fun, and mine was in not walking out when I'd started to, regardless of her hysterics. Had I done so I'd have preserved my own tranquillity and allowed Miss Rankin to regain hers by despising me instead of both of us. I had remained, I think, both out of a sense of chivalry, to which I often inclined though I didn't *believe* in it, and out of a characteristic disinclination to walk out on any show, no matter how poor or painful, once I'd seen the first act.

But there was a length of time beyond which I could not bear to be actively displeased with myself, and when that time began to announce its approach – about seven-fifteen – I went to sleep. Only the profundity and limited duration of my moods kept me from being a suicide: as it was, this practice of mine of going to bed when things got too awful, this deliberate termination of my day, was itself a kind of suicide, and served its purpose as efficiently. My moods were little men, and when I killed them they stayed completely dead.

The buzzer from the front door woke me at nine o'clock, and by the time I got up and put a robe on, Joe Morgan and his wife were at my door. I was surprised, but I invited them in cheerfully, because I knew as soon as I opened my eyes that sleep had changed my emotional scenery: I felt fine. Rennie Morgan, to whom I was introduced, was by no means my idea of a beautiful woman; she looked like an outdoorsman's wife. Rather large-framed, blond, heavier than I, strong-looking, and exuberant, she was not the type of woman whom one (or at least *this* one) thinks of instinctively in sexual terms. Yet of course there I was, appraising her in sexual terms: no doubt my afternoon's adventure influenced both the nature and the verdict of my appraisal.

'Can I offer you anything to eat?' I asked her, and I was pleased to see that both of them were apparently in good spirits.

'No, thanks,' Joe smiled; 'we've eaten enough for three already.'

'We saw your car out front,' Rennie said, 'and wondered whether the plane had gotten in from Baltimore yet.'

'You Morgans will track a man to his very lair!' I protested.

Because we all seemed to be feeling friendly, and because Joe and Rennie had the good sense not to make a *cause célèbre* out of a *fait accompli*, if I may say so, I fetched bottles of ale from the case I had on ice down in the kitchen and told them the story of my day, omitting none but the most indelicate details (and those more from my own embarrassment than from Rennie's, who seemed able to take it straight), by way of entertainment.

We got on extremely well. Rennie Morgan, though lively, seemed to be a trifle unsure of herself; her mannerisms – like the habit of showing excruciating hilarity by squinting her eyes shut and whipping her head from side to side, or her intensely excited gestures when speaking – were borrowed directly from Joe, as were both the matter and the manner of her thinking. It was clear that in spite of the progress she'd evidently made toward being indistinguishable from her husband, she was still apprehensive about the disparity between them. Whenever Joe took issue with a statement she'd made, Rennie would argue the point as vigorously as possible, knowing that that was what he expected her to do, but there was in her manner the same nervous readiness to concede that one might expect in a boy sparring with his gym teacher. The metaphor, in fact, if you add to it a touch of Pygmalion and Galatea, pretty well covers everything about their relationship that I could see that evening, and though I'd no ultimate objection at all to such a relationship – after all, Galatea *was* a remarkable woman, and some uneasy young pugilists grow up to be Gene Tunney – the presence of two so similarly forceful people was overwhelming: I several times caught myself whipping *my* head from side to side as they did, at some especially witty remark, or gesticulating excitedly after their fashion while making a point.

As for Joe, the first hour of conversation made it clear that he was brilliant, one of the most brilliant people I'd met. He spoke slowly and softly as a rule, with a slight Southern accent, but one had always the feeling that this slowness did not come naturally to him; that they were controls that he maintained over his normal ebullience. Only when the turn of the conversation excited him did his speech rise in volume and rapidity: at these times he was likely to scratch his head vigorously, jab his spectacles hard back on his nose, and gesture eloquently with his hands. I learned that he'd taken his bachelor's and master's degrees at Columbia – the one in literature, the other in philosophy – and had completed all the requirements except the dissertation for a doctorate in history at Johns Hopkins. Wicomico was Rennie's home town and WTC her alma mater: the Morgans were staying there while Joe made a leisurely job of the dissertation. Talking with him for an evening was tremendously stimulating – I was continually impressed by his drive, his tough intellectuality, and his deliberateness – and, like any very stimulating thing, it was exhausting.

We took to each other at once: it was clear in a very short time that if I remained in Wicomico we would be friends. My initial estimate of him I had completely to revise; it turned out that those activities of his and aspects of his personality about which I had found it easy to make commonplace criticisms were nearly always the result of very careful, uncommon thinking. One understood that Joe Morgan would never make a move or utter a statement, if he could help it, that he hadn't considered deliberately and penetratingly beforehand, and he had, therefore, the strength not to be much bothered if his move proved unfortunate. He would never have allowed himself to get into a position like Miss Rankin's, for example, or like mine when I was circling around the college driveway on Monday. Indecision of that sort was apparently foreign to him: he was always sure of his ground; he acted quickly, explained his actions lucidly if questioned, and would have regarded apologies for missteps as superfluous. Moreover, four of my least fortunate traits – shyness, fear of appearing ridiculous, affinity for many sorts of nonsense, and almost complete inconsistency – he seemed not to share at all. On the other hand, he was, at least in the presence of a third party, somewhat prudish (he didn't enjoy my story) and, despite his excitability, seemingly lacking in warmth and spontaneity, though he doubtless had as clear reasons for being so as he had for being a scoutmaster – he was a man whom it was exceedingly difficult to criticize. Finally, for better or worse he seemed completely devoid of craft or guile, and in that sense ingenuous, though by no means naïve, and had no interest in any sort of career as such.

All this was exhausting, most exhausting, to encounter. We talked concentratedly until one-thirty in the morning (I could not begin to remember what about), and when the Morgans left I felt that the evening had been the pleasantest I'd spent in months; that in Joe I'd found an extremely interesting new acquaintance; and that I had no special wish to see this interesting new acquaintance of mine again for at least a week.

As they were leaving, Rennie happened to say, 'Oh, Jake, we forgot to congratulate you about your job.' (This sort of oversight, I later learned, was characteristic of the Morgans.)

'You're jumping the gun, aren't you?'

'What do you mean?' Joe asked. 'Didn't Dr Schott ever get hold of you?'

'Nope.'

'Well, you got the job. The Committee met this morning and decided. I guess Schott called while you were in Ocean City, or while you were asleep this evening.'

They both congratulated me, awkwardly – for they were unable to express affection, friendship, or even congratulation easily – and then left. I still felt too fine to sleep, so I read my *World Almanac* for a while and listened to Mozart's *Ein Musikalischer Spass* on the record player. I was beginning to feel at home in my room and in Wicomico; the Morgans pleased me; and I was still in an unusual state of excitement from the afternoon's sexual adventure and Joe's intelligence. But I must have been thoroughly fatigued by these things, too, and from my day on the beach, for at six-thirty in the morning I woke with a start, having dropped unintentionally into a sound sleep. The *World Almanac* was still in my lap, open to page 96: 'Air Line Distances Between Principal Cities of the World'; *Ein Musikalischer Spass* was playing for what must have been the fiftieth time; and the sun, just rising between two dark brick houses across the street, shot a blinding beam directly over my lap into Laocoön's face, contorted noncommittally in bright plaster.

Chapter Four
I got up, stiff from sleeping in the chair

I got up, stiff from sleeping in the chair, showered, changed my clothes, and went out for breakfast. Perhaps because the previous day had been, for me, so unusually eventful, or perhaps because I'd had relatively little sleep (I must say I take no great interest in causes), my mind was empty. All the way to the restaurant, all through the meal, all the way home, it was as though there were no Jacob Horner today. After I'd eaten I returned to my room, sat in my rocker, and rocked, barely sentient, for a long time, thinking of nothing.

Once I had a dream in which it became a matter of some importance to me to learn the weather prediction for the following day. I searched the newspapers for the weather report, but couldn't find it in its usual place. I turned the radio on, but the news broadcasters made no mention of tomorrow's weather. I dialed the Weather number on the telephone (this dream took place in Baltimore), but although the recording described the current weather conditions it told me nothing about the forecast for the next day. Finally I called the Weather Bureau directly, but it was late at night and no one answered. I happened to know the chief meteorologist's name, and so I called his house. The telephone rang many times before he answered; it seemed to me that I detected an uneasiness in his voice.

'What is it?' he asked.

'I want to know what weather we'll be having tomorrow,' I demanded. 'It's terribly important.'

'There's no use your trying to impress me,' the meteorologist said. 'No use at all. What made you suspicious?'

'I assure you, sir, I just want to know what the weather will be tomorrow. I can't say I see anything suspicious in that question.'

'There isn't going to be any weather tomorrow.'

'What?'

'You heard me. There isn't going to be any weather to-morrow. All our instruments agree. No weather.'

'But that's impossible!'

'I've said what I've said,' the weatherman grumbled. 'No weather tomorrow, and that's that. Leave me alone; I have to sleep.'

That was the end of the dream, and I woke up very much upset. I tell it now to illustrate a difference between moods and the weather, their usual analogy: a day without weather is unthinkable, but for me at least there were frequently days without any mood at all. On these days Jacob Horner, except in a meaningless metabolistic sense, ceased to exist, for I was without a personality. Like those microscopic specimens that biologists must dye in order to make them visible at all, I had to be colored with some mood or other if there was to be a recognizable self to me. The fact that my successive and discontinuous selves were linked to one another by the two unstable threads of body and memory; the fact that in the nature of Western languages the word *change* presupposes something upon which the changes operate; the fact that although the specimen is invisible without the dye, the dye is not the specimen – these are considerations of which I was aware, but in which I had no interest.

On my weatherless days my body sat in a rocking chair and rocked and rocked and rocked, and my mind was as nearly empty as interstellar space. Such was the day after the Morgans' visit: I sat and rocked from eight-thirty in the morning until perhaps two in the afternoon. If I looked at Laocoön at all, it was without recognition. But at two o'clock the telephone rang and startled into being a Jacob Horner, who jumped from the chair and answered it.

'Hello?'

'Jacob? This is Rennie Morgan. Will you have dinner with us tonight?'

'*Why*, for God's sake?' This Jacob Horner was an irritable type.

'Why?'

'Yes. Why the hell are you all so anxious to feed me a dinner?'

'Are you angry?'

'No, I'm not angry. I just want to know why you're all so anxious to feed me a dinner.'

'Don't you want to come?'

'I didn't say that. Why are you all so anxious to feed me a dinner? That's all I asked.'

There was a pause. Rennie was one who took all questions seriously; she would not offer an answer simply to terminate a situation, but must search herself for the truth. This, I take it, was Joe's doing. Another person would have asked pettishly, 'Why does anybody ask anybody for dinner?' and thereby cloaked ignorance in the garb of self-evidence. After a minute she replied in a careful voice, as though examining her answer as she spoke.

'Well, I think it's because Joe's pretty much decided that he wants to get to know you well. He enjoyed the conversation last night.'

'Didn't you?' I interrupted out of curiosity. I didn't really see how she could have, for we had talked of nothing but abstract ideas, and Rennie's determined but limited participation had been under what struck me as a tacit but very careful scrutiny from her husband. I don't mean to suggest that there was anything ungenuine in Rennie's interest, though it was awfully *deliberate*, or anything of the husband embarrassed by his wife's opinions in Joe's concern about her statements; his attention was that of a tutor listening to his favorite protégé, and when he questioned her opinions he did so in an entirely impersonal, unarrogant, and unpedantic manner. Joe was not a pedant.

'Yes, I believe I did. Do you think that there ought to be a kind of waiting period between visits, Jacob?'

I was amazed. 'What do *you* think?'

Again a short pause, and then a solemn opinion.

'It seems to me that there wouldn't be any reason for it unless one of us just happened to feel like not seeing the other for a while. I think sometimes a person feels that way. Is that how you feel, Jake?'

'Well, now, let me see,' I said soberly, and paused. 'It seems to me that you do right to question the validity of social conventions, like waiting a certain time between visits, but you have to keep in mind that they're all ultimately unjustifiable. But it doesn't follow that because a thing is unjustifiable it's without value. And you have to remember that *dispensing* with a convention, even a silly one, always involves the risk of being made to feel unreasonably guilty, simply because the conventions *do* happen to be conventions. Take drinking beer for breakfast, for instance, or going through red lights late at night, or committing adultery with your husband's approval, or performing a euthanasia . . .'

'Are you making fun of me?' Rennie demanded mildly, as though asking purely for information.

'I am indeed!'

'You know, it seems to me that lots of times a person makes fun of another person because the other person's opinions make him uncomfortable but he doesn't really know how to refute them. He feels that he *ought* to know how, but he doesn't, and instead of admitting that to himself and studying the problem and working out a real refutation, he just sneers at the other person's argument. It's too easy to sneer at an argument. I feel that way a lot about you, Jake.'

'Yes. Joe said the same thing.'

'Now you *are* making fun of me, aren't you?'

I was resolved not to let Mrs Rennie Morgan make me uncomfortable again. That was too easy.

'Listen, I'll come eat your dinner tonight. I'll come at six o'clock, after you've put your kids to bed, as you said.'

'We neither one want you to come if you don't feel like it, Jake. You have to be –'

'Now wait a minute. *Why* don't you want me to come even if I don't feel like it?'

'What?'

'I said why don't you want me to come even if I don't feel like it? You see, the only grounds you'd have for breaking the custom of waiting a proper interval between visits would be if you took the position that social conventions might be necessary for stability in a social group, but that they aren't absolutes and you can dispense with them in special situations where your end justifies it. In other words, you're willing to have me to dinner tonight anyhow as long as that's what we all want – social stability isn't your end in this special situation. Well, then, suppose your end was to have another conversation and you had reason to believe that once I got there I'd talk to you whether I'd really wanted to come or not – most guests would – then it shouldn't matter to you whether I wanted to come or not, since your ends would be reached anyway.'

'You're still making fun of me.'

'Oh, now, that's too easy an out. It's beside the point whether I'm making fun of you or not. You're evading the question.'

No answer.

'Now, I'm coming to dinner at six o'clock, whether I want to or not, and if you aren't ready to answer my argument by then, I'm going to tell Joe.'

'Six-thirty is when the kids go to bed,' Rennie said in a slightly injured voice, and hung up. I went back to my rocker and rocked for another forty-five minutes. From time to time I smiled inscrutably, but I cannot say that this honestly reflected any sincere feeling on my part. It was just a thing I found myself doing, as frequently when walking alone I would find myself repeating over and over in a judicious, unmetrical voice, *Pepsi-Cola hits the spot; twelve full ounces: that's a lot* – accompanying the movement of my lips with a wrinkled brow, distracted twitches of the corner of my mouth, and an occasional quick gesture of my right hand. Passers-by often took me for a man lost in serious problems, and sometimes when I looked behind me after passing one I'd see him, too, make a furtive movement with his right hand, trying it out.

At four-fifteen Dr Schott telephoned and confirmed my appointment to the faculty of the Wicomico State Teachers College as a teacher of grammar and composition, at a starting salary of $3200 per year.

'You know,' he said, 'we don't pay what they pay at the big universities! Can't afford it! But that doesn't mean we're not choosy about our teachers! We're a pretty dedicated bunch, frankly, and we hired you because we believe you share our feelings about the importance of our job!'

I assured him that I did indeed share that feeling, and he assured me that he was sure I did. I was not pleased at being asked to teach composition as well as grammar – I was supposed to be strictly a prescriptive-grammar man – but, pending advice from the Doctor, I thought it best to accept the job anyway.

As a matter of fact I drove out to the Morgans' place at five-thirty, for no particular reason. My day was no longer weatherless, but I was quiescent. I found Joe and Rennie having a leisurely catch with a football on the lawn in front of their house, although the afternoon was fairly warm. They showed no great surprise at seeing me, greeted me cordially, and invited me to join their game.

'No, thanks,' I said, and went over to where their two sons, ages three and four, were throwing their own little football at each other – adeptly for their age. I sat on the grass and watched everybody.

'I didn't mean to get upset on the phone today, Jake,' Rennie said cheerfully between passes.

'Ah, don't pay attention to what I say on telephones,' I said. 'I can't talk on telephones.'

I've never seen a girl who could catch and throw a football properly except Rennie Morgan. As a rule she was a clumsy animal, but in any sort of strenuous physical activity she was completely at ease and even graceful. She caught and threw the ball in the same manner and with the same speed and accuracy as a practiced man.

'What have you changed your mind about that you said, then?' Joe asked, keeping his eyes on the ball.

'I don't even remember what I said.'

'You don't? Rennie remembers the whole conversation. Do you really not remember, or are you trying not to make her uncomfortable?'

'I really don't remember at all,' I said, with some truth. 'I've learned by now that you all don't believe in avoiding discomfort. The fact is I can never remember arguments, my own or anybody else's. I can remember conclusions, but not arguments.'

This observation, which I thought arresting enough, seemed to disgust Joe. He lost interest in the conversation and stopped to correct the older boy's way of gripping the football. The kid attended his father's quiet advice as though it were coming from Knute Rockne; Joe watched him throw the ball correctly three times and then turned away.

'Here, Jake,' he said tossing me the other ball. 'Why don't you pitch a few with Rennie while I put supper on, and then we'll have a drink. No use to wait till six-thirty, since you're here.'

I was, as I said before, quiescent. I would not voluntarily have joined the game, but neither would I go out of my way to avoid playing. Joe went on into the house, the two boys following close behind, and for the next twenty minutes Rennie and I threw the football to each other. Luckily – for as a rule I dreaded being made to look ridiculous – I was no novice at football myself; though not so adept a passer as Joe, I was able to throw at least as accurately and unwobblingly as Rennie. She seemed to have nothing special to say to me, nor did I to her, and so the only sound heard on the lawn was the rush of passing-arms, the quiet spurts of running feet on the grass, the soft smack of catches, and our heavy breathing. It was all neither pleasant nor unpleasant.

Presently Joe called to us from the porch, and we went in to dinner. The Morgans rented half of the first floor of the house. Their apartment was very clean; what furniture they owned was the most severely plain modern, tough and functional, but there was very little of it. In fact, because the rooms were relatively large they seemed quite bare. There were no rugs on the hardwood floors, no curtains or drapes on the polished windows, and not a piece of furniture above the necessary minimum; a day bed, two sling chairs, two lamps, a bookcase, and a writing table in the living room; a small dining table and four metal folding chairs in the kitchen; and a double bunk, two bureaux, and a work table with benches in the single bedroom, where the boys slept. Because the walls and ceiling were white, the light pouring through the open venetian blinds made the living room blindingly bright. I squinted; there was too much light in that room for me.

While we drank a glass of beer, the children went into the bedroom, undressed themselves and actually bathed themselves without help in the water that Joe had already drawn for them. I expressed surprise at such independence at ages three and four. Rennie shrugged.

'We make pretty heavy demands on them for physical efficiency,' Joe admitted. 'What the hell, in New Guinea the kids are swimming before they walk, and paddling bamboo logs out in the ocean at Joey's age. We figured the less they're in our hair the better we'll get along with each other.'

'Don't think we drive them,' Rennie said. 'We don't really give a damn. But I guess we demand a lot tacitly.'

Joe listened to this remark with casual interest.

'Why do you say you don't give a damn?' he asked her.

Rennie was a little startled at the question, which she had not expected.

'Well – I mean *ultimately*. Ultimately it wouldn't matter one way or the other, would it? But *immediately* it matters because if they weren't independent we'd have to go through the same rigmarole most people go through, and the kids would be depending on all kinds of crutches.'

'Nothing matters one way or the other ultimately,' Joe pointed out. 'The other importance is all there is to anything.'

'That's what I meant, Joe.'

'What I'm trying to say is that you shouldn't consider a value less real just because it isn't absolute, since less-than-absolutes are all we've got. That's what's implied when you say you don't *really* give a damn.'

Well, it was Rennie's ball – I watched them over my beer much as I'd watched them out on the lawn – but the game was interrupted by the timer bell on the kitchen stove. Rennie went out to serve up the dinner while Joe dried the two boys and assisted them into their pajamas: their physical efficiency apparently didn't extend to fastening their own snaps in the back.

'Why don't you have them snap each other up in the back?' I suggested politely. Rennie flashed me an uncertain look from the kitchen, where she was awkwardly dishing out rice with a spoon too small for the job, but Joe laughed easily and unsnapped both boys' pajama shirts so that they could try it. It worked.

Since there were only four chairs in the kitchen, Rennie

and the two boys and I ate at the table while Joe ate standing up at the stove. There would have been no room at the table for one of the sling chairs, and anyhow it did not take long to eat the meal, which consisted of steamed shrimp, boiled rice, and beer for all hands. The boys – husky, well-mannered youngsters – were allowed to dominate the conversation during dinner; they were as lively and loud as any other bright kids their age, but a great deal more physically co-ordinated and self-controlled than most. As soon as we finished eating they went to bed, and though it was still quite light outside, I heard no more from them.

The Morgans had an arrangement with their first-floor neighbor whereby they could leave open a door connecting the two apartments and listen for each other's children if one couple wished to go out for the evening. Taking advantage of this, we went walking through a clover field and a small stand of pines behind the house after the supper dishes were washed. The Morgans tended to walk vigorously, and this did not fit well with my quiescent mood, but neither did refusing to accompany them. Rennie, an amateur natural-ist, remarked on various weeds, bugs, and birds as we bounded along, and Joe confirmed her identifications. I can't say I enjoyed the walk, although the Morgans enjoyed it almost fiercely. When it was over, Rennie went inside the house to write a letter, and Joe and I sat outside on the lawn in the two sling chairs. Our conversation, by his direction, dealt with values, since they'd come up earlier.

'Most of what you told Rennie on the phone this afternoon was sensible,' Joe granted. 'I'm glad you talked to her, and I'm glad you told her it was beside the point whether you were making fun of her or not. That's exactly what she needs to learn. She's too sensitive about that.'

'So are you,' I said. 'Remember the Boy Scouts.'

'No, I'm not, really,' Joe denied, in a way that left you no special desire to insist that he was. 'The only reason I caught it up about the Scouts was that I'd decided I wanted to know you a little bit, and it seemed to me that too much of that might stand in the way of any sensible talking. It doesn't matter at all outside of that.'

'Okay.' I offered him a cigarette, but he didn't smoke.

'What really pleases me is that in spite of your making fun of Rennie you seem willing to take her seriously. Almost no man is willing to take any woman's thinking seriously, and that's what Rennie needs more than anything else.'

'It's none of my business, Joe,' I said quiescently, 'but if I were Rennie I'd object like hell having anybody so concerned over my *needs*. You talk about her as if she were a patient of yours.'

He laughed and jabbed his spectacles back on his nose. 'I guess I do; I don't mean to. When Rennie and I were married we understood that neither of us wanted to make a permanent thing of it if we couldn't respect each other in every way. Certainly I'm not sold on marriage-under-any-circumstances, and I'm sure Rennie's not either. There's nothing intrinsically valuable about marriage.'

'Seems to me you put a pretty high value on *your* marriage,' I suggested.

Joe squinted at me in disappointment, and I felt that had I been his wife he would have corrected me more severely than he did.

'Now you're making the same error Rennie made a while ago, before supper: the fallacy that because a value isn't intrinsic, objective, and absolute, it somehow isn't *real*. What I said was that the marriage relationship isn't any more of an absolute than anything else. That doesn't mean that I don't value it; in fact I guess I value my relationship with Rennie more than anything else in the world. All it means is that once you admit it's no absolute, you have to decide for yourself the conditions under which marriage is important to you. Okay?'

'Suits me,' I said indifferently.

'Well, do you agree or not?'

'Sure, I agree.' And, so cornered, I suppose I *did* agree, but there was something in me that would have recoiled from so systematic an analysis of things even if I'd had it straight from God that such happened to be the case.

'Well,' Joe said, 'I'm not a man who needs to be married under any circumstances – in fact, under a lot of circumstances I couldn't tolerate being married – and one of my conditions for preserving any relationship at all, but particularly a marriage relationship, would be that the parties involved be able to take each other seriously. If I straighten Rennie out now and then, or tell her that some statement of hers is stupid as hell, or even slug her one, it's because I respect her, and to me that means not making a lot of kinds of allowances for her. Making allowances might be Christian, but to me it would always mean not taking seriously the person you make allowances for. That's the only objection I have to your making fun of Rennie: not that it might hurt her feelings, but that it means you're making allowances for her being a *woman*, or some such nonsense as that.'

'Aren't you regarding this take-us-seriously business as an absolute?' I asked. 'You seem to want you and Rennie to take each other seriously under any circumstances.'

This observation pleased Joe, and to my chagrin I noticed that I was unaccountably happy that I'd said something he considered bright.

'That's a good point,' he grinned, and began his harangue. 'The usual criticism of people like me is that somewhere at the end of the line is the *ultimate* end that gives the whole chain its relative value, and this ultimate end is rationally unjustifiable if there aren't any absolute values. These ends can be pretty impersonal, like "the good of the state", or else personal, like taking your wife seriously. In either case if you're going to defend these ends at all I think you have to call them subjective. But they'd never be *logically* defensible; they'd be in the nature of psychological *givens*, different for most people. Four things that I'm not impressed by,' he added, 'are unity, harmony, eternality, and universality. In my ethics the most a man can ever do is be right from his point of view; there's no general reason why he should even bother to defend it, much less expect anybody else to accept it, but the only thing he can do is operate by it, because there's nothing else. He's got to expect conflict with people or institutions who are also right from *their* points of view, but whose points of view are different from his.

'Suppose it were the essence of my nature that I was completely jealous of Rennie, for instance,' he went on. 'Now it happens that that's not the case at all, but suppose it were true that because of my psychological make-up, marital fidelity was one of the *givens*, the subjective equivalent of an absolute, one of the conditions that would attach to any string of ethical propositions I might make for myself. Then suppose Rennie committed adultery behind my back. From my point of view the relationship would have lost its *raison d'être*, and I'd probably walk out flat, if I didn't actually shoot her or shoot myself. But from the state's point of view, for example, I'd still be obligated to support her, because you can't have a society where people just walk out flat on family relationships like that. From their point of view I should be forced to pay support money, and I would have no reason to complain that their viewpoint isn't the same as mine: it couldn't be. In the same way, the state would be as justified in hanging me or jailing me for shooting her as I would be in shooting her – do you see? Or the Catholic Church, if I were officially a Catholic, would be as justified from their point of view in refusing me sacred burial ground as I'd be in committing suicide if the marriage relationship had been one of the *givens* for my whole life. I'd be a fool if I expected the world to excuse my actions simply because I can explain them clearly.

'That's one reason why I don't apologize for things,' Joe said finally. 'It's because I've no right to expect you or anybody to accept anything I do or say – but I can always *explain* what I do or say. There's no sense in apologizing, because nothing is ultimately defensible. But a man can act coherently; he can act in ways that he can explain, if he wants to. This is important to me. Do you know, for the first month of our marriage Rennie used to apologize all over herself to friends who dropped in, because we didn't have much furniture in the house. She knew very well that we didn't want any more furniture even if we could have afforded it, but she always apologized to other people for not having their point of view. One day she did it more elaborately than usual, and as soon as the company left I popped her one on the jaw. Laid her out cold. When she came to, I explained to her very carefully why I'd hit her. She cried, and apologized to me for having apologized to other people. I popped her again.'

There was no boastfulness in Joe's voice when he said this; neither was there any regret.

'What the hell, Jake, the more sophisticated your ethics

get, the stronger you have to be to stay afloat. And when you say good-by to objective values, you really have to flex your muscles and keep your eyes open, because you're on your own. It takes *energy*: not just personal energy, but cultural energy, or you're lost. Energy's what makes the difference between American pragmatism and French existentialism – where the hell else but in America could you have a cheerful nihilism, for God's sake? I suppose it was rough, slugging Rennie, but I saw the moment as a kind of crisis. Anyhow, she stopped apologizing after that.'

'Ah,' I said.

Now it may well be that Joe made no such long coherent speech as this all at once; it is certainly true that during the course of the evening this was the main thing that got said, and I put it down here in the form of one uninterrupted whiz-bang for convenience's sake, both to illustrate the nature of his preoccupations and to add a stroke or two to my picture of the man himself. I heard it all quiescently; despite the fact that I was accustomed to expressing certain of these opinions myself at times (more hopefully than honestly), arguments against nearly everything he said occurred to me as he spoke. Yet I would by no means assert that he couldn't have refuted my objections – I daresay even I could have. As was usually the case when I was confronted by a really intelligent and lucidly exposed position, I was as reluctant to give it more than notional assent as I was unable to offer a more reasonable position of my own. In such situations I most often adopted what in psychology is known as the 'non-directive technique': I merely said, 'Oh?' or 'Ah,' and gave the horse his head.

But I was interested in the story of Rennie's first encounter with the Morgan philosophy, and the irresistible rhetoric Joe had employed to open her eyes to the truth about apologies. It demonstrated clearly that philosophizing was no game to Mr Morgan; that he lived his conclusions down to the fine print; and Rennie became a somewhat more interesting figure to me. Indeed, I should say that that particular little anecdote was doubtless the main thing that made me amenable to a proposal that Joe made later on, after Rennie had joined us out on the lawn.

'Do you like horseback-riding, Jake?' Rennie had happened to ask.

'Never rode before, Rennie.'

'Gee, it's fun; you'll have to try it with me sometime.'

I raised my eyebrows. 'Yes, I suppose it would be better to do that before I tried it with a horse.'

Rennie giggled, whipping her head from side to side, and Joe laughed loudly, but not, I think, enthusiastically. Then I saw his frowning forehead suddenly illuminate.

'Hey, that's an idea!' he exclaimed to Rennie. 'Teach Jake how to ride!' He turned to me. 'Rennie's folks have riding horses on their farm, down the road, but I seldom get a chance to ride and Rennie hates to ride by herself. I'm busy nearly all day reading for my thesis before school starts. Why don't you let Rennie teach you to ride? It'll give her a chance to get outdoors more, and you all will be able to do some talking.'

I was embarrassed both by Joe's deliberate enthusiasm for his project and by his poor taste in implying that talking to me would do Rennie good. It pleased me, perversely, to see Rennie squirm a little, too: she was apparently not yet so well educated by her husband that his ingenuousness did not sometimes embarrass her, though she was careful to conceal her discomfort from Joe.

'What do you think?' he demanded of her.

'I think it's a swell idea, if Jake wants to learn,' Rennie said quickly.

'*Do* you?' Joe asked me.

I shrugged. 'Doesn't make a damn to me.'

'Well, if it doesn't make a damn to you, and Rennie and I think it's a good idea, then it's settled,' Joe laughed. 'In fact, whether you want to learn or not it's settled, if you're not willing to refuse, just like this dinner business!'

We all chuckled, and the subject was dropped, Joe explaining to me happily that as a matter of fact my statement on the telephone (that I would come to dinner whether I wanted to or not) was unintelligible.

'Rennie would've told you if you hadn't flustered her by making fun of her,' he smiled; 'the only demonstrable index to a man's desires is his acts, when you're speaking of past time: what a man did is what he wanted to do.'

'What?'

'Don't you see?' asked Rennie, and Joe sat back and relaxed. 'The idea is that you could have conflicting desires – say, the desire not to have dinner with us and the desire not to offend us. If you end by coming to dinner it's because the second desire was stronger than the first: other things being equal, you wouldn't want to eat with us, but other things never are equal, and actually you'd rather eat with us than insult us. So you eat with us – that's what you *finally* wanted to do. You shouldn't say you'll eat with us whether you want to or not; you should say you'll eat with us if it satisfies desires in you stronger than your desire *not* to eat with us.'

'It's like combining plus one hundred and minus ninety-nine,' Joe said. 'The answer is just barely plus, but it's completely plus. That's another reason why it's silly for anybody to apologize for something he's done by claiming he didn't really want to do it: what he *wanted* to do, in the end, was what he did. That's important to remember when you're reading history.'

I observed that Rennie colored slightly at the reference to apologizing.

'Mmm,' I replied to Joe, non-directively.

Chapter Five
The clumsy force of Rennie was a thing that attracted me

The clumsy force of Rennie was a thing that attracted me during the weeks following this dinner of shrimp, rice, beer, and values that the Morgans had fed me. It was a clumsiness both of action and of articulation – Rennie lurched and blurted – and I was curious to know whether what lay behind it was ineptitude or graceless strength.

At least this was my attitude when we began my riding lessons. My mood was superior, in that I regarded myself as the examiner and her as the subject, but it was not supercilious, and there was a certain sympathy in my curiosity. That I felt this special superiority is fortunate, because it got me through the first lessons on horseback, which otherwise would have been difficult to face indeed. I hated not the work but the embarrassment of learning new things, the ludicrousness of the tyro, and I can't imagine ever having learned to ride horses (for I had only the most vagrant interest in riding) without this special curiosity and special superiority feeling to salve my pride.

Rennie was an excellent rider and a most competent teacher. We rode mostly in the mornings, fairly early, and occasionally after supper, and we rode every day unless it was raining very hard. I would drive to the Morgans' place at seven-thirty or eight in the morning, sometimes earlier, and have breakfast with them; then Joe would begin his day's reading and note taking, and Rennie, the boys, and I would drive the four miles out to her parents' farm. Mrs Mac-Mahon, her mother, took charge of the children, and Rennie and I went riding. Her horse was a spirited five-year-old dun stallion of fifteen hands (her description) named Tom Brown, and mine a seven-year-old chestnut mare with a white race down her face, sixteen hands high, named Susie, whom both Rennie and her father described as gentle, although she was plenty lively enough for me. Rennie's father kept the two horses for his own pleasure but rarely had a chance to exercise them properly, and so was pleased with Joe's project. The first thing he said to Rennie when he saw us approach in our riding outfits (Rennie had insisted that I purchase cotton jodhpurs and riding boots) was 'Well, Ren, I see Joe recruited you a companion!'

'This is Jake Horner, Dad,' Rennie said briskly. 'I'm going to teach him how to ride.' She was aware that her father's remark had told me something I wasn't especially intended to know – that Joe's project hadn't occurred to him on the spur of the moment, but had been premeditated – and being conscious of this made her awkward. She moved off immediately to the paddock where the two horses were grazing, leaving her father and me to shake hands and make pleasantries as best we could.

There is no need for me to go into any detail about my instruction: it is uninteresting and has little to do with my observation of Rennie. About the only prior knowledge I had of horses was that one mounted them from the 'near', or left, side, and even that little piece of equine lore I found to be not so invariably true as I'd believed. I was introduced to the mysteries of Pelhams and hackamores, snaffles and curbs, of collected and extended gaits, of the aids and the leads. I made all the mistakes that beginners make – hanging on by the reins, clinging with my legs, lounging in the saddle – and slowly corrected them. That I was at first very much afraid of my animal is irrelevant, since I'd not under any circumstances have shown my fear to Rennie.

She herself was a 'strong' rider – she applied the aids heavily and kept frisky Tom Brown as gentle as a lap dog – but most of her abrupt instructions to me were aimed at making me use them lightly.

'Stop digging her in the barrel,' she'd blurt out as we trotted along. 'You're telling her to go with your heels and holding her back with your hands.'

Hour after hour I practiced riding at a walk, a trot, and a canter (both horses were three-gaited), bareback and without holding the reins. I learned how to lead a horse who doesn't care to follow; how to anticipate and prevent shying and bucking and running away; how to saddle and bridle and currycomb.

Susie, my mare, had a tendency to nip me when I tightened her girth.

'Slap her hard on the nose,' Rennie ordered, 'and next time hold your left arm stiff up on her neck and she won't turn her head.'

Tom Brown, her stallion, liked to rear high two or three times just out of the stable. Once when he did this I was horrified to see Rennie lean as far back as she could on the reins, until Tom was actually overbalanced and came toppling over backwards, whinnying and flailing. Rennie sprang dextrously out of the saddle and out of the way a second before eleven hundred pounds of horse hit the ground: she caught Tom's reins before he was up, and in a few seconds, by soft talking, had him quiet.

'That'll fix him,' she grinned.

But 'It's your own fault,' she told me when Susie once tried the same trick. 'She knows you're just learning. No need to flip her over; she'll behave when you've learned to ride her a little more strongly.' Thank heaven for that, because if Rennie had told me to flip Susie over, my pride would have made me attempt it. I scared easily; in fact, I was extremely timid as a rule, but my vanity usually made this fact beside the point.

At any rate, I became a reasonably proficient horseman and even learned to be at ease on horseback, but I never became an enthusiast. The sport was pleasant, but not worth the trouble of learning. Rennie and I covered a good deal of countryside during August; usually we rode out for an hour and a half, dismounted for a fifteen- or twenty-minute rest, and then rode home. By the time we finished unsaddling, grooming, and feeding the animals it was early afternoon: we would pick up the boys, ride back to Wicomico, and eat a late lunch with Joe, during which, bleary-eyed from reading, he would question Rennie or me about my progress.

But the subject at hand is Rennie's clumsy force. On horseback, where there are traditional and even reasonable rules for one's posture every minute of the time, it was a pleasure to see her strong, rather heavy body sitting perfectly controlled in the saddle at the walk or posting to the trot, erect and easy, her cheeks ruddy in the wind, her brown eyes flashing, her short-cropped blond hair bright in the sun. At such times she assumed a strong kind of beauty. But she could not handle her body in situations where there were no rules. When she walked she was continually lurching ahead. Standing still, she never knew what to do with her arms, and she was likely to lean all her weight on one leg and thrust the other awkwardly out at the side. During our brief rest periods, when we usually sat on the ground and smoked cigarettes, she was simply without style or grace: she flopped and fidgeted. I think it was her self-consciousness about this inability to handle her body that prompted her to talk more freely and confidentially during our rides than she would have otherwise, for both Morgans were normally unconfiding people, and Rennie was even inclined to be taciturn when Joe was with us. But in these August mornings we talked a great deal – in that sense, if not in some others, Joe's program was successful – and Rennie's conversation often displayed an analogous clumsy force.

One of our most frequent rides took us to a little creek in a loblolly-pine woods some nine miles from the farm. There the horses could drink on hot days, and often we wore bathing suits under our riding gear and took a short swim when we got there, dressing afterwards, very properly, back in the woods. This was quite pleasant: the little creek was fairly clean and entirely private, shaded by the pines, which also carpeted the ground with a soft layer of slick brown shats. I remarked to Rennie once that it was a pity Joe couldn't enjoy the place with us.

'That's a silly thing to say,' she said, a little upset.

'As all politeness is silly,' I smiled. 'I feel politely sorry for him grinding away at the books while we gallop and splash around.'

'Better not tell him that; he hates pity.'

'That's a silly way to be, isn't it?' I said mildly. 'Joe's funny as hell.'

'What do you mean, Jake?' We were resting after a swim; I was lying comfortably supine under a tree beside the water, chewing on a green pine needle and squinting over at Susie and Tom Brown, tethered nearby. Rennie had been slouched back like a sack of oats against the same tree, smoking, but now she sat up and stared at me with troubled eyes. 'How can you possibly call Joe silly, of all people?'

'Do you mean how can I of all people call Joe silly, or how can I call Joe of all people silly?'

'You know what I mean: how can you call Joe silly? Good God!'

'Oh,' I laughed. 'What could be sillier than getting upset at politeness? If I really felt sorry for him it would be my business, not his; if I'm just saying I feel sorry for him to be polite, there's even less reason to be bothered, since I'm just making so much noise.'

'But that kind of noise is absurd, isn't it?'

'Sure. Where did you and Joe get the notion that things should be scrapped just because they're absurd? That's a silly one for you. For that matter, what could be sillier than this whole aim of living coherently?'

Now I know very well what Joe would have answered to these remarks: let me be the first to admit that they are unintelligible. My purpose was not to make a point, but to observe Rennie. She was aghast.

'You're not serious, Jake! Are you serious?'

'And boy oh boy, what could *possibly* be sillier than his notion that two people in the same house can live that way!'

Rennie stood up. Her expression, I should guess, was that of the Athenians on the morning they discovered that Alcibiades had gelded every marble god in town. She was speechless.

'Sit down,' I said, laughing at her consternation. 'The point is, Rennie, that anybody's position can be silly if you want to think of it that way, and the more consistent, the sillier. It's not silly from Joe's point of view, of course, granted his ends, whatever they are. But frankly I'm appalled that he expects anybody else to go along with him.'

'He doesn't!' Rennie cried. 'That's the whole idea!'

'Why did he cork you once for apologizing, then – twice, I mean. Just for the exercise? Why wouldn't you dare tell him you felt sorry for him even if you did?'

I asked these things without genuine malice, only as a sort of tease, but Rennie, to my surprise, burst into tears.

'Whoa, now!' I said gently. 'I'm terribly sorry I hurt your feelings, Rennie.' I took her arm, but she flinched as if I too had struck her.

'Whoops, I'm sorry I said I'm sorry.'

'Jake, stop it!' she cried, and I observed that the squint-eyed head-shaking was used to express pain as well as hilarity, and this it did quite effectively. When she had control of herself she said, 'You certainly must think our marriage is a strange one, don't you?'

'Damnedest thing I ever saw,' I admitted cheerfully. 'But hell, that's no criticism.'

'But you think I'm a complete zero, don't you?'

Ah. Something in me responded very strongly to this not-especially-moving question of Rennie's.

'I don't know, Rennie. What's your opinion?'

By way of answer Rennie began what turned out to be the history of her alliance with Joe. Her face, chunky enough to begin with, was red and puffy from crying, and in a more critical mood I would have found her unpleasing to look at just then, but it happened that I was really impressed by her breakdown, and the curious sympathy that I'd felt from the time I first heard of her knockout – a sympathy that had little to do with abstract pity for women – was now operating more noticeably in me. This sympathy, too, I observed impersonally and with some amusement from another part of myself, the same part that observed me being not displeased by Rennie's tearful, distracted face. Here is what she told me, edited and condensed:

'You know, I lived in a complete fog from the day I was born until after I met Joe,' she said. 'I was popular and all that, but I swear it was just like I was asleep all through school and college. I wasn't really interested in anything, I never thought about anything, I never even particularly wanted to *do* anything – I didn't even especially enjoy myself. I just dreamed along like a big blob of sleep. If I thought about myself at all, I guess I lived on my potentialities, because I never felt dissatisfied with myself.'

'Sounds wonderful,' I said, not sincerely, because in fact

it sounded commonplace. It interested me only because it fitted well with the unharnessed animal that I had sometimes thought I glimpsed in Rennie.

'You shouldn't say that,' Rennie said flatly. 'It wasn't anything, wonderful or otherwise. When I got out of college I went to New York to work, just because my roommate had a job there and wanted me to go along with her, and that's where I met Joe – he was taking his master's degree at Columbia. We dated for a while, pretty casually: I wasn't much interested in him, and I didn't think he saw much in me. Then one night he grinned at me and told me he wouldn't be taking me out any more. I asked him why not, and he said, "Don't think I'm threatening you; I just don't see any point to it." I said, "Is it because I don't sleep with you?" and he said, "If that was it I'd have gotten a Puerto Rican girl in the first place instead of wasting my time with you."'

'A good line,' I remarked.

'He said he just didn't feel any need for female companionship in itself: companionship to him meant a real exchange of everything on the same level, and sex meant sex, and I wasn't offering him either. You'll have to take my word for it that he wasn't just feeding me a line. He meant it. He said he thought I could probably be wonderful, but that I was shallow as hell as I was, and he didn't expect me to change just for his sake. He couldn't offer me a thing in return that would fit the values I had then, and he wasn't interested in me as I was, so that was that.'

'Did you fling yourself at him then?'

'No. I was hurt, and I told him he wasn't so hot himself.'

'Good!'

'You're silly to say that, Jake.'

'I retract it.'

'Don't you see that right now you're doing all the things that Joe would never do? Those pointless remarks, half teasing me. Joe just shrugged his shoulders at what I said and walked off, leaving me on the bench – he didn't give a damn for courtesy.'

'On the bench?'

'I forgot to tell you. The night all this happened my roommate and I were having a party for some reason or other, and all our New York friends were there – just ordinary people. We'd been drinking and talking silly and horsing around and all: I can't even remember what we did, because I was still in my fog then. About halfway through the evening Joe had said he wanted to go walking, and I hadn't especially wanted to leave the party, but I went anyhow. We walked around in Riverside Park for a while, and when we sat on the bench I thought he was going to neck. He'd never bothered much with that before, and I was kind of surprised. But he came out with this other instead and then walked off. I realized then for the first time what a complete blank I was!

'I went back to the party and got as drunk as I could, and the drunker I got, the more awful everybody seemed. I discovered that I'd never really listened to people before, what they said, and now when I heard them for the first time it was amazing! Everything they said was silly. My roommate was the worst of all – I'd thought she was a pretty bright kid, but now that I was listening to her she talked nothing but nonsense. I thought if I heard another word of their talk I'd die.

'Finally, when I was good and drunk, my roommate tried to get me to take a fellow to bed with me. Everybody else had gone but two fellows – my roommate's boy friend and this other guy – and they'd made up their minds to sleep with us. My roommate was willing if I was willing, and you know, I was disgusted with her, not because of what she wanted to do but because she was too dumb to do anything clearly. But Joe had made me feel so awful and useless, once he'd opened my eyes, that I just didn't give a damn what happened to me; I assumed he was gone for good.

'It was funny as hell, Jake. I was a virgin, but that had never meant anything to me one way or the other. This fellow wasn't a bad guy, just a thin, plain-looking boy who worked in an office somewhere, and with the liquor in him he was pawing and poking me like a real he-man. When I decided I didn't care what happened to me I grabbed him by the hair with both hands and rubbed noses with him. I was bigger than he was, and he fell right off the couch!

'My roommate and her boy friend were already in the bedroom, so I helped the guy take his pants down right in the living room. He was scared to death of me! He wanted to turn off the lights and turn on the music and undress me in the dark and spend a half hour necking before he started and this and that and the other – I called him a fairy and pulled him right down on the rug and bit him till the blood came. You know what he did? He just lay there and hollered!'

'Lord, I don't blame him!' I said.

'Well, I knew if he didn't do something quick it would be too late, because I was hating myself more every second. But the poor boy passed out on the floor. I thought it would be fun to straddle him as he was and give him artificial respiration –'

'My God!'

'I was drunk too, remember. Anyhow, I couldn't make it work right, and to top things off I got sick all over him.'

I shook my head.

'Then I was so disgusted I walked out of the place and went over to Joe's room – I lived on a Hundred and Tenth and he lived on a Hundred and Thirteenth, right near Broadway. I didn't give a damn what *he* did to me then, after this other guy.'

'I won't ask you what he did.'

'What he did was to take one look at me and throw me in the shower, clothes and all: remember I'd vomited all over myself. He turned the cold water on and let me sit there while he fixed some soup and tomato juice, and then he put pajamas and a robe on me and I ate the soup. That was all. I even slept with him that night –'

'Hey, Rennie, you don't have to tell me all this.'

Rennie looked at me, surprised.

'No, I mean *slept*. He didn't make love to me, but he'd never have slept in a chair all night just for propriety's sake. Don't you want to hear this?'

'Sure I do, if you want to tell it to me.'

'I do want to tell it to you. I've never told anybody this stuff before, and Joe and I have never even mentioned it, but nobody ever suggested to me before that our marriage might look silly, and I think it's important to me to tell you about it. I don't believe I ever even thought about it until you started making fun of us.'

'I admire Joe's restraint,' I said uncomfortably.

'Jake, he *is* a Boy Scout in some ways, I guess, but he had another reason, too. When I was sober he told me he just wasn't so hard up he had to take advantage of me when I was helpless. He said he'd like to make love to me, but not just for that – anything we did together we had to do on the same level, understanding it in the same way, for the same purpose, nobody making allowances for anybody else, or he just wasn't interested. But he told me he'd like a more or less permanent relationship.

'"Do you mean marry me?" I said. He said, "It doesn't make a damn to me, Rennie. I'd rather get married, because I don't like the horseshit that goes with most mistress-lover relationships, but you'd have to understand what I mean by a more or less permanent arrangement." What he meant was that we'd stay together as long as each of us could respect everything about the other, absolutely everything, and working for that respect would be our first interest. He wasn't much interested in just having a wife or a mistress, but this other thing he was intensely interested in.

'Do you know what we did? We talked about it almost steadily for two days and two nights, and all that time he wouldn't touch me or let me touch him. I didn't go to work and he didn't go to class, because we both knew this was more important than anything else we'd ever done. He explained his whole attitude toward things, all of it, and asked me more questions about myself than I'd ever been asked before. "The world is full of tons and tons of horseshit, and without any purpose," he said. "Only a few things could ever be valuable to me, and this is one of them." We agreed that on every single subject, no matter how small or apparently trivial, we'd compare our ideas absolutely impersonally and examine them as sharply as we could, at least for the first few years, and he warned me that until I got into the habit of articulating very clearly all the time – until I learned *how* to do that – most of the more reasonable-sounding ideas would be his. We would just try to forget about my ideas . . . He wanted me to go back to school and learn a lot of things, not because he thought scholarship was so all-important, but because that happened to be his field, and if I stayed ignorant of it we'd just get farther and farther apart all the time. There was to be no such thing as shop talk, no such thing as *my* interests and *his* interests. What one of us took seriously both ought to be able to take seriously, and our relationship was first on the list, over any career or ambition or anything else. He told me that he would expect me to make the same heavy demands on myself and on him that he made on himself and would make on me, and that they always had to be the same demands.'

'God!'

'Do you see what that meant? Joe had no friends, because he would expect a lesser degree of the same kind of thing from a friend – expect them to be sharp and clear all the time. So I scrapped every last one of my friends, because you had to make all kinds of allowances for them; you couldn't take them as seriously as all that. I had to completely change my mind not only about my parents, but about my whole childhood. I'd thought it was a pretty ideal childhood, but now I saw it as just so much cottonwool. I threw out every opinion I owned, because I couldn't defend them. I think I completely erased myself, Jake, right down to nothing, so I could start over. And you know, the thing is I don't think I'll ever really get to be what Joe wants – I'll always be uncertain, and he'll always be able to explain his positions better than I can – but there's nothing else to do but what I've done. As Joe says, it's all there is.'

I shook my head. 'Sounds bleak, Rennie.'

'It's not!' she protested. 'Joe's wonderful; I wouldn't go back if I could. Don't forget I chose to do this: I could walk out any time, and he'd support the kids and me.'

But it seemed to me that she chose it as I chose my position in the Progress and Advice Room.

'Joe's remarkable,' I agreed, 'if you go for that sort of thing.'

'Jake, he's wonderful!' Rennie repeated. 'I've never seen anybody anything like Joe, I swear. He thinks as straight as an arrow about everything. Sometimes I think that nothing Joe could think about would ever be worth the sharpness of his mind. This will sound ridiculous to you, Jake, but I think of Joe as I'd think of God. Even when he makes a mistake, his reasons for doing what he did are clearer and sharper than anybody else's. Don't laugh at that.'

'He's intolerant,' I suggested.

'So is God! But you know *why* Joe's intolerant: he's only intolerant of stupidity in people he cares about! Jake, I'm better off now than I was; I wasn't anything before. What have I lost?'

I grinned. 'I suppose I should say something about your individuality. People are supposed to mention individuality at times like this.'

'Joe and I have talked about that, Jake. God, please of all things don't accuse him of being naïve! He says that one of the hardest and most essential things is to be aware of all the possible alternatives to your position.'

'How did he mention it?'

'First of all, suppose everyone's personality *is* unique. Does it follow that because a thing is unique it's valuable? You're saying that it's better to be a real Rennie MacMahon than an imitation Joe Morgan, but that's not self-evident, Jake; not at all. It's just romantic. I'd rather be a lousy Joe Morgan than a first-rate Rennie MacMahon. To hell with pride. This unique-personality business is another thing that's no absolute.'

'To quote the gospel to you, Rennie,' I said: 'it doesn't follow either that because a thing's not absolute it isn't valuable.'

'Stop it, Jake!' Rennie was getting upset again.

'Why? You could just as well take the position that even though Rennie MacMahon wasn't intrinsically valuable, she was all there was. Let me ask you a question, Rennie: why do you think Joe is interested in me? He must know I'm not going to go along with any program of his. I make allowances for everybody, most of all for myself. God, do I make allowances for Joe! And certainly *he's* been making allowances for that. Why was he so anxious to have me talk to you? Didn't he know I'd tell you I think this whole business is either funny or appalling, depending on my mood?'

'Jake, you haven't seen how strong Joe is, I guess. That's the finest thing of all: his strength. He's so strong that he wouldn't want me if anybody could convince me I was making a mistake.'

'I don't see much strength in this premeditated horseback-riding thing. Anybody who didn't know better would think he was trying to fix me up with you.'

Rennie didn't flinch. 'He's so strong he can afford to look weak sometimes, Jake. Nobody is as strong as Joe is.'

'He's an Eagle Scout, all right,' I said cheerfully.

'Even that,' Rennie said; 'he's so strong he can even afford to be a caricature of his strength sometimes, and not care. Not many people are that strong.'

'Am I supposed to be a devil's advocate, then? I'd be a damned good one.'

Now Rennie was uneasy. 'I don't know. I guess this will insult you, Jake. I honestly don't know why Joe's so taken with you. He's never been interested in anybody before – we haven't had any friends, or wanted any – but he said after your interview that he was interested in you, and after your first few conversations he was pretty much excited. What he told me was that it would be good for me to get to know a first-rate mind that was totally different from his, but there must have been more to it than that.'

'I'm flattered,' I said, and to my mild annoyance I really was. 'You think there must be more to it than that because you can't see anything first-rate about me?'

'Never mind that. What scares me sometimes is that in a lot of ways you're *not* totally different from Joe: you're just like him. I've even heard the same sentences from each of you at different times. You work from a lot of the same premises.' Rennie had been getting more nervous all the time she spoke. Now she shuddered. 'Jake, I don't like you!'

This calmed me: my own discomfort disappeared at this pronouncement, and my mood changed as if by magic. I was now a strong, quiet, half-sinister Jacob Horner, nothing like the wise-cracking fop who'd heard the earlier part of Rennie's history. I smiled at Rennie.

'I wish Joe hadn't thought of this idea,' she said. 'I don't like anything about it. I don't want to be unfair to you, Jake, but I think I was much happier a month ago, before we met you.'

'Tell Joe about it.'

The squint-eyed head-whipping, not in hilarity.

'Joe thinks I've come farther than I have,' she said tersely.

63

'Already I feel guilty about telling you so much. That was weak; almost like I've been dishonest with him.'

'I'll tell him we've talked about it,' I said.

Rennie breathed shakily and shook her head.

'That's it, see? I can't tell you not to tell him, but if you did I'd be lost. I'd never catch up again.'

I could see that easily enough: it was a little germ of Rennie MacMahon that had made the confidences.

'You must have realized that some people would think the whole Morgan plan was just plain funny.'

'Of course I did. But they were just "some people". What scares me is that anybody could grant all of Joe's premises – our premises – understand them and grant them and *then* laugh at us.'

'Maybe that's what Joe was after.'

'It could be, but if it was he overestimated me! I can't take it. He could take it and not worry – you remember when he was talking about the kids' physical efficiency and you suggested that they snap each other's pajamas? That's what I meant when I said he's strong enough to be a caricature of himself – all the things about him that you've made fun of. When you suggested that, it scared me, really scared me. I didn't know what he'd do. God, Jake, he can be violent! But he just laughed and had the kids do what you said.'

'He's got you scared to death, Rennie. Is it because of the time he socked you?'

Every time I mentioned this Rennie wept. That blow had struck harder than God imagined.

'I'm not that strong, Jake!' she cried; 'it's my fault, but I'm not strong enough for him.'

Said I, 'I understand that God is a bachelor.'

Like Joe's earlier disquisition on values, this history of the Morgans' domestic problems was not delivered to me all in so handy a piece as I've presented it here. What happened was that, once it got started, our daily equitations changed their character. Now we generally rode silently and with amusing purposefulness directly to the little creek in the pine grove for our talk, and spent as much as an hour there instead of twenty minutes. It is interesting to note that Rennie never spoke of the matter while riding: in fact it was with ill-concealed lack of relish that she mounted Tom Brown every morning. But we always headed for the grove – the horses would doubtless have gone there without our direction, and I will admit that more than once Susie and I took the initiative in heading that way.

Back at the Morgan apartment Rennie would clam up completely unless Joe questioned her directly about our morning. This he did often, and when it became necessary Rennie would lie grimly to him about the nature of our conversation. Grimly and clumsily: it was not pretty to watch. Joe listened carefully, and, as a rule, noncommittally, and sometimes smiled. Probably he knew she was lying, although it is hard for one who is aware of the truth to judge effectively its disguise. But if he knew, it didn't worry him. He was indeed very strong.

He and I got along better all the time. He argued exuberantly with me about politics, history, music, integrity, logic – everything; we played tennis and gin rummy together, and I proofread two or three improperly split infinitives out of the manuscript of his dissertation – an odd, brilliant study of the saving roles of innocence and energy in American political and economic history. My attitude toward Joe, Rennie, and all the rest of the universe changed as frequently as Laocoön's smile: some days I was a stock left-wing Democrat, other days I professed horror at the very concept of reform in anything; some days I was ascetic, some days Rabelaisian; some days super-rational, some days anti-rational. Each time I defended myself vehemently (except on my uncommunicative days), and Joe laughed and took me to pieces. It was a pleasant enough way to kill the afternoons, I thought, but Rennie grew increasingly morose as August progressed. At the pine grove she shuddered, rationalized, talked, and wept.

She was caught.

As for me, I was still undecided whether what I had learned of her unusual self-effacement evidenced a great weakness or an extraordinary strength; there is no way to gauge such things when they are carried out so completely. But I found her altogether, if inconsistently, more attractive, I believe, and the observing part of me now thought that it pretty well understood the attracted part (many, many other 'parts' were totally unaffected one way or the other): I think Rennie's attraction for me lay in the fact that, alone of all the women I knew, if not all the people, she had peered deeply into herself and had found *nothing*. When such is the case, the question of integrity becomes meaningless.

On August 31, 1953, her attitude seemed to have changed. It had rained until early afternoon, and so we took our ride after supper, while Joe was at his Boy Scout meeting in Wicomico. That evening she held Tom Brown to a walk – rode him almost apprehensively, I thought, without force or style, and chatted idly about nothing during the ride. But in the pine grove she was calm.

'Everything's okay, Jake.' She smiled, not warmly.

'What's okay?'

'I'm still sorry I ran at the mouth so, but that's over with now.'

'Oh?'

'You know, I really was frightened at you for a while. Sometimes it seemed to me that I couldn't really say to myself that Joe was stronger than you. Whenever his arguments were ready to catch you, you weren't there any more, and worse than that, even when he destroyed a position of yours it seemed to me that he hadn't really touched *you* – there wasn't that much of you in any of your positions.'

'You're getting very sharp,' I laughed.

'That, right there,' she said, catching me up: 'all you'd do was laugh when he took the props out of your argument. Then just lately I began to wonder, "If his opinions aren't him, what *is* him?"'

'Bad grammar.'

Rennie ignored me. 'You know what I've come to think, Jake? I think you don't exist at all. There's too many of you. It's more than just masks that you put on and take off – we all have masks. But you're different all the way through, every time. You cancel yourself out. You're more like somebody in a dream. You're not strong and you're not weak. You're nothing.'

I thought it appropriate to say nothing.

'Two things have happened, Jake,' Rennie said coolly. 'One is that I'm pretty sure I'm pregnant again – my period is a week late, and I'm usually regular. The other thing is that I've decided I don't have to think about you or deal with you any more, because you don't exist. That's Joe's superiority.

'One day last week,' she went on, 'I either had a dream, or else I was just daydreaming, that for the past few weeks Joe had become friendly with the Devil, and was having fun arguing with him and playing tennis with him, to test his own strength. Don't laugh.'

'I'm not laughing.'

'I thought Joe had invited the Devil to test me, too – probably it was because you mentioned *devil's advocate* that time. But this Devil scared me, because I wasn't that strong yet, and what was a game for Joe was a terrible fight for me.' Here Rennie faltered a bit. 'Then when Joe saw how it was, he told me that the Devil wasn't real, and that he had conjured up the Devil out of his own strength, just as God might do. Then he made me pregnant again so I'd know *he* was the one who was real and I wouldn't be scared, and so –'

(This pretty conceit Rennie had started calmly, but as she told it she grew more and more emotional – it was a thing she'd obviously worked out for herself with care to salve the hurt of her lying – until at the end her apparent new control was gone, and she shook with tears.)

' – and so I'd grow to be just as strong as he is, and stronger than somebody who isn't even real!'

But she wasn't. I stroked her hair. Her teeth were actually chattering.

'Oh, God, I wish Joe was here!' she cried.

'You know what he'd say, Rennie. Crying is one of the things that are beside the point: you're just evading the question. This Devil business is too easy. It lets you get rid of me on false pretenses.'

'You're not *real* like Joe is! He's the same man today he was yesterday, all the way through. He's genuine! That's the difference.'

She was sitting on the ground, her head on her knees, and still I stroked her hair.

'But not me,' I said.

'No!'

'How about you?'

For answer she whipped her head from side to side shortly.

'I don't know. Joe's strong enough to take care of me, I guess. I don't care.'

This was absurd and we both knew it. I confined my argument to stroking her hair, which made her shudder. We sat thus for perhaps five minutes without saying anything. Then Rennie got up.

'I hope to Christ you know what you're doing to us, Jake,' she said.

I made no reply.

'Joe's real enough to handle you,' she said. 'He's real enough for both of us.'

'Nothing plus one is one,' I said agreeably.

Now Rennie was tight-lipped, and rubbed her stomach nervously. 'That's right,' she said.

But a most curious thing happened shortly afterwards. We took the horses back to the stable and drove home, neither of us saying an unnecessary word. It was as though a great many things were suspended in delicate equilibrium – the rapid crowding on of dusk upon an entirely empty summer sky, with its attendant noiseless rush as of the very planet plunging, doubtless helped – and one felt hushed, for a word might knock the cosmos out of kilter. It was dark when we parked in front of the Morgans' apartment and I escorted Rennie across the deep lawn.

'Joe's home,' I said, observing a light behind the closed blinds of the living room. I heard Rennie, beside me, sniff, and realized that she'd been crying some more.

'We'd better wait a minute before you go in, don't you think?'

Rennie made no answer, but she stopped and we stood quietly just outside the door. I had no desire to touch her. I bounced idly on my heels, singing to myself *Pepsi-Cola hits the spot*. I noticed that although the venetian blind was closed, it was not lowered completely: a bar of light streamed across the grass from an inch-high slit along the window sill.

'Want to eavesdrop?' I whispered impulsively to Rennie. 'Come on, it's great! See the animals in their natural habitat.'

Rennie looked shocked. 'What for?'

'You mean you never spy on people when they're alone? It's wonderful! Come on, be a sneak! It's the most unfair thing you can do to a person.'

'You disgust me, Jake!' Rennie hissed. 'He's just reading! You don't know Joe at all, do you?'

'What does that mean?'

'*Real* people aren't any different when they're alone. No masks. What you see of them is authentic.'

'Horseshit. Nobody's authentic. Let's look.'

'No.'

'I am.' I tiptoed over to the window, stooped down, and peered into the living room. Immediately I beckoned to Rennie.

'What is it?' she whispered.

'Come here!' A sneak should snicker: I snickered.

Reluctantly she came over to the window and peeped in beside me.

It is indeed the grossest of injustices to observe a person who believes himself to be alone. Joe Morgan, back from his Boy Scout meeting, had evidently intended to do some reading, for there were books lying open on the writing table and on the floor beside the bookcase. But Joe wasn't reading. He was standing in the exact center of the bare room, fully dressed, smartly executing military commands. About *face!* Right *dress!* 'Ten-*shun!* Parade *rest!* He saluted briskly, his cheeks blown out and his tongue extended, and then proceeded to cavort about the room – spinning, pirouetting, bowing, leaping, kicking. I watched entranced by his performance, for I cannot say that in my strangest moments (and a bachelor has strange ones) I have surpassed him. Rennie trembled from head to foot.

Ah! Passing a little mirror on the wall, Joe caught his own eye. What? What? Ahoy there! He stepped close, curtsied to himself, and thrust his face to within two inches of the glass. Mr Morgan, is it? Howdy do, Mr Morgan. Blah bloo blah. *Oo-o-o-o* blubble thlwurp. He mugged antic faces at himself, sklurching up his eye corners, zbloogling his mouth about,

69

glubbling his cheeks. Mither Morgle. Nyoing nyang nyumpie. Vglibble vglobble vglup. Vgliggy*bloo*! Thlucky thlucky, thir.

He jabbed his spectacles back on his nose. Had he heard some sound? No. He went to the writing table and apparently resumed his reading, his back turned to us. The show, then, was over. Ah, but one moment – yes. He turned slightly, and we could see: his tongue gripped purposefully between his lips at the side of his mouth, Joe was masturbating and picking his nose at the same time. I believe he also hummed a sprightly tune in rhythm with his work.

Rennie was destroyed. She closed her eyes and pressed her forehead against the window sill. I stood beside her, out of the light from the brilliant living room, and stroked and stroked her hair, speaking softly in her ear the wordless, grammarless language she'd taught me to calm horses with.

Chapter Six
In September it was time to see the Doctor

In September it was time to see the Doctor again: I drove out to the Remobilization Farm one morning during the first week of the month. Because the weather was fine, a number of the Doctor's other patients, quite old men and women, were taking the air, seated in their wheel chairs or in the ancient cane chairs along the porch. As usual, they greeted me a little suspiciously with their eyes; visitors of any sort, but particularly of my age, were rare at the farm, and were not welcomed cordially. Ignoring their stony glances, I went inside to pay my respects to Mrs Dockey, the receptionist-nurse. I found her in consultation with the Doctor himself.

'Good day, Horner,' the Doctor beamed.

'Good morning, sir. Good morning, Mrs Dockey.'

That large, masculine woman nodded shortly without speaking – her custom – and the Doctor told me to wait for him in the Progress and Advice Room, which, along with the dining room, the kitchen, the reception room, the bathroom, and the Treatment Room constituted the first floor of the old frame house. Upstairs the partitions between the original bedrooms had been removed to form two dormitories, one for the men and one for the women. The Doctor had his own small bedroom upstairs too, and there were two bathrooms. I did not know at the time where Mrs Dockey slept, or whether she slept at the farm at all. She was a most uncommunicative woman.

I had first met the Doctor quite by chance – a fortunate chance – on the morning of March 17, 1951, in what passes for the grand concourse of the Pennsylvania Railroad Station in Baltimore. It happened to be the day after my twenty-eighth birthday, and I was sitting on one of the benches in the station with my suitcase beside me. I was in an unusual condition: I couldn't move. On the previous day

I had checked out of my room in the Bradford Apartment Hotel, an establishment on St Paul and Thirty-third streets owned by the Johns Hopkins University. I had roomed there since September of the year before, when, half-heartedly, I matriculated as a graduate student at the university and began work on the degree that I was scheduled to complete the following June.

But on March 16, my birthday, with my oral examination passed but my master's thesis not even begun, I packed my suitcase and left the room to take a trip somewhere. Because I have learned to be not much interested in causes and bio-graphies, I ascribe this move to simple birthday despond-ency, a phenomenon sufficiently familiar to enough people so that I need not explain it further. Birthday despondency, let us say, had reminded me that I had no self-convincing reason for continuing for a moment longer to do any of the things that I happened to be doing with myself as of seven o'clock in the evening of March 16, 1951. I had thirty dollars and some change in my pocket: when my suitcase was filled I hailed a taxi, went to Pennsylvania Station, and stood in the ticket line.

'Yes?' said the ticket agent when my turn came.

'Ah – this will sound theatrical to you,' I said with some embarrassment, 'but I have thirty dollars or so to take a trip on. Would you mind telling me some of the places I could ride to from here for, say, twenty dollars?'

The man showed no surprise at my request. He gave me an understanding if unsympathetic look and consulted some sort of rate scales.

'You can go to Cincinnati, Ohio,' he declared. 'You can go to Crestline, Ohio. And let's see, now – you can go to Dayton, Ohio. Or Lima, Ohio. That's a nice town. I have some of my wife's people up around Lima, Ohio. Want to go there?'

'Cincinatti, Ohio,' I repeated, unconvinced. 'Crestline, Ohio; Dayton, Ohio; and Lima, Ohio. Thank you very much. I'll make up my mind and come back.'

So I left the ticket window and took a seat on one of the benches in the middle of the concourse to make up my mind. And it was there that I simply ran out of motives, as a car runs out of gas. There was no reason to go to Cincinnati, Ohio. There was no reason to go to Crestline, Ohio. Or Dayton, Ohio; or Lima, Ohio. There was no reason, either, to go back to the Bradford Apartment Hotel, or for that matter to go anywhere. There was no reason to do anything. My eyes, as Winckelmann said inaccurately of the eyes of the Greek statues, were sightless, gazing on eternity, fixed on ultimacy, and when that is the case there is no reason to do anything – even to change the focus of one's eyes. Which is perhaps why the statues stand still. It is the malady *cosmopsis*, the cosmic view, that afflicted me. When one has it, one is frozen like the bullfrog when the hunter's light strikes him full in the eyes, only with cosmopsis there is no hunter, and no quick hand to terminate the moment – there's only the light.

Shortsighted animals all around me hurried in and out of doors leading down to the tracks; trains arrived and departed. Women, children, salesmen, soldiers, and redcaps hurried across the concourse toward immediate destinations, but I sat immobile on the bench. After a while Cincinnati, Crestline, Dayton, and Lima dropped from my mind, and their place was taken by that test pattern of my consciousness, *Pepsi-Cola hits the spot*, intoned with silent oracularity. But it, too, petered away into the void, and nothing appeared in its stead.

If you look like a vagrant it is difficult to occupy a train-station bench all night long, even in a busy terminal, but if you are reasonably well dressed, have a suitcase at your side, and sit erect, policemen and railroad employees will not disturb you. I was sitting in the same place, in the same position, when the sun struck the grimy station windows next morning, and in the nature of the case I suppose I would have remained thus indefinitely, but about nine o'clock a small, dapper fellow in his fifties stopped in front of me and stared directly into my eyes. He was bald, dark-eyed, and dignified, a Negro, and wore a graying mustache and a trim tweed suit to match. The fact that I did not stir even the pupils of my eyes under his gaze is an index to my condition, for ordinarily I find it next to impossible to return the stare of a stranger.

'Weren't you sitting here like this last night?' he asked me sharply. I did not reply. He came close, bent his face down toward mine, and moved an upthrust finger back and forth about two inches from my eyes. But my eyes did not follow his finger. He stepped back and regarded me critically, then suddenly snapped his fingers almost on the point of my nose. I blinked involuntarily, although my head did not jerk back.

'Ah,' he said, and regarded me again. 'Does this happen to you often, young man?'

Perhaps because of the brisk assuredness of his voice, the *no* welled up in me like a belch. And I realized as soon as I deliberately held my tongue (there being in the last analysis no reason to answer his question at all) that as of that moment I was artificially prolonging what had been a genuine physical immobility. Not to choose at all is unthinkable: what I had done before was simply choose not to act, since I had been at rest when the situation arose. Now, however, it was harder – 'more of a choice' – to hold my tongue than to croak out something that filled my mouth, and so after a moment I said, 'No.'

Then, of course, the trance was broken. I was embarrassed, and rose quickly and stiffly from the bench to leave.

'Where will you go?' my examiner asked with a smile.

'What?' I frowned at him. 'Oh – get a bus home, I guess. See you around.'

'Wait.' His voice was mild, but entirely commanding. I stopped. 'Won't you have coffee with me? I'm a physician, and I'd be interested in discussing your case with you.'

'I don't have any case,' I said awkwardly. 'I was just – sitting there for a minute or so.'

'No. I saw you there last night at ten o'clock when I came in from New York,' the doctor said. 'You were sitting in the same position. You *were* paralyzed, weren't you?'

I laughed shortly. 'Well, if you want to call it that, but there's nothing wrong with me. I don't know what came over me.'

'Of course you don't, but I do. My specialty is various sorts of physical immobility. You're lucky I came by this morning.'

'Oh, you don't understand –'

'I brought you out of it, didn't I?' he said cheerfully.

'Here.' He took a fifty-cent piece from his pocket and handed it to me – I accepted it before I realized what he'd done. 'I can't go into that lounge over there. Get two cups of coffee for us and we'll sit here a minute and decide what to do.'

'No, listen, I –'

'Why not?' he laughed. 'Go on, now. I'll wait here.'

Why not, indeed?

'I have my own money,' I protested lamely, offering him his fifty-cent piece back, but he waved me away and lit a cigar.

'Now hurry up,' he ordered calmly, around the cigar. 'Move fast, or you might get stuck again. Don't think of anything but the coffee I've asked you to get.'

'All right.' I turned and walked with dignity toward the lounge, just off the concourse.

'Fast!' the doctor laughed behind me. I flushed, and impulsively quickened my step.

While I waited for the coffee I tried to feel the curiosity about my invalidity and my rescuer that it seemed appropriate I should feel, but I was too weary in mind and body to wonder at anything. I do not mean to suggest that my condition had been unpleasant – it was entirely anesthetic in its advanced stage, and even a little bit pleasant in its inception – but it was fatiguing, as an overlong sleep is fatiguing, and one had the same reluctance to throw it off that one has to finally get out of bed when one has slept around the clock. Indeed, as the Doctor had warned (it was at this time, not knowing my benefactor's name, that I began to think of him with a capital *D*), to slip back into immobility at the coffee counter would have been extremely easy: I felt my mind begin to settle into rigidity, and only the clerk's peremptory 'Thirty cents, please,' brought me back to action – luckily, because the Doctor could not have entered the white lounge to help me. I paid the clerk and took the paper cups of coffee back to the bench.

'Good,' the Doctor said. 'Sit down.'

I hesitated. I was standing directly in front of him.

'Here!' he laughed. 'On this side! You're like the donkey between two piles of straw!'

I sat where ordered and we sipped our coffee. I rather

75

expected to be asked questions about myself, but the Doctor ignored me.

'Thanks for the coffee,' I said uncertainly. He glanced at me impassively for a moment, as though I were a hitherto silent parrot who had suddenly blurted a brief piece of nonsense, and then he returned his attention to the crowd in the station.

'I have one or two calls to make yet before we catch the bus,' he announced without looking at me. 'Won't take long. I wanted to see if you were still here before I left town.'

'What do you mean, catch the bus?'

'You'll have to come over to the farm – my Remobilization Farm over near Wicomico – for a day or so, for observation,' he explained coldly. 'You don't have anything else to do, do you?'

'Well, I should get back to the university, I guess. I'm a student.'

'Oh,' he chuckled. 'Might as well forget about that for a while. You can come back in a few days if you want to.'

'Say, you know, really, I think you must have a misconception about what was wrong with me a while ago. I'm not a paralytic. It's all just silly, really. I'll explain it to you if you want to hear it.'

'No, you needn't bother. No offense intended, but the things you think are important probably aren't even relevant at all. I'm never very curious about my patients' histories. Rather not hear them, in fact – just clutters things up. It doesn't much matter what caused it anyhow, does it?' He grinned. 'My farm's like a nunnery in that respect – I never bother about why my patients come there. Forget about causes; I'm no psychoanalyst.'

'But that's what I mean, sir,' I explained, laughing uncomfortably. 'There's nothing physically wrong with me.'

'Except that you couldn't move,' the Doctor said. 'What's your name?'

'Jacob Horner. I'm a graduate student up at Johns Hopkins –'

'Ah, ah,' he warned. 'No biography, Jacob Horner.' He finished his coffee and stood up. 'Come on, now, we'll get a cab. Bring your suitcase along'

'Oh, wait now!'

'Yes?'

I fumbled for protests: the thing was absurd.

'Well – this is absurd.'

'So?'

I hesitated, blinking, wetting my lips.

'Think, think!' the Doctor said brusquely.

My mind raced like a car engine when the clutch is disengaged. There was no answer.

'Well, I – are you sure it's all right?' I had no idea what my question signified.

The Doctor made a short, derisive sound (a sort of 'Huf!') and turned away. I shook my head – at the same moment aware that I was watching myself act bewildered – and then fetched up my suitcase and followed after him, out to the line of taxicabs at the curb.

Thus began my *alliance* with the Doctor. He stopped first at an establishment on North Howard Street, where he ordered two wheel chairs, three pairs of crutches, and certain other apparatus for the farm, and then at a pharmaceutical supply house on South Paca Street, where he also made some sort of order. Then we went to the W.B. & A. bus terminal on Howard and Redwood streets and took the Red Star bus to the Eastern Shore. The Doctor's Mercury station wagon was parked at the Wicomico bus depot; he drove to the little settlement of Vineland, about three miles south of Wicomico, turned off on to a secondary road, and finally drove up a long, winding dirt lane to the Remobilization Farm, an aged but clean-painted white clapboard house in a clump of oaks on a knoll overlooking some creek or other. The patients on the porch, senile men and women, welcomed the Doctor with querulous enthusiasm, and he returned their greeting. Me they regarded with open suspicion, if not hostility, but the Doctor made no explanation of my presence – for that matter, I should have been hard put to explain it myself.

Inside I was introduced to the muscular Mrs Dockey and taken to the Progress and Advice Room for my first interview. I waited alone in that clean room, bare, but not really clinical-looking – just an empty white room in a farmhouse – for some ten minutes, and then the Doctor entered and took his seat very much in front of me. He had donned a white medical-looking jacket and appeared entirely official and competent.

'I'll make a few things clear very quickly, Jacob,' he said, leaning forward with his hands on his knees and rolling his cigar around in his mouth between sentences. 'The farm, as you can see, is designed for the treatment of paralytics. Most of my patients are old people, but you mustn't infer from that that this is a nursing home for the aged. It's not. Perhaps you noticed when we drove up that my patients like me. It has happened several times in the past that for one reason or another I have seen fit to change the location of the farm. Once it was outside of Troy, New York; another time near Fond du Lac, Wisconsin; another time near Biloxi, Mississippi. And we've been other places, too. Nearly all the patients I have on the farm now have been with me at least since Fond du Lac, and if I should have to move tomorrow to Helena, Montana, or Far Rockaway, most of them would go with me, and not because they haven't anywhere else to go. But don't think I have an equal love for them. They're just more or less interesting problems in immobility, for which I find it satisfying to work out therapies. I tell this to you, but not to them, because your problem is such that this information is harmless. And for that matter, you've no way of knowing whether anything I've said or will say is the truth, or just a part of my general therapy for you. You can't even tell whether your doubt in this matter is an honestly founded doubt or just a part of your treatment: access to the truth, Jacob, even belief that there is such a thing, is itself therapeutic or antitherapeutic, depending on the problem. The reality of your problem itself is all that you can be sure of.'

'Yes, sir.'

'Why do you say that?' the Doctor asked.

'Say what?'

'"Yes, sir." Why do you say "Yes, sir"?'

'Oh – I was just acknowledging what you said before.'

'Acknowledging the truth of what I said or merely the fact that I said it?'

'Well,' I hesitated, flustered, 'I don't know, sir,'

'You don't know whether to say you were acknowledging

the truth of my statements, when actually you weren't, or to say you were simply acknowledging that I said something, at the risk of offending me by the implication that you don't agree with any of it. Eh?'

'Oh, I agree with *some* of it,' I assured him.

'What parts of it do you agree with? Which statements?'

'I don't know: I guess –' I searched my mind hastily to remember even one thing that he'd said. He regarded my floundering coldly for a minute and then went on as if the interruption hadn't occurred.

'Agapotherapy – devotion therapy – is often useful with older patients,' he said. 'One of the things that work toward restoring their mobility is devotion to some figure, a doctor or other kind of administrator. It keeps their allegiances from becoming divided. For that reason I'd move the farm occasionally even if other circumstances didn't make it desirable. It does them good to decide to follow me. Agapotherapy is one small therapy in a great number, some consecutive, some simultaneous, which are exercised on the patients. No two patients have the same schedule of therapies, because no two people are ever paralyzed in the same way. The authors of medical textbooks,' he added with some contempt, 'like everyone else, can reach generality only by ignoring enough particularity. They speak of paralysis, and the treatment of paralytics, as though one read the textbook and then followed the rules for getting paralyzed properly. There is no such thing as *paralysis*, Jacob. There is only paralyzed Jacob Horner. And I don't *treat* paralysis: I schedule therapies to mobilize John Doe or Jacob Horner, as the case may be. That's why I ignore you when you say you aren't paralyzed as the people out on the porch are paralyzed. I don't treat your paralysis; I treat paralyzed you. Please don't say, "Yes, sir."'

The urge to acknowledge is almost irresistible, but I managed to sit silent and not even nod.

'There are several things wrong with you, I think. I daresay you don't know the seating capacity of the Cleveland Municipal Stadium, do you?'

'*What?*'

The Doctor did not smile. 'You suggest that my question is

absurd, when you have no grounds for knowing whether it is or not – you obviously heard me and understood me. Probably you want to delay my learning that you *don't* know the seating capacity of Cleveland Municipal Stadium, since your vanity would be ruffled if the question *weren't* absurd, and even if it were. It makes no difference whether it is or not, Jacob Horner: it's a question asked you by your doctor. Now, is there any ultimate reason why the Cleveland Stadium shouldn't seat fifty-seven thousand, four hundred eighty-eight people?'

'None that I can think of,' I grinned.

'Don't pretend to be amused. Of course there's not. Is there any reason why it shouldn't seat eighty-eight thousand, four hundred seventy-five people?'

'No, sir.'

'Indeed not. Then as far as Reason is concerned its seating capacity could be almost anything. Logic will never give you the answer to my question. Only Knowledge of the World will answer it. There's no ultimate reason at all why the Cleveland Stadium should seat exactly seventy-seven thousand, seven hundred people, but it happens that it does. There's no reason in the long run why Italy shouldn't be shaped like a sausage instead of a boot, but that doesn't happen to be the case. *The world is everything that is the case*, and what the case is is not a matter of logic. If you don't simply *know* how many people can sit in the Cleveland Municipal Stadium, you have no real reason for choosing one number over another, assuming you can make a choice at all – do you understand? But if you have some Knowledge of the World you may be able to say, "Seventy-seven thousand, seven hundred," just like that. No choice is involved.'

'Well,' I said, 'you'd still have to choose whether to answer the question or not, or whether to answer it correctly, even if you knew the right answer, wouldn't you?'

The Doctor's tranquil stare told me my question was somehow silly, though it seemed reasonable enough to me.

'One of the things you'll have to do,' he said dryly, 'is buy a copy of the *World Almanac* for 1951 and begin to study it scrupulously. This is intended as a discipline, and you'll have to pursue it diligently, perhaps for a number of years.

Informational Therapy is one of a number of therapies we'll have to initiate at once.'

I shook my head and chuckled genially. 'Do all your patients memorize the *World Almanac*, Doctor?'

I might as well not have spoken.

'Mrs Dockey will show you to your bed,' the Doctor said, rising to go. 'I'll speak to you again presently.' At the door he stopped and added, 'One, perhaps two, of the older men may attempt familiarities with you at night up in the dormitory. They're on Sexual Therapy, and I find it useful and convenient in their cases to suggest homosexual affairs rather than heterosexual ones. But unless you're accustomed to that sort of thing I don't think you should accept their advances. You should keep your life as uncomplicated as possible, at least for a while. Reject them gently, and they'll go back to each other.'

There was little I could say. After a while Mrs Dockey showed me my bed in the men's dormitory. I was not introduced to my roommates, nor did I introduce myself. In fact (though since then I've come to know them better), during the three days that I remained at the farm not a dozen words were exchanged between us, much less homosexual advances. When I left they were uniformly glad to see me go.

The Doctor spent two or three one-hour sessions with me each day. He asked me virtually nothing about myself; the conversations consisted mostly of harangues against the medical profession for its stupidity in matters of paralysis, and imputations that my condition was the result of defective character and intelligence.

'You claim to be unable to choose in many situations,' he said once. 'Well, I claim that that inability is only theoretically inherent in situations, when there's no chooser. Given a particular chooser, it's unthinkable. So, since the inability *was* displayed in your case, the fault lies not in the situation but in the fact that there was no chooser. Choosing is existence: to the extent that you don't choose, you don't exist. Now, everything we do must be oriented toward choice and action. It doesn't matter whether this action is more or less reasonable than inaction; the point is that it is its opposite.'

'But why should anyone prefer it?' I asked.

'There's no reason why you should prefer it,' he said, 'and no reason why you shouldn't. One is a patient simply because one chooses a condition that only therapy can bring one to, not because any one condition is inherently better than another. All my therapies for a while will be directed toward making you conscious of your existence. It doesn't matter whether you act constructively or even consistently, so long as you act. It doesn't matter to the case whether your character is admirable or not, so long as you think you have one.'

'I don't understand why you should choose to treat anyone, Doctor,' I said.

'That's my business, not yours.'

And so it went. I was charged, directly or indirectly, with everything from intellectual dishonesty and vanity to nonexistence. If I protested, the Doctor observed that my protests indicated my belief in the truth of his statements. If I only listened glumly, he observed that my glumness indicated my belief in the truth of his statements.

'All right, then,' I said at last, giving up. 'Everything you say is true. All of it is the truth.'

The Doctor listened calmly. 'You don't know what you're talking about,' he said. 'There's no such thing as truth as you conceive it.'

These apparently pointless interviews did not constitute my only activity at the farm. Before every meal the other patients and I were made to perform various calisthenics under the direction of Mrs Dockey. For the older patients these were usually very simple – perhaps a mere nodding of the head or flexing of the arms – although some of the old folks could execute really surprising feats: one gentleman in his seventies was an excellent rope climber, and two old ladies turned agile somersaults. For each Mrs Dockey prescribed different activities; my own special prescription was to keep some sort of visible motion going all the time. If nothing else, I was constrained to keep a finger wiggling or a foot tapping, say, during mealtimes, when more involved movements would have made eating difficult. And I was told to rock from side to side in my bed all night long: not an unreasonable request, as it happened, for I did this habitually anyhow – a habit carried over from childhood.

'Motion! Motion!' the Doctor would say, almost exalted. 'You must be always *conscious* of motion!'

There were special diets and, for many patients, special drugs. I learned of Nutritional Therapy, Medicinal Therapy, Surgical Therapy, Dynamic Therapy, Informational Therapy, Conversational Therapy, Sexual Therapy, Devotional Therapy, Occupational and Preoccupational Therapy, Virtue and Vice Therapy, Theotherapy and Atheotherapy – and, later, Mythotherapy, Philosophical Therapy, Scriptotherapy, and many, many other therapies practiced in various combinations and sequences by the patients. Everything, to the Doctor, is either therapeutic, anti-therapeutic, or irrelevant. He is a kind of super-pragmatist.

At the end of my last session – it had been decided that I was to return to Baltimore experimentally, to see whether and how soon my immobility might recur – the Doctor gave me some parting instructions.

'It would not be well in your particular case to believe in God,' he said. 'Religion will only make you despondent. But until we work out something for you it will be useful to subscribe to some philosophy. Why don't you read Sartre and become an existentialist? It will keep you moving until we find something more suitable for you. Study the *World Almanac*: it is to be your breviary for a while. Take a day job, preferably factory work, but not so simple that you are able to think coherently while working. Something involving sequential operations would be nice. Go out in the evenings; play cards with people. I don't recommend buying a television set just yet. If you read anything outside the *Almanac*, read nothing but plays – no novels or non-fiction. Exercise frequently. Take long walks, but always to a previously determined destination, and when you get there, walk right home again, briskly. And move out of your present quarters; the association is unhealthy for you. Don't get married or have love affairs yet: if you aren't courageous enough to hire prostitutes, then take up masturbation temporarily. Above all, act impulsively: don't let yourself get stuck between alternatives, or you're lost. You're not that strong. If the alternatives are side by side, choose the one on the left; if they're consecutive in time, choose the earlier. If neither of these applies, choose the alternative whose name begins with the earlier letter of the alphabet. These are the principles of Sinistrality, Antecedence, and Alphabetical Priority – there are others, and they're arbitrary, but useful. Good-by.'

'Good-by, Doctor,' I said, a little breathless, and prepared to leave.

'If you have another attack, contact me as soon as you can. If nothing happens, come back in three months. My services will cost you ten dollars a visit – no charge for this one. I have a limited interest in your case, Jacob, and in the vacuum you have for a self. That *is* your case. Remember, keep moving all the time. Be *engagé*. Join things.'

I left, somewhat dazed, and took the bus back to Baltimore. There, out of it all, I had a chance to attempt to decide what I thought of the Doctor, the Remobilization Farm, the endless list of therapies, and my own position. One thing seemed fairly clear: the Doctor was operating either outside the law or on its very fringes. Sexual Therapy, to name only one thing, could scarcely be sanctioned by the American Medical Association. This doubtless was the reason for the farm's frequent relocation. It was also apparent that he was a crank – though perhaps not an ineffective one – and one wondered whether he had any sort of license to practice medicine at all. Because – his rationalizations aside – I was so clearly different from his other patients, I could only assume that he had some sort of special interest in my case: perhaps he was a frustrated psychoanalyst. At worst he was some combination of quack and prophet – Father Divine, Sister Kenny, and Bernarr MacFadden combined (all of them quite effective people), with elements of faith healer and armchair Freud thrown in – running a semi-legitimate rest home for senile eccentrics; and yet one couldn't easily laugh off his forcefulness, and his insights frequently struck home. As a matter of fact, I was unable to make any judgement one way or the other about him or the farm or the therapies.

A most extraordinary Doctor. Although I kept telling myself that I was just going along with the joke, I actually did move from the Bradford down to East Chase Street; I took a job as an assembler on the line of the Chevrolet factory out on Broening Highway, where I operated an air wrench that bolted leaf springs on the left side of Chevrolet chassis, and I joined the U.A.W. I read Sartre but had difficulty deciding how to apply him to specific situations. (How did existentialism help one decide whether to carry one's lunch to work or buy it in the factory cafeteria? I had no head for philosophy.) I played poker with my fellow assemblers, took walks from Chase Street down to the waterfront and back, and attended B movies. Temperamentally I was already pretty much of an atheist most of the time, and the proscription of women was a small burden, for I was not, as a rule, heavily sexed. I applied Sinistrality, Antecedence, and Alphabetical Priority religiously (though in some instances I found it hard to decide which of those devices best fitted the situation). And every quarter for the next two years I drove over to the Remobilization Farm for advice. It would be idle for me to speculate further on why I assented to this curious alliance, which more often than not is insulting to me – I presume that anyone interested in causes will have found plenty to pick from by now in this account.

I left myself sitting in the Progress and Advice Room, I believe, in September of 1953, waiting for the Doctor. My mood on this morning was an unusual one; as a rule I am almost 'weatherless' the moment I enter the farmhouse, and I suppose that weatherlessness is the ideal condition for receiving advice, but on this morning, although I felt unemotional, I was not without weather. I felt dry, clear, and competent, for some reason or other – quite sharp and not a bit humble. In meteorological terms, my weather was *sec Supérieur*.

'How are you these days, Horner?' the Doctor asked affably as he entered the room.

'Just fine, Doctor,' I replied breezily. 'How's yourself?'

The Doctor took his seat, spread his knees, and regarded me critically, not answering my question.

'Have you begun teaching yet?'

'Nope. Start next week. Two sections of grammar and two of composition.

'Ah.' He rolled his cigar around in his mouth. He was

studying me, not what I said. 'You shouldn't be teaching composition.'

'Can't have everything,' I said cheerfully, stretching my legs out under his chair and clasping my hands behind my head. 'It was that or nothing, so I took it.' The Doctor observed the position of my legs and arms.

'Who is this confident fellow you've befriended?' he asked. 'One of the other teachers? He's terribly sure of himself!'

I blushed: it occurred to me that I *was* imitating Joe Morgan. 'Why do you say I'm imitating somebody?'

'I didn't,' the Doctor smiled. 'I only asked who was the forceful fellow you've obviously met.'

'None of your business, sir.'

'Oh, my. Very good. It's a pity you can't take over that manner consistently – you'd never need my services again! But you're not stable enough for that yet, Jacob. Besides, you couldn't act like him when you're in his company, could you? Anyway I'm pleased to see you assuming a role. You do it, evidently, in order to face up to me: a character like your friend's would never allow itself to be insulted by some crank with his string of implausible therapies, eh?'

'That's right, Doctor,' I said, but much of the fire had gone out of me under his analysis.

'This indicates to me that you're ready for Mythotherapy, since you seem to be already practising it without knowing it, and therapeutically, too. But it's best you be aware of what you're doing, so that you won't break down through ignorance. Some time ago I told you to become an existentialist. Did you read Sartre?'

'Some things. Frankly I really didn't get to be an existentialist.'

'No? Well, no matter now. Mythotherapy is based on two assumptions: that human existence precedes human essence, if either of the two terms really signifies anything; and that a man is free not only to choose his own essence but to change it at will. Those are both good existentialist premises, and whether they're true or false is of no concern to us – they're *useful* in your case.'

He went on to explain Mythotherapy.

'In life,' he said, 'there are no essentially major or minor characters. To that extent, all fiction and biography, and most historiography, are a lie. Everyone is necessarily the hero of his own life story. *Hamlet* could be told from Polonius's point of view and called *The Tragedy of Polonius, Lord Chamberlain of Denmark*. He didn't think he was a minor character in anything, I daresay. Or suppose you're an usher in a wedding. From the groom's viewpoint he's the major character; the others play supporting parts, even the bride. From your viewpoint, though, the wedding is a minor episode in the very interesting history of *your* life, and the bride and groom both are minor figures. What you've done is choose to *play the part* of a minor character: it can be pleasant for you to *pretend to be* less important than you know you are, as Odysseus does when he disguises as a swineherd. And every member of the congregation at the wedding sees himself as the major character, condescending to witness the spectacle. So in this sense fiction isn't a lie at all, but a true representation of the distortion that everyone makes of life.

'Now, not only are we the heroes of our own life stories – we're the ones who conceive the story, and give other people the essences of minor characters. But since no man's life story as a rule is ever one story with a coherent plot, we're always reconceiving just the sort of hero we are, and consequently just the sort of minor roles that other people are supposed to play. This is generally true. If any man displays almost the same character day in and day out, all day long, it's either because he has no imagination, like an actor who can play only one role, or because he has an imagination so comprehensive that he sees each particular situation of his life as an episode in some grand over-all plot, and can so distort the situations that the same type of hero can deal with them all. But this is most unusual.

'This kind of role-assigning is myth-making, and when it's done consciously or unconsciously for the purpose of aggrandizing or protecting your ego – and it's probably done for this purpose all the time – it becomes Mythotherapy. Here's the point: an immobility such as you experienced that time in Penn Station is possible only to a person who for some reason or other has ceased to participate in Mythotherapy. At that time on the bench you were neither a major nor a minor character: you were no character at all. It's because this has happened once that it's necessary for me to explain to you something that comes quite naturally to everyone else. It's like teaching a paralytic how to walk again.

'Now many crises in people's lives occur because the hero role that they've assumed for one situation or set of situations no longer applies to some new situation that comes up, or – the same thing in effect – because they haven't the imagination to distort the new situation to fit their old role. This happens to parents, for instance, when their children grow older, and to lovers when one of them begins to dislike the other. If the new situation is too overpowering to ignore, and they can't find a mask to meet it with, they may become schizophrenic – a last-resort mask – or simply shattered. All questions of integrity involve this consideration, because a man's integrity consists in being faithful to the script he's written for himself.

'I've said you're too unstable to play any one part all the time – you're also too unimaginative – so for you these crises had better be met by changing scripts as often as necessary. This should come naturally to you; the important thing for you is to realize what you're doing so you won't get caught without a script, or with the wrong script in a given situation. You did quite well, for example, for a beginner, to walk in here so confidently and almost arrogantly a while ago, and assign me the role of a quack. But you must be able to change masks at once if by some means or other I'm able to make the one you walked in with untenable. Perhaps – I'm just suggesting an offhand possibility – you could change to thinking of me as The Sagacious Old Mentor, a kind of Machiavellian Nestor, say, and yourself as The Ingenuous But Promising Young Protégé, a young Alexander, who someday will put all these teachings into practice and far outshine the master. Do you get the idea? Or – this is repugnant, but it could be used as a last resort – The Silently Indignant Young Man, who tolerates the ravings of a Senile Crank but who will leave this house unsullied by them. I call this repugnant because if you ever used it you'd cut yourself off from much that you haven't learned yet.

'It's extremely important that you learn to assume these

masks wholeheartedly. Don't think there's anything behind them: there isn't. *Ego* means *I*, and *I* means *ego*, and the ego by definition is a mask. Where there's no ego – this is you on the bench – there's no *I*. If you sometimes have the feeling that your mask is *insincere* – impossible word! – it's only because one of your masks is incompatible with another. You mustn't put on two at a time. There's a source of conflict, and conflict between masks, like absence of masks, is a source of immobility. The more sharply you can dramatize your situation, and define your own role and everybody else's role, the safer you'll be. It doesn't matter in Mythotherapy for paralytics whether your role is major or minor, as long as it's clearly conceived, but in the nature of things it'll normally always be major. Now say something.'

I could not.

'Say something!' the Doctor ordered. 'Move! Take a role!'

I tried hard to think of one, but I could not.

'Damn you!' the Doctor cried. He kicked back his chair and leaped upon me, throwing me to the floor and pounding me roughly.

'Hey!' I hollered, entirely startled by his attack. 'Cut it out! What the hell!' I struggled with him and, being both larger and stronger than he, soon had him off me. We stood facing each other warily, panting from the exertion.

'You watch that stuff!' I said belligerently. 'I could make plenty of trouble for you if I wanted to, I'll bet!'

'Anything wrong?' asked Mrs Dockey, sticking her head into the room. I would not want to tangle with her.

'No, not now,' the Doctor smiled, brushing the knees of his white trousers. 'A little Pugilistic Therapy for Jacob Horner. No trouble.' She closed the door.

'Shall we continue our talk?' he asked me, his eyes twinkling. 'You were speaking in a manly way about making trouble.'

But I was no longer in a mood to go along with the whole ridiculous business. I'd had enough of the old lunatic for this quarter.

'Or perhaps you've had enough of The Old Crank for today, eh?'

'What would the sheriff in Wicomico think of this farm?'
I grumbled uncomfortably. 'Suppose the police were sent
out to investigate Sexual Therapy?'

The Doctor was unruffled by my threats.

'Do you intend to send them?' he asked pleasantly.

'Do you think I wouldn't?'

'I've no idea,' he said, still undisturbed.

'Do you dare me to?'

This question, for some reason or other, visibly upset him:
he looked at me sharply.

'Indeed I do not,' he said at once. 'I'm sure you're quite
able to do it. I'm sorry if my tactic for mobilizing you just
then made you angry. I did it with all good intent. You *were*
paralyzed again, you know.'

'Horseshit!' I sneered. 'You and your paralysis!'

'You *have* had enough for today, Horner!' the Doctor said.
He too was angry now. 'Get out! I hope you get paralyzed
driving sixty miles an hour on your way home!' He raised
his voice. 'Get out of here, you damned moron!'

His obviously genuine anger immediately removed mine,
which after the first instant had of course been only a novel
mask.

'I'm sorry, Doctor,' I said. 'I won't lose my temper again.'
We exchanged smiles.

'Why not?' he laughed. 'It's both therapeutic and pleasant to lose your temper in certain situations.' He relit his
cigar, which had been dropped during our scuffle. 'Two
interesting things were demonstrated in the past few minutes,
Jacob Horner. I can't tell you about them until your next
visit. Good-by, now. Don't forget to pay Mrs Dockey.'

Out he strode, cool as could be, and a few moments later
out strode I: A Trifle Shaken, But Sure Of My Strength.

Chapter Seven
The dance of sex: if one had no other reason for choosing to subscribe

The dance of sex: if one had no other reason for choosing to subscribe to Freud, what could be more charming than to believe that the whole vaudeville of the world, the entire dizzy circus of history, is but a fancy mating dance? That dictators burn Jews and businessmen vote Republican, that helmsmen steer ships and ladies play bridge, that girls study grammar and boys engineering all at behest of the Absolute Genital? When the synthesizing mood is upon one, what is more soothing than to assert that this one simple yen of humankind, poor little coitus, alone gives rise to cities and monasteries, paragraphs and poems, foot races and battle tactics, metaphsyics and hydroponics, trade unions and universities? Who would not delight in telling some extragalactic tourist, 'On our planet, sir, males and females copulate. Moreover, they enjoy copulating. But for various reasons they cannot do this whenever, wherever, and with whomever they choose. Hence all this running around that you observe. Hence the world?' A therapeutic notion!

My classes commenced on the seventh of September, a tall blue day as crisp as the white starched blouses of the coeds who filed into my classroom and nervously took their seats. Standing behind the lectern at eight o'clock sharp, suit fresh-pressed and chin scraped clean, I felt my nostrils flare like a stud's at the nubby tight sex of them, flustered and pink-scrubbed, giggling and moist; my thighs flexed, and I yawned ferociously. The boys, too, lean and green, smooth-chinned and resilient, shivered and stretched at the mere nearness of young breasts and buttocks as hard as new pears. In a classroom on the first day of a new term the air's electric with sex like ozone after a summer storm, and all sensed it, if all couldn't name it: the rubby sweet friskies twitched in their seats and tugged their skirts down dimpled white knees;

the springy fresh men flexed and slouched, passed quick hands over crew cuts; I folded arms and tightened hams, and leaning against the desk, let its edge press calmingly against my trouser fly like a steadying hand. Early blue morning is an erotic time, the commencement of school terms an erotic season; little's to be done but nod to Freud on such a day.

We looked one another over appraisingly. What I said, with professorial succinctness, was: 'My name's Jacob Horner; my office is in Room Twenty-seven, around the corner. There's a list of my office hours on the door.' I assigned texts and described the course; that was all, and that was enough. My air of scholarly competence, theirs of studious attention (they wrote my name and office number as frowningly as if I'd pronounced the Key to the Mystery) were so clearly feigned, we were all so conscious of playing school, that to attempt a lesson would have been preposterous. Why, confronted with that battery of eager bosoms and delicious behinds, a man cupped his hands in spite of himself; the urge to drop the ceremonious game and leap those fine girls on the spot was simply terrific. The national consternation, if on some September morn every young college instructor in the land cried out what was on his mind – 'To hell with this nonsense, men: let's take 'em!' – a soothing speculation!

'That's all for today. Buy the books and we'll start right off next time with a spelling test, for diagnostic purposes.'

Indeed! One hundred spelling words dictated rapidly enough to keep their heads down, and I, perched high on my desk, could diagnose to my heart's content every bump of femininity in the room (praised be American grade schools, where little girls learn to sit up front!). Then, perhaps, having ogled my fill, I could get on with the business of the course. For as a man must grow used to the furniture before he can settle down to read in his room, this plenitude of girlish appurtenances had first to be assimilated before anyone could concentrate attention on the sober prescriptions of English grammar.

Four times I repeated the ritual pronouncements – at eight and nine in the morning and at two and three in the afternoon. Between the two sessions I lounged in my office with a magnificent erection, wallowing in my position, and watched with proprietary eye the parade of young things passing my door. I had nothing at all to do but spin indolent daydreams of absolute authority – Nerotic, Caligular authority of the sort that summons up officefuls of undergraduate girls, hot and submissive – leering professorial dreams!

By four o'clock, when my first working day ended, I had so abandoned myself to the dance that I was virtually in pain. I tossed my empty brief case into the car and drove directly across town to the high school, to seek out Miss Peggy Rankin; after some inquiry at the principal's office I caught up with her just as she was leaving the teachers' lounge.

'Come on!' I said urgently. 'I have to see you right away!'

She recognized me, blushed, and fumbled for protests.

'Come *on* !' I grinned. 'I can't tell you here how important it is!' I took her arm and escorted her swiftly outside.

'What's the matter, Jake? Where are we going?'

'Wherever you want to,' I said, holding the car door open for her.

'Jake, for God's sake, are you just picking me up again?' she asked incredulously.

'What do you mean, *just*? There's nothing just about this, girl.'

'There certainly isn't! It's fantastic! What do you think I am, for heaven's sake?'

I stepped on the accelerator. 'Shall we go to your place or to mine?'

'Mine!' she said furiously. 'And just as fast as you can! I've never in my life met such a monster as you are! You're simply a *monster* !'

'I'm not simply a monster, Peggy: I'm *also* a monster.'

'You're an incredible cad! That exactly describes you – you're a complete cad! You're so wrapped up in yourself that you don't have a shred of respect for anyone else on earth! Turn left right here.'

I turned left.

'The fourth house up on the right-hand side. Yes.'

I parked the car.

'Now look at me, Jake. *Look* at me!' she cried. 'Don't you

realize I'm just as much of a human being as you are? How in the *world* could you even look me in the eye again after last time? I'd have been shocked if you'd even had the gall to face up and apologize to me, but *this* – '

'Listen, Peggy,' I said sharply. 'You say I don't respect you. Is that because I didn't bother to flatter you at Ocean City, or apologize afterwards, or call up yesterday to make a date for today?'

'Of course it is! What do you *think* I mean? You haven't got the slightest bit of common courtesy in you; not even common civility! I'm – I'm astonished! You're not a man at all.'

'I'll explain this only once,' I said solemnly; 'I assumed you were mature enough to understand it without explanation, as these things should be understood.'

'What on earth are you getting at?'

'I'm afraid I overestimated you, Peggy,' I declared. 'I thought after I met you that you might actually be the superior woman you give the first impression of being. But you know, you're turning out to be one hundred per cent ordinary.'

She was speechless.

'Don't you understand,' I smiled, my testicles aching, 'that I'm probably less interested in sex than any other man you've ever met?'

'Oh, my *God*!'

'I enjoy it, all right, just as I'd enjoy having a lot of money, but I'm not willing to put up with any nonsense to get either.'

'Not even a common respect for a woman's dignity!'

'That's it, right there,' I said soberly: 'a common respect, a common courtesy, a common this, a common that. Add it all up and what it gives you is a common relationship, and that's a thing I've no use for. You don't seem to be my kind of girl, Peggy, and I could have sworn you were. My kind of girl doesn't want common respect; she wants uncommon respect, and that means a relationship where nobody makes the common allowances for anybody else.'

'I don't believe you,' Peggy said, aghast and troubled.

'You're testifying against yourself, then,' I said quietly.

'Don't you understand that all this rigmarole of flattery and chivalry – the whole theatrical that men perform for women – is *disrespect?* Any lie is disrespect, and a relationship based on that nonsense is a lie. Chivalry is a fiction invented by men who don't want to be bothered with taking women seriously. The minute a man and woman assent to it they stop thinking of each other as individual human beings: they assent to it precisely so they won't have to think about their partners. Which is completely useful, of course, if sex is the only thing that's on your mind. I may as well tell you, Peggy, now that it's too late, that you're the only woman I ever dared try to respect before, and take completely seriously, on my own terms, just as I'd take myself. No lies, no myths, no allowances, no hypocrisy. That's the only kind of relationship with a woman that I could ever stay interested in vertically as well as horizontally.'

Peggy burst into nervous laughter.

'You musn't laugh at that, Peggy,' I said gravely.

'Oh, my God!' she laughed. 'Oh, my *God*!'

I turned from the wheel and very carefully socked her square on the cheek. The blow threw her head back against the window, and immediately she began crying.

'As you see, I'm still taking you seriously,' I said.

'Oh!'

'Try to understand, Peggy, that I'm *just not that interested* in laying women. I can do without. But I will not have my Deepest Values thrown in my face! I'm not a man who strikes girls. To hell with girls. What I want is a female human being that I can take as seriously as myself. If you're not interested, get out, but don't laugh at the only man who's ever taken you seriously in your whole life.'

'Jake, for God's sake!' Peggy sobbed, embracing my lap. Fresh tears. 'What a horrible spot a woman's in!'

I patted her head. 'Our society makes sincerity sound like the greatest hypocrisy of all.'

'Jake?'

'What?'

Because she'd lost her summer tan, her red eyes looked redder than they had in July.

'I'll die if you say it's too late.'

I smoothed her hair. 'I socked you, didn't I? Nothing's less chivalrous than that.'

'Thank God you did!' She inspected the welt on her cheek in the mirror. 'I wish it would never go away.'

'I really *was* just bringing you home, you know, Peggy,' I smiled, playing the kicker at the end of my hand. 'When can I see you?'

She was properly amazed. 'Jake?'

'What?'

'Oh, Jake, *now*! You've got to come up to my apartment right now!'

I made a mental salute to Joseph Morgan, *il mio maestro*, and another to Dr Freud, caller of the whole cosmic hoedown: up to Miss Peggy's flat we tripped. A *pas de deux*, an *entrechat*, and that was that. I left on promises of greater things to come, which I had no special plans to keep.

He having stood me in such excellent stead that afternoon, it was rather a pity that, come nightfall and my first really clandestine visit to Rennie, I was no longer prepared to be Joe Morgan or any other sort of dancer. I was never highly sexed. For me the intervals between women were long, as a rule, and I was not normally disturbed by doing without sexual intercourse. A condition of erotic excitement such as I'd entertained during most of this first school day was almost as rare as a manic with me, and almost as easily dissipated. After the one game I was good for, I was as unarousable as a gelding.

That, I think, is not how Rennie had found me on the evening of our first adultery, shortly after we'd played Peeping Tom on Joe – the sheer energy required to be the spirited lover is difficult, but not entirely impossible, for me to muster – but that's how I felt on this evening when I went to her. I was neither bored nor fatigued nor sad, nor excited nor fresh nor happy: merely a placid, undesiring animal.

The initial act had been a paradigm of assumed inevitability. Three days after our eavesdropping Joe went to Washington to do research in the Library of Congress, and before leaving he asked me to keep Rennie company during his absence – a very Morganesque request. I went out there and spent the afternoon playing with the boys. It was not *necessary* for me to do this at all, but neither was it obviously compromising. Rennie quite unsuggestively invited me to stay for dinner, and I did, though I had no special reason not to eat as usual in a restaurant. We scarcely spoke to each other. Rennie said once, 'I feel lost without Joe', but I could think of no appropriate reply, and for that matter I was not certain how extensive was the intended meaning of her observation. After dinner I volunteered to oversee the boys' bath, spun them a bedtime story, and bade them good night. I could have left then, but my staying to drink ale with Rennie during the evening certainly had no clear significance. We talked impersonally and sporadically – much of the time nothing was said, but mutual silences were neither unusual nor uncomfortable with Rennie – and I truly remember little of our conversation, except that Rennie mentioned being weary and thanked me for having helped with the children that day.

The point I want to make is that on the face of it there was no overt act, no word or deed that unambiguously indicated desire on the part of either of us. I shall certainly admit that I found Rennie attractive that day. Her whole manner was one of exhausted strength: throughout the afternoon her movements had been heavy and deliberate, like those of a laborer who has worked two straight shifts; in the evening she sat for the most part without moving, and frequently upon blinking her eyes she would keep them shut for a full half minute, opening them at last with a wide stare and a heavy expiration of breath. All this I admired, but really rather abstractly, and any sexual desire that I felt was also more or less abstract. We spoke little of Joe, and not at all about what we'd seen through the living-room window.

Then at nine-thirty or thereabouts Rennie said, 'I'm going to take a shower and go to bed, Jake,' and I said, 'All right.' To reach the bathroom, she had to go through a little hallway off the living-room; to get my jacket, I had to go to an open closet in this same hallway, and so it is still not quite necessary to raise an eyebrow at the fact that we got up from our chairs and went to the hallway together. There, if she turned to face me for a slight moment at the door to the bathroom, who's to say confidently that good nights were not on the tips of tongues? It happened that we embraced each other instead before we went our separate ways – but I think a slow-motion camera would not have shown who moved first – and it happened further (but I would not say *consequently*) that our separate ways led to the same bed. By that time, if we had been consciously thinking of first steps – and I for one certainly wasn't – I'm sure we both would have assumed that the first steps, whoever made them, had already been made. I mention this because it applies so often to people's reasoning about their behavior in situations that later turn out to be regrettable: it is possible to watch the sky from morning to midnight, or move along the spectrum from infrared to ultraviolet, without ever being able to put your finger on the precise point where a qualitative change takes place; no one can say, 'It is exactly *here* that twilight becomes night,' or blue becomes violet, or innocence guilt. One can go a long way into a situation thus without finding the word or gesture upon which initial responsibility can handily be fixed – such a long way that suddenly one realizes the change has already been made, is already history, and one rides along then on the sense of an inevitability, a too-lateness, in which he does not really believe, but which for one reason or another he does not see fit to question.

I could illustrate this phenomenon, in the case at hand, clear up to the point – well, up to the point where the cuckolding of Joe Morgan was pretty much an accomplished fact; but delicacy, to which I often incline, forbids. We spent a wordless, tumultuous night together, full of tumblings and flexings and shudders and such, exciting enough to experience but boring to describe; for the neighbors' sake I left before sunrise.

It is with reason that I say no more than this about our adultery: the whole business was without significance to me. I had no idea what was on Rennie's mind – and no wish to penetrate until afterwards her characteristic taciturnity – but I know that my own was empty. It was not a case of weatherlessness; my mood was one of first general and later specific desire, combined with a definite but not inordinate masculine curiosity: in other words, first I wanted to copulate, then I wanted to copulate with Rennie and in addition to learn not only 'what she was like in bed', but also what the intimate relationship (I do not mean sexual relationship) would be like which I presumed would be established by our intercourse. Although I was not often gregarious or even very sociable, I could maintain a thoroughgoing curiosity about one or two people at a time.

That was all. Other than these half-articulated sentiments there was nothing on my mind. Rennie, a bed partner rather too athletic for my current taste, more than satisfied my desires, both general and specific, and my curiosity was satisfied that it would be satisfied as time went on. I cannot call my share in the act gratuitous in the sense of its being unmotivated – I knew why I went along with it – but I would call it both specifically (if not generally) unpremeditated and entirely unreflective. The fellow who committed it was not thinking ahead of his desire.

The next day I became engrossed in reading several volumes of plays that I'd borrowed from the college library at the Doctor's behest, and gave the matter no more thought of any sort. It was insignificant, unimportant, and, as far as I was concerned, inconsequential. I didn't read often, but when I got a fit on I read voraciously; for the next four days I scarcely left my room except to eat, and I read seven collections of plays – some seventy or eighty plays in all. The day after I finished the last volume was the first day of the school term, the day of this chapter, and it was, I think, not at all my love-making of five days earlier, but the release from my heavy diet of vicarious emotions, that induced my highly erotic mood.

In the evening, after supper, I felt tortoise-like, even lichen-like, and, left to myself, I'd have sat rocking in my chair, buried in comfortable torpidity, until bedtime. This inertia, which must be distinguished from both weatherlessness and Penn Station-type immobility, is mildly euphoric – my mind is neither empty nor still, but disengaged, and the idle race of fugitive thoughts that fill it spins past against a kind of all-pervasive, cosmic *awareness*, almost palpable and audible, which I can compare only to the text 'I feel the breath of other planets blowing', from Schönberg's Second String Quartet, or, less esoterically but about as accurately, to the atmospheric rustle on a radio receiver when the volume is turned on full. It is a state from which I can remove myself at will, but I'm usually reluctant to do so. It turned out that, as in the case of my July manic, a telephone call from Rennie dispelled it.

'Jake, I think you'd better come over here,' she said. 'I have to see you.'

'All right.' I had no feeling about going, except the special, non-urgent curiosity previously mentioned. 'When?'

'Now. Joe's at his Scout meeting.'

'All right.'

I readily assumed that what was in the offing was a polishing of the crown of horns we'd already placed on Joe's brow; as I drove out to the Morgans' I attempted, half heartedly, to be pleased by the irony of my friend's being at a Boy Scout meeting at the time. But it didn't work. Indeed, I was somewhat irritable, not a bit desirous; felt commonplace, conventional; *wanted* to feel conventional; didn't want to think about myself. Perhaps as a result, for the very first time since I'd met the Morgans, I experienced a sudden, marvelous sensation of guilt.

And, following immediately on this sensation, the guilt poured in with a violent shock that slacked my jaw, dizzied me at the wheel, brought sweat to my forehead and palms, and slightly sickened me. What in heaven's name was I doing? What, for God's sake, had I done? I was appalled. Does Jacob Horner betray the only man he can think of as a friend, and then double the felony by concealing the betrayal? I was anguished, as never before in my life. What is more, my anguish was pretty much unselfconscious: I was not aware of watching Jacob Horner suffer anguish. Had I been, I believe I'd have seen a face very like Laocoön's.

The instant assumption of this burden of guilt crushed me. I wanted to turn back, or, better, keep on going, out of Maryland, and not come back. This was a new feeling for me, and I had not the strength or courage, or the complexity, even to be curious about it, as I usually am about my rare moments of intense feeling. But I hadn't nerve enough to escape. I parked in front of Rennie's house, and after a while went inside. I had no idea what to do: certainly I was incapable of repeating the offense.

Rennie answered the door, dead white. As soon as she saw me she tried to say something, choked on it, and burst into tears.

'What's the matter, Rennie?' I took her shoulders and would have embraced her, only to steady both of us, but she jerked away, horrified, and fell into a chair. The intensity of her agitation increased my nausea: cold sweat ran under my clothes; I felt weak-kneed and ready to vomit.

'It's incredible, Rennie!' I cried. She looked up at me but couldn't speak, and tears sprang to my eyes. I had to sit down.

'God, I feel *weak*!' I said. The enormity of the injury I'd done Joe was almost too painful to bear. He never looked finer or stronger to me than at that moment when I thought of him at the Boy Scout meeting. 'What in the world was I *thinking* of? Where in hell *was* I?'

Rennie closed her eyes and whipped her head from side to side. After a moment she calmed herself somewhat and wiped her eyes with the top of her wrist.

'What are we going to do, Jake?'

'Does he know yet?'

She shook her head, pressing the butt of her hand against her brow.

'He worked terribly hard in Washington, to get enough material to last him awhile, and then when he came home' – she choked on it – 'he was sweeter to me than he's ever been before. I wanted to die. And when I thought – how I was carrying his child when it happened –'

I burned with shame.

'Do you know what I did? I went to our doctor this morning and asked him for Ergotrate to abort it. He was terrible to me. He's known me since I was little, and he got angry and told me I should be ashamed.'

'Oh, God.'

'Then it turned out I didn't need it. This afternoon I started menstruating. I wasn't even pregnant; I was just late.'

She broke down again; apparently the fact that she wasn't pregnant somehow made things worse.

'Will you tell Joe?' I asked.

'I don't know,' she said dully. 'I can't imagine *never* telling him. God, the last thing we'd do is hide anything from each other! These five days have been terrible, Jake. I've had to pretend to be gay and alert all the time. I swear, the only reason I haven't killed myself is that that would just be cheating him more.'

'How would he take it?'

'I don't know! That's the terrible thing. I can imagine him doing anything from just laughing to shooting both of us. What's terrible is that I don't know *what* he'd do, and that's because neither of us would ever dream of doing anything like this to the other! Do you think I should tell him?'

'I don't know,' I said, but so unnerved was I by my guilt that the prospect terrified me.

'You're afraid of him, aren't you?' Rennie asked.

It was fortunate that she asked this, because although the taunt in her voice was slight – the real sense being that she too was afraid – nevertheless it was fundamental, perhaps the most fundamental taunt one human being can throw at another. I steadied at once.

'I'm afraid of violence,' I said. 'I'm always afraid of any kind of violence, even violent emotions. But you have to understand that when anything that matters is concerned, I wouldn't go an inch out of my way to avoid violence. Fear is different from cowardice. If I don't want you to tell Joe it's because I'm afraid of possible violence, but I'd never say a word to talk you out of telling him. There's nothing a man can do about fear, but he has to choose to be cowardly.'

This was pretty much true; at least I felt it was at the time. I would not normally be cowardly unless taken by surprise. But I felt weak, pitifully weak: weak to have gone to bed with Rennie in the first place; weak not to have told Joe at once afterwards; weak now at being so afraid of his finding out. The violence was one thing; just as intense was my fear of his disappointment in me, his disapproval of me, and his disgust with me – I felt weak at being afraid of these things, which ordinarily would not bother me. I could account for all except the original weakness in having unthinkingly betrayed Joe, because one weakness spawns other weaknesses as one strength spawns other strengths; but there was no excusing that original one. I was miserable.

After a while Rennie said, 'Joe will be coming home in a few minutes.'

I rose to leave.

'Rennie – God, I'm sorry. Do whatever you think is best.'

She didn't look at me.

'I don't know what to do. Sometimes I wake up in the morning feeling wonderful: he – we always sleep with our arms around each other – ' This overwhelmed her for a moment. 'Then I remember it, against my will, and I want to die. I wish I'd never waked up. I hardly believe it happened. I guess I don't really believe it *did* happen. It *couldn't* have happened, Jake: I couldn't have hurt him like that.'

'That's how I feel,' I said. I almost reminded her how much it would hurt him to find out, and checked myself just in time, afraid that if I said it she'd think I was trying to talk her out of telling him – precisely the truth – and therefore tell him. With all my heart I didn't want her to tell him.

'Do whatever you have to do,' I said. 'Be strong as you can.'

I left and drove back to my room. It was useless to try to read or sleep: there was no slipping into someone else's world or otherwise escaping my own, which had me by the throat. All I could think of was Rennie there in the house with Joe, perhaps in bed with him; I wondered how long her strength would last against his embraces, his sleeping with her in his arms, his new sweetness. My heart was filled equally with profound sympathy for Rennie, whom I felt I'd placed in that position, and with fear that she'd tell him what we'd done. He must have walked in about ten minutes after I left – I perspired to think I'd got out just in time.

It occurred to me that, granted all this profound sympathy, tenderness, and general concern for Rennie, I could have stayed to face Joe directly myself and tell him everything. Every passing minute added to my deception. So, then, it seemed I had to admit that I *was* a coward after all: an adulterer, a deceiver, a betrayer of friends, and a coward. And now I was self-conscious again; I watched myself refuse to recognize that beside my bed was a telephone by means of which one could call Joe Morgan; that parked out front was a Chevrolet by means of which one could drive out there. Cowardice, apparently, is as proliferous as is weakness. The act of will required to make the tiny motion of lifting the telephone was beyond me.

My curiosity returned with my self-consciousness. I placed my hand on the telephone and for some time studied with interest the blushing, uncomfortable fellow who would not pick it up.

Chapter Eight
Such guilt as I felt could not be sustained, nor could such self-contempt

Such guilt as I felt could not be sustained, nor could such self-contempt.
Killing it with sleep was out of the question, because I
couldn't sleep, except fitfully. No great activity or overwhelming new mood appeared, to remove it from my mind.
The loathing that I felt for myself soured my digestion, so
that food lay like clay in my stomach; poisoned my consciousness, so that attempts at diversion – books or movies –
were agonizing, and acting the professor was a bitter farce.
As though to complement my mood, it rained for the next
three days: one got soaked running from cars to buildings and
from buildings to cars; the classrooms smelled of wet clothing,
chalk dust, and stale air; students stared sullenly out the
windows. To hear my own voice, prating of adverbs and
prepositions like an insane parrot, sickened me; no one paid
attention. Penned in my room alone with myself, I was
frantic.

I believe a week of such self-revulsion would have brought
me to suicide: certainly that was what occupied my mind a
great deal of the time. I envied all dead things – the fat earth-
worms that lay squashed upon the wet sidewalks, the animals
whose fried bodies I chewed at mealtimes, people decom-
posing in muddy cemeteries – but I had at hand no means of
self-destruction that I was courageous enough to use.

Stendhal claims to have once postponed suicide simply out
of curiosity about the contemporary political situation in
France: he wanted to see what would happen next. And,
apart from cowardice, there was a similar thing that stayed
my hand – since the evening of my last interview with Rennie,
Joe had not been to school. Shirley, Dr Schott's secretary,
announced that Mr Morgan was ill, but was expected to
return to work any day. The suspense involved in his absence
was torturous, to be sure: was he actually ill, or had Rennie

confessed her adultery? What was the specific connection between her confession and his absence? Most important of all, what would his reaction be? These were terrifying questions, but while they made me shrink at the thought of finally coming face to face with him, they also worked counter to any suicidal impulses; I could not kill myself at least until they were answered, if for no other reason than that from one very special point of view I would never learn whether doing away with myself had been *called for*.

On the third day, after lunch, Joe appeared at school and taught his afternoon classes. I paled when accidentally I met him in the main hallway between periods; my nervousness was made more excruciating by the fact that we had time to do no more than say hello to each other. He was entirely calm, but my feelings must have shown all over my face. I've no idea how I managed my last two classes.

At four o'clock I went to my office to grade my first batch of compositions, and a few minutes later Joe walked in. The two men who shared the office had gone home. Joe sat on the edge of the desk next to mine.

'How's it going?' he asked.

I shook my head, aching to tell him everything before he could tell me he already knew; but by this time I was so demoralized and confirmed in my weakness that all I could see was the remote possibility that he still didn't know. As long as this possibility still existed I was not strong enough to confess, and yet I knew very well that whatever happened to remove it would at the same time render my confession pointless.

'First batch of themes,' I said, keeping my eyes on them. 'How do you feel? Shirley said you've been sick.'

'I have,' Joe said. No doubt his face would have told me how to understand this reply, but I couldn't look him in the face. I pretended to examine a theme paper, and clutched at the hope that he was speaking literally.

'How about you?' he asked; there was no sarcasm in his voice, only curiosity. My heart lifted.

'Oh, as usual.'

'No colds from all this rain?'

'Nope. I don't take cold easily.' I could have laughed aloud with relief! Shame I would doubtless feel later, but just then the narrowness of my escape exhilarated me. He didn't know! Silently I thanked Rennie with all my heart – almost loved her at that moment.

'What'd you have?' I asked, more steadily and cheerfully. 'Mononucleosis or gonorrhea?' Now I even dared glance at him to see his response to my slight joke.

'Horner,' he said painfully, 'why in the name of Christ did you fuck Rennie?'

The question was like a blow to the head: I grew dizzy, and my stomach knotted up. For a moment it was impossible to talk. He waited, regarding me with, I think, fascinated disgust.

'Lord, Joe – 'I croaked. At the first sound of my voice, at the sheer effort of speaking, tears filled my eyes, and I blushed and sweated. I had nothing to say.

Joe pushed his glasses back on his nose.

'Why'd you want to do it? What was your reason?'

'Joe, I can't talk now.'

'Yes, you can,' he said evenly. 'You talk now, or I'll knock the crap out of you.'

This, I should say, while entirely in keeping with his frank nature, was a double tactical error on Joe's part. In the first place, although the threat of violence frightened me, it also put me immediately on the defensive, and if defensiveness is an indication of guilt feelings, it is at the same time a release from them: a murderer bent on escaping punishment has little time to contemplate the vileness of his deed. Second, it seems to me that, generally speaking, the only way for a person to get truly honest answers from another person, and be confident of their honesty, is to create the suggestion that any answer will be received cordially, without punishment.

'I didn't *want* to do it, Joe. I don't know why I did it.'

'Horseshit. Maybe you don't *approve* of what you did, but you obviously wanted to do it, or you wouldn't have done it. What a man ends up doing is what he has to take responsibility for having wanted to do. Why did you *think* you were doing it?'

'I wasn't thinking, Joe. If I'd been thinking I wouldn't have done it.'

'Did you think I'd like the idea? What kind of a guy did you think I was?'

'I didn't think, Joe.'

'You're being deliberately obtuse, Horner, and that irritates me.'

'Maybe obtuse, but not deliberately. I don't know what unconscious motives I might have had, Joe, but whatever they were, they were unconscious, so I can't know anything about them.' And, I was thinking, can't be held responsible for them. 'But I swear I had no conscious motives at all.'

'Don't you *want* to be held responsible?' Joe asked incredulously.

'I do, Joe, believe me,' I said halfheartedly. 'But I can't give you reasons when I didn't have any. Do you want me to make up reasons?'

'What kind of picture did you have of Rennie and me, for God's sake?' Joe said, exasperated. 'The thing that appalls me most is what you must have thought of our relationship, to pull a stunt like that! I know you made fun of a lot of things about us – I always had to excuse a lot of your crap because I was interested in you. Did you decide that Rennie was easy game because I was driving her hard, or what? And don't you draw any distinctions between easy game and fair game? Did you really think you could split her off from me to the point where she'd keep something like that a secret?'

'Joe, for God's sake, I know it was a hell of a thing to do! I'm not defending adultery and deception.'

'But you committed them. Why did you do it? Do you think I care what you think about the seventh commandment? I'm not objecting to adultery and deception as sins, Horner; I object to your screwing Rennie and then trying to get her to hide the fact from me. Listen, I don't give a damn about you. You've already forfeited any claims you might have thought you had to my friendship. On that level I'm through with you. It may be that I'm through with Rennie, too, but I can't tell until I've heard the whole story. I want to hear your version of the business, if you've got one. I've already heard Rennie's – that's what I've been doing for the last three days. But her memory's not perfect, and like anybody else's it's selective. Naturally, what I've heard puts the

st possible interpretation on what she did, and perhaps the
orst possible on what you did. Remember, boy, *I wasn't
ere*. Rennie's not playing innocent, but I want all the facts
nd all the interpretations of the facts.'

'What can I say, Joe?'

He sprang down lightly from the desk. 'I'll be up to see you
ter supper,' he said. 'I'd rather hear what you have to say
ithout Rennie around. Don't worry,' he added with some
ontempt; 'I won't shoot you, Jake. I wouldn't have men-
oned violence if Rennie hadn't said you expected it.'

Well, I ate an uneasy meal. Nevertheless, the notion of
uicide no longer entered my head. As if to symbolize my
eather change, the rain let up during the late afternoon,
nd by six o'clock ceased altogether, though the sky was still
vercast. Indeed, I even found myself adding my former
ntense guilt feeling to the list of my other weaknesses, and
onsequently regretting it along with the rest. I felt no better
bout what I'd done – fornicating with their wives behind
my friends' backs and then deceiving them about it were
vils in terms of my own point of view whenever I could be
aid to have a point of view – but I felt *differently* about it.
ow that it was out in the open I felt truly relieved, and deal-
ng concretely with Joe shifted the focus of my attention from
my guilt to what I could do toward salvaging my self-respect.
f I was going to live, I had to live with myself, and because
much of the time I was a moral animal, the salvage job was
he first order of business. What had been done had been
one, but the past, after all, exists only in the minds of those
who are thinking about it in the present, and therefore in the
nterpretations which are put upon it. In that sense it is never
oo late to *do* something about the past. Not that I wanted to
ecreate the incident, *à la* Moscow, in a way favorable to
myself: my difficulty, precisely, was that I hadn't the desire
o defend what I'd done, or the ability to explain it. The
acob Horner that I felt a desperate desire to defend was not
he one who had tumbled stupidly on Joe Morgan's bed with
oe Morgan's wife or the one who had burned in shame and
kulking fear for days afterwards, but the one who was now
he object of Joe's disgust – the Horner of the present moment

and all the Horners to come. And, for better or worse, th
fellow who rose to the defense was still contrite – profoundl
contrite – but no longer humble.

Joe came up to my room shortly after seven and sat no
quite at ease in one of my grotesque chairs. The very fact o
his coming there instead of asking me to come to his place
while no doubt the only way to operate, was, it seemed to me
another tactical error – at least his manner was more sub
dued than it had been that afternoon. But, as he would hav
observed at once had I been in a position to point this out
Joe by his very nature had no tactic. It was, of course, th
simple fact that he wasn't interested in prosecuting any cas
against me which made the job of defending myself mor
difficult, if not impossible.

'Let me explain my position in this, Jake,' he began.

'God, Joe, yours is the only position that doesn't need it!

'That's not right. The fact that you don't realize it's no
right is part of your misunderstanding of Rennie and me.'

'Joe, I realize perfectly well that you'd have been com
pletely justified in beating the daylights out of me or ever
shooting me. I don't question my guilt.'

'And I'm not interested in your guilt,' he said. 'Thi
business of harping on your guilt and my right to be outraged
is an oversimplification of the problem. By pretending tha
all the fuss is over broken commandments, you allow your
self not to take any of it very seriously, because you know a
well as I do that those things aren't absolutes. I'm not inter
ested in blaming anybody for anything. If you really under
stood us you'd realize that – but of course if you really
understood us this wouldn't have happened.'

'I wish to Christ it hadn't,' I said fervently.

'That's silly. If anything I'm glad it did happen, because i
uncovered real problems that I didn't know existed. Try to
remember that I'm not the least bit interested in or concerned
about you. If that hurts your pride, all I can say is that you
pride isn't the most important thing on my mind right now
If I can explain our problem to you, maybe you'll understand
what's relevant and what isn't.'

And so he explained it:

'The most important thing in the world to me – one of my

absolutes, I suppose – is the relationship between Rennie and me. Rennie's already told me all the stuff she could remember having told you about us during your horseback rides. The fact that she told you is one of my problems, but since she did it's probably best to hear my end of it too.

'You know I met Rennie in New York while I was at Columbia. What attracted me to her was that she was the most *self-sufficient* girl I'd ever met; maybe the only one – our culture doesn't turn them out too generously. She was popular enough, but she didn't seem to need popularity or even friendship at all. If she ever felt lonely back then, I believe it was because she didn't always understand her own self-sufficiency – certainly she didn't feel lonely very often. That's what attracted me. I had been in the Army before Columbia, and in a college fraternity before that, and I'd done plenty enough horsing around with women not to confuse one kind of attraction with another. Have you laid very many women, Jake?'

'Not very many,' I replied modestly.

'I only asked because I wonder if that mixing-up of attractions might not be involved in your part of this business. Possibly it was in Rennie's: she'd never slept with any man but me before.'

I squirmed with contrition.

'It was because of this self-sufficiency I thought I saw in her that I was able to imagine having the kind of relationship with her that she described to you – a more or less permanent relationship. It would only be possible between two pretty independent people who had a complete respect for each other's self-sufficiency. The fact that we didn't *need* each other in any of the ordinary "basic" ways seemed to me to mean that we could be damned good for each other in all kinds of other ways. But I think you've heard all this. It explains, incidentally, why Rennie's telling you all that stuff in the pine grove surprised me and bothered me – not that privacy is so important in itself, but it's an indication of the kind of independence we thought we had.

'Now you must realize that I don't have any theories about sexual morality, for Christ's sake. Rennie and I never talked about it at all. But I believe we both tacitly assumed that any

kind of extramarital sex was out of the question for us in th
same way that lying or homosexuality was out of the question
we hadn't the slightest need for it. Not only don't I have an
philosophy about sexual morals – I don't seem to have an
automatic feelings about them, either. But Rennie did. Ver
strong ones. I'm sure she couldn't have defended them ration
ally – no ethical program can be defended rationally clea
down the line. Probably it was a carryover from her hom
life. But the fact that she felt strongly about marital fidelit
was enough to make it our way of operating: her feeling didn
conflict with any private notions of my own, and for tha
matter it kind of suited the relationship we wanted, becaus
it kept everything intramural.

'So that was my ideal of Rennie: self-sufficiency, strengt
(I could tell you a lot about her strength), and privacy. An
there's our problem. According to my version of Renni
what happened couldn't have happened. According to he
version of herself, it couldn't have happened. And yet it hap
pened. That's why even now we have a hard time believin
it really *did* happen: we not only have to accept the fact tha
she did what she did, but also the fact that she *wanted* to do i
– don't think I'm accusing you of rape. Accepting those fact
makes it necessary to correct our version of Rennie, and righ
now we can't see how any version that allows for what hap
pened would also allow for the kind of relationship w
thought we had. And that relationship was the orientatio
post that gave every other part of our lives – everything we di
– its values. It's more important to me than being a grea
scholar or a great anything else. If we have to scrap it, al
these other things lose their point. There's nothing emotiona
about all this – it's as coherent a picture as I can make of th
way I see what Rennie and I were doing, and why every
thing's got to be held in suspension now until we decide th
significance of what happened. Rennie feels the same way
It's what we've been talking about for the last three days
and it's what we'll talk about for a long time to come, if sh
doesn't do away with herself while I'm up here with you.'

My heart went out to him.

'I'm sorry, Joe.'

'But that's beside the point!' he laughed, not humorously

The only reason I'm interested in your share of this – the reason I keep asking you why you did it and what you thought of Rennie and me to give you the idea of trying her out – is that I have to know to what extent your actions influenced her actions.'

'Joe, I swear, I take full responsibility for everything that happened.'

'But I see you're not willing to help me. Do you take full responsibility for the fact that she was on top the first time? Was it you that bit yourself on your own left shoulder? Damn it, I told you Rennie wasn't playing innocent! What she and I want out of each other isn't possible unless we assume that we're free agents – *pretend* we are even when we suspect we aren't. Why do you insist on playing games like this, Jake? I'm obviously being as honest as I can. Just once, for God's sake, drop all the acting and be straight with me!'

'I'm doing my best, Joe,' I declared uncomfortably.

'But you refuse to forget about yourself even for a minute! What do you want? If you're trying to make me feel good about you, I swear this isn't the way. I don't know whether anything you say will work that way, but the only chance at all is to be absolutely honest now.'

'Well, it seems to me that you won't accept anything as honest except whatever it is that you want to hear, and I'm not sure what that is or I'd say it. Ask me questions, and I'll answer them.'

'Why'd you screw Rennie?'

'I don't *know*!'

'What reasons do you think you might have had?'

'I couldn't give any reason that I think would be true.'

'Hell, Horner, you don't just *do* things. What was on your mind?'

'Nothing was on my mind.'

Joe began to show anger.

'Listen, Joe,' I pleaded. 'You've got to allow for the fact that people – maybe yourself excluded – aren't going to have conscious motives for everything they do. There'll always be a few things in their autobiography that they can't account for. Now when that happens the person could still make up conscious reasons – maybe in your case they'd spring to mind

the first time you thought about an act after you did it – bu[t]
they'd always be rationalizations after the fact.'

'That's all right,' Joe insisted. 'If I went along with every[-]
thing you just said, I'd still have to say that even the ratio[n-]
alizing after the fact has to be done, and the person has to b[e]
held responsible – has to hold *himself* responsible – for h[is]
rationalizings, if he wants to be a moral actor.'

'Then you'll have to go further still and allow that som[e]
times a man won't even be able to rationalize. Nothing come[s]
to mind. You don't accept it when I take full responsibilit[y]
for everything that happened, and you won't accept it if [I]
don't take any responsibility. But in this business I don't se[e]
what's in between.'

I lit a cigarette. I was nervous, and happy and unhappy a[t]
the same time about the fact that despite my nervousness [I]
felt pretty good, pretty sure of my mind, pretty satisfied at m[y]
ability to play a role that struck me as being at once som[e]
what abhorrent and yet apparently ineluctable. That is, [I]
felt it to be a role, but I wasn't sure that anything els[e]
wouldn't also be a role, and I couldn't think of any othe[r]
possible roles for me anyhow. If, as may be, this is the be[st]
anyone can do – at least the best I could do – why, then, it'[s]
as much as can ever be signified by the term *sincerity*.

'That's all beside the point,' Joe said. 'I'm not intereste[d]
in how much responsibility you're willing to assume. What [I]
want to know is what happened, so I'll know how muc[h]
responsibility to hand out all around, whether you accept i[t]
or not. When did you get the idea you could make out wit[h]
Rennie?'

'I don't know. Maybe not till we were in bed, maybe a[s]
soon as I met you all, maybe sometime in between. I wasn'[t]
aware of getting the idea.'

'What did she do or say that gave you the idea?'

'I'm not sure I *had* the idea. The afternoon and evening
was out there, while you were gone, I could interpret every[-]
thing she said and didn't say as evidence that she was pre[-]
pared to make love with me, or I could interpret none of i[t]
as evidence. At the time I don't believe I was interpretin[g]
at all.'

'What was said?'

'God, I can't remember conversations! Didn't Rennie tell you?'

'Sure she did. Can't you remember, or are you playing obtuse again?'

'I can't remember.'

'Well, what the hell am I going to do?' Joe cried. 'You claim you didn't have any conscious motives. You aren't aware of any unconscious motives. You won't rationalize. You didn't make any conscious interpretations of anything Rennie did. And you can't remember any conversations. Have I got to agree with Rennie that you don't even exist? What else makes a man a human being except these things?'

I shrugged. 'I could add some more things to the list of my inabilities.'

'Don't bother. Don't you see, Horner, if you could convince me that very much of what Rennie did was under your influence, it wouldn't be good, because she shouldn't have been in a position to be influenced very much. And if you convinced me that very little if any of it was your influence, it still wouldn't be good, because by our picture of her she couldn't have chosen to do it. So it's not that I'm trying to solve the problem by passing the buck. The thing is, I can't be sure just what the problem is that has to be solved until I know just what happened and why each thing happened.'

I felt strong enough by this time to say, 'I don't think you'd have as much of a problem if you had more respect for the answer "I don't know". It can be an awfully honest answer, Joe. When somebody close to you injures you unaccountably, and you say, "Why in the world did you do that?" and they say, "I don't know", it seems to me that that answer can be worthy of respect. And if it's somebody you love or trust who says it, and they say it contritely, I think it could even be acceptable.'

'But once they've said it,' Joe said, 'once they're in a position to *have* to say it, how do you tell whether the love and trust that make it acceptable were justified?'

How indeed? All I could have replied is that I personally couldn't imagine ever having to reach that question, but I could certainly imagine Joe reaching it.

'Well, that could never do, Jake,' Joe said, getting ready

to go. 'If that has to be your answer, I can't see how to deal with you, and if it's got to be Rennie's I can't see how to deal with her either. That answer simply doesn't come up in the Morgan cosmos. Maybe I'm in the wrong cosmos, but it's the only one I can see setting up serious relationships in. You ought to know, boy, that Rennie blames you for nearly everything that happened.'

I was a little surprised, but I simply wrinkled my forehead and made a quick *tch* in the left corner of my mouth.

'I don't see why you shouldn't believe her,' I declared.

'But you think it's pretty ordinary of her, don't you? The kind of thing you'd expect a *woman* to do?'

'I don't have any opinion,' I said. 'Or rather, I have both opinions at once.'

This observation nearly clenched Joe's fists in disgust, and he left my room.

I could say that this conversation left me disturbed, but it seems more accurate to say that it left me stimulated: my disturbance was the disturbance of stimulation more than of guilt, the same disturbance that a complicated argument always produces – the disturbance, neither pleasant nor unpleasant, but invariably exhilarating, effected by any duel of articulations, where the duelists have things of sufficient value at stake to make the contest, if after all a game, at least a serious game.

Articulation! There, by Joe, was *my* absolute, if I could be said to have one. At any rate, it is the only thing I can think of about which I ever had, with any frequency at all, the feelings one usually has for one's absolutes. To turn experience into speech – that is, to classify, to categorize, to conceptualize, to grammarize, to syntactify it – is always a betrayal of experience, a falsification of it; but only so betrayed can it be dealt with at all, and only in so dealing with it did I ever feel a man, alive and kicking. It is therefore that, when I had cause to think about it at all, I responded to this precise falsification, this adroit, careful myth-making, with all the upsetting exhilaration of any artist at his work. When my mythoplastic razors were sharply honed, it was unparalleled sport to lay about with them, to have at reality.

In other senses, of course, I don't believe this at all.

Chapter Nine
One of the things I did not see fit to tell Joe Morgan

One of the things I did not see fit to tell Joe Morgan (for to do so would have been to testify further against myself) is that it was never very much of a chore for me, at various times, to maintain with perfectly equal unenthusiasm contradictory, or at least polarized, opinions at once on a given subject. I did so too easily, perhaps, for my own ultimate mobility. Thus it seemed to me that the Doctor was insane, and that he was profound; that Joe was brilliant and also absurd; that Rennie was strong and weak; and that Jacob Horner – owl, peacock, chameleon, donkey, and popinjay, fugitive from a medieval bestiary – was at the same time giant and dwarf, plenum and vacuum, and admirable and contemptible. Had I explained this to Joe he'd have added it to his store of evidence that I did not exist: my own feeling was that it was and was not such evidence. I explain it now in order to make as clear as I can what I mean when I say that I was shocked and not surprised, disgusted and amused, excited and bored, when, the evening after the conversation just recorded, Rennie came up to my room. I'd had a brilliant day with my students, explaining gerunds, participles, and infinitives, and my eloquence had brought me around to feeling both guilty and nonchalant about the Morgan affair.

'Well, I'll be damned!' I said when I saw her. 'Come on in! Have you been excommunicated, or what?'

'I didn't want to come up here,' Rennie said tersely. 'I didn't want to see you again at all, Jake.'

'Oh. But people want to do the things they do.'

'Joe drove me in, Jake. He told me to come up here.'

This was intended as a bombshell, I believe, but I was not in an explodable mood.

'What the hell for?'

Rennie had started out with pretty firm, solemn control,

but now she got choky and couldn't, or wouldn't, answer the question.

'Has he turned you out?'

'No. Can't you understand why he sent me up here? Please don't make me explain it!' Tears were imminent.

'Honestly, I couldn't guess, Rennie. Are we supposed to reenact the crime in a more analyzable way, or what?'

Well, that finished her control; the head-whipping began. Rennie, incidentally, looked great to me. She'd obviously been suffering intensely for the past few days, and, like exhausted strength, it lent her the sexual attractiveness that tormented women occasionally have. Tender, lovelike feelings announced their presence in me.

'Everything that's happened wrenches my heart,' I said to her, laying my hand on her shoulder. 'You've no idea how much I sympathize with Joe, and how much more with you. But he sure is making a Barnum and Bailey out of it, isn't he? This sending you up here is the damndest thing I ever heard of. Is it supposed to be punishment?'

'It's not ridiculous unless you're determined to see it that way,' Rennie said, tearfully but vehemently. 'Of course *you'd* say it was, just so you won't have to take Joe seriously.'

'What's it all about, for heaven's sake?'

'I didn't want to see you again, Jake. I told Joe that. He told me everything you said to him last night, and at first I thought you were lying all the way. I guess you know I've hated you ever since we made love; when I told Joe about it, I didn't leave out anything we did – not a single detail – but I blamed you for everything.'

'That's okay. I don't have any real opinion on the subject.'

'I can't blame you any more,' Rennie went on. 'It's too easy, and it doesn't really solve anything. I guess I don't have any opinion either – and Joe doesn't either.'

'He doesn't?'

'He's heartbroken. So am I. But he's determined not to evade the question in any way, or take a stand just to cover up the hurt. You don't realize what an obsession this is with him! Sometimes I've thought we'd both lose our minds this past week. This thing is tearing us up! But Joe would rather be torn up than falsify the trouble in any way. That's why I'm here.'

'Why?'

She hung her head.

'I told him I couldn't stand to see you again, whether you were responsible or not. He got angry and said I was being melodramatic, evading the question. I thought he was going to hit me again! But instead he calmed down and – even made love to me, and explained that if we were ever going to end our trouble we'd have to be extra careful not to make up any versions of things that would keep us from facing the facts squarely. If anything, we had to do all we could to throw ourselves as hard as possible against the facts, and as often as possible, no matter how much it hurt. He said that as it stands now we're defeated, and the only possible chance to save anything is never to leave the problem for a minute. I told him I'd die if I had to live with it much longer the way I've been doing, and he said he might too, but it's the only way. I guess you think this is ridiculous, too.'

'No opinion,' I said, meaning I felt contradictory opinions.

'One of the things he thinks we mustn't do is drop you yet, or let you drop us. That's why he brought me up here. Refusing to see you again is – evading the issue.'

'Well, I'm happy as hell to see you, but I must say I'm all in favor of evading any issue if it's both painful and insoluble. Aren't you?'

With all her heart, I could see, she was indeed.

'No,' she said determinedly. 'I agree with Joe completely.'

'Well, what are we supposed to do? Talk philosophy?'

Head-whipping. 'Jake, for Christ's sake, tell me *honestly* what you think of Joe.'

'I honestly have a number of opinions,' I smiled.

'What are they?'

'Well, in the first place – not first in order of intensity – he's noble as the dickens.'

Rennie laughed and cried at once.

'He's noble, strong, and brave, more than anybody I've ever seen. A disaster for him is a disaster for reason, intelligence, and civilization, because he's the quintessence of these things. There's nobody else like him in the United States. I believe this.'

Rennie so melted that, had I chosen, I could have embraced her at that moment without protest.

'In the second place,' I said, 'he's completely ridiculous. Contemptible. A buffoon, a sophist, and a boor. Arrogant, small, intolerant, a little bit cruel, and even stupid. He uses logic and this childish honesty as a club and a shield at the same time. Or you could say he's just insane, a monomaniac: he's fixed in the delusion that intelligence will solve all problems.'

'But you know very well he could reply to that!'

'Sure, he can defend his position and his method, but he can't solve this problem happily in terms of it. But you know, all these versions of him are complimentary, because they're extreme. My last opinion, which I don't hold any more strongly than the others, is that he's a little bit of all these things, but mainly just a pretty unremarkable guy, more pathetic than tragic, and more amusing than contemptible. Faintly grotesque and in the last analysis not terribly charming or even pleasant. Kind of silly and awfully naïve. That's our Joseph. Not a man to take too seriously, because he simply doesn't represent his position brilliantly enough or even coherently enough. I should add that I feel all these things about myself, too, and some more besides.'

'Jake, you know he could answer all those charges.'

'Sure. The beauty of it is that it doesn't make any difference whether he can or not. They're not charges: they're opinions. Hell, Rennie, don't get the wrong idea: I like Joe all right.'

'You're acting awfully superior.'

I laughed. 'One of my opinions, along with the one that I'm inferior to Joe in most ways, is that I'm superior to him in most ways. You be honest with me now: what does Joe really have on his mind in sending you up here?'

'We've had to agree that even if you're the one who started the whole thing, I couldn't have allowed you to influence me if I hadn't wanted to be influenced. You took advantage of a weak time in my life, but you didn't rape me. I can't deny Joe's statement that if I ended up in bed with you it's because when all's said and done I *wanted* to, no matter how repugnant the idea is now. So Joe insists that all my dislike for you now is beside the point. He asked me how I'd have felt three weeks ago if he'd suggested that I make love to you, and I had to say, "I don't know." Then he asked me how I'd feel if he suggested it now, and I told him I was horrified and repelled by the idea. He said that's the sort of reaction we have to guard against, because it obscures the problem. We have to be as honest as possible about what we really believe, and not confuse it with what we think is safe or prudent to believe, and we have to act on our real beliefs so we can know where we stand. And apparently – this is what Joe said – I believe it's all right for me to make love to other men, at least to you, whether I want to admit it to myself or not, since I did it.'

'Good Lord!'

'Jake – he sent me up here to do it again.'

'But you disagree with him about this, don't you?'

She did, of course, as much as she'd disagreed about the necessity of not evading the whole issue, but she'd already committed herself to agreeing with him on that, and for that matter on everything else. It took her a moment to answer.

'I hate the idea, Jake! Everything in me recoils at the idea. But that hate is just like my feelings about you. Nobody has to point that out to me. I'm lost, Jake! I'm not as strong as Joe or even you. I'm not strong enough to get caught in this!'

Well, now. It occurred to me that Joe's position, while entirely illogical (Rennie's single adultery, of course, did not at all necessarily imply that she believed extramarital sex was *generally* 'all right' with either other men in general or me in particular: at most it implied that she'd been willing to do it just once), afforded me a chance to really persecute her if I wanted to. It was a great temptation to cut short the conversation and say, 'Okay, babe, there's the bed'; but I was not in a Rennie-torturing mood.

'Are you willing to do it, then?' I asked her.

'No! God, it's the last thing in the world I could ever do again!'

'Joe's insane. You know, I could say this strikes me as being perverted on his part.'

'Go ahead and say it. Then you won't have to try to understand him.'

'That's a wonderful line,' I laughed. 'It cancels out any possible criticism anyone could ever make of him! That line and the one about his being strong enough to be a caricature of himself – those two defenses make anybody unassailable.'

'But in his case they're true,' Rennie insisted.

'What time is he picking you up?'

'We assumed you'd drive me home afterwards,' she said glibly.

'After we'd finished?'

'Stop it, please!'

'Well, are you ready to go? Home, I mean?'

She looked at me, bewildered.

'He's not going to examine you each time, is he?' I grinned. 'He couldn't tell anyhow. All you have to do is swear on your scout's honor we did our duty.'

Now for the first time she saw the real nature of her dilemma: she had to choose between going to bed with me, which was repugnant to her, and lying to Joe, which was also repugnant to her, since the third alternative – asserting her own opinion by simply refusing to comply with his policy decisions at all – was apparently beyond her strength.

'Oh, God! What would you do if you were me, Jake?'

'I'd have told him to go to hell!' I said cheerfully. 'I wouldn't have come up here in the first place. But since you did, if I were you I wouldn't hesitate to lie to him. Give him a string of gory details. Tell him we made love five times and committed sodomy twice. He's asking for it. I'll bet he won't send you up here again if you make it sound hot enough. It's the old trick of getting rid of a bad law by overenforcing it.'

Rennie bit her knuckle and whipped her head shortly.

'I can't lie to him. I can't ever do that again.'

'Then tell him to go to hell.'

'You don't understand how this thing has affected him, Jake. He's not insane; I couldn't even call him neurotic. I believe he's thinking more clearly and intensely than he ever has in his life. But this is a life-and-death business with him. With both of us. It's the biggest crisis we ever had.'

'What could he do if you just said you won't string along with him on this one thing?'

'I can imagine him walking out flat, for good, or killing himself or all of us. I can even imagine him bringing me right back up here and coming up himself to make sure –'

'To make sure you do what you're supposed to want to do? God, this is funny!'

'He'd think I was letting him down completely. Throwing up my hands.'

'Well, then, for Christ's sake let's go to bed. If you can't pretend to take him seriously, let's really take him seriously I guarantee he won't send you up here again.' I stood up. 'Come on, girl: you can tell him all the things I said before and be telling the truth. We'll give old Joe an object lesson.'

'How can you even *think* of it?' Rennie cried.

To tell the truth, my feelings were ambivalent as usual. Rennie's conflict was the classical one between what she liked and what she approved of – rather, between her dislike of further adultery and her disapproval of lying to Joe – but mine was between two things that I approved of and also between two things that I liked. I approved of disengaging myself from any further participation in the business that had so disrupted the Morgans' extraordinary relationship (which, I might as well add, I regarded as an admirable one, as a matter of fact, but which I knew better than to think I could have enjoyed personally in very many of my moods) yet at the same time I approved of the idea of going along with Joe on this point, both because I had pledged my co-operation and because I really believed that one good dose of his medicine would make him change his prescription. Also, though I was at times entirely capable of enjoying sexual sadism, I was not just then in a frame of mind to like an intercourse that would be pure torture for Rennie; nevertheless, as I mentioned earlier, her suffering exerted a powerful physical attraction on me. My guilt feelings, incidentally, although I'd still have agreed to their propriety, had got lost in the melodrama of Joe's new step. I was too entirely astonished and intrigued by his action to devote much attention to feeling guilty.

'I'm not taking a stand,' I declared. 'I'm an issue evader

from way back. I'll go along with you any way you want.'

'I can't do it!' Rennie wailed.

'Let's go home, then.'

'I *can't*! Please, *please*, either throw me out or rape me, Jake! I can't do anything!'

'I'm not going to make up your mind,' I said.

This too, I suppose, was sadistic, but it was pretty much honest; I really couldn't have done very wholeheartedly either of the things she requested, and it is easier to sit still halfheartedly than to do dramatic things halfheartedly. Rennie sobbed for a full two minutes, huddled in her chair: this affair was indeed tearing her up.

Ah me, and there were so many other ways it could have been handled. Perhaps, I reflected, what would eventually destroy both Morgans, after all, was lack of imagination. I glanced up at Laocoön: his agony was abstract and un-suggestive.

Chapter Ten
The disintegration of Rennie that September
was not often an entertaining spectacle

The disintegration of Rennie that September was not often an entertaining spectacle to observe, for although, as she pointed out, it is not self-evident that every personality is valuable simply because it's unique, nevertheless I could seldom enjoy contributing to the unhappiness of people whom I'd come to know at all well. There is no humanitarianism in this fact: for humankind in general I had no feeling one way or the other, and the plight of some specific people, Peggy Rankin for example, I must say concerned me not at all. This is merely a description of my reactions – I wouldn't attempt to defend it as an assumed position.

The trouble, I suppose, is that the more one learns about a given person, the more difficult it becomes to assign a character to him that will allow one to deal with him effectively in an emotional situation. Mythotherapy, in short, becomes increasingly harder to apply, because one is compelled to recognize the inadequacy of any role one assigns. Existence not only precedes essence: in the case of human beings it rather defies essence. And as soon as one knows a person well enough to hold contradictory opinions about him, Mythotherapy goes out the window, except at times when one is no more than half awake.

There were such times, but they were few. The latter part of the evening just described was one: when at length I carried Rennie to the bed (excited by her heaviness) I was able to do so only because, for better or worse, enough of my alertness was gone to permit me to dramatize the situation as part of a romantic contest between symbols. Joe was The Reason, or Being (I was using Rennie's cosmos); I was The Unreason, or Not-Being; and the two of us were fighting without quarter for possession of Rennie, like God and Satan for the soul of Man. This pretty ontological Manichaeism would certainly stand no close examination, but it had the triple virtue of excusing me from having to assign to Rennie any essence more specific than The Human Personality, further of allowing me to fornicate with a Mephistophelean relish, and finally of making it possible for me not to question my motives, since what I was doing was of the essence of my essence. Does one look for introspection from Satan?

As for Rennie, she had by that time very nearly reached the condition of paralysis, and it was, I believe, with something like relief that she allowed me to cast her in the role of Mankind; what drama was on *her* mind I couldn't say. I took her home afterwards.

'Aren't you going to come in for a while?' she asked numbly.

But my little play had dissipated with my sexual ardor, and I was vegetable.

'Nope. I'll see you around.'

For the rest, I felt mostly a generalized pity for the Morgans, especially for Rennie. Joe, after all, was behaving pretty consistently with his position, and that knowledge can be comforting even in cases where the position leads to defeat or disaster, as when a bridge player plays out a losing hand perfectly or an Othello loves not wisely but too well. But Rennie no longer had a position to act consistently with, not even the position of acting inconsistently, and yet, unlike my own, her personality was such that it seemed to require a position in order to preserve itself.

She came to my room three times during September and once in October. The first visit I've already described. The second, on Wednesday of the following week, was quite different: Rennie seemed warm, strong, even gay and a little wild. We made love zestfully at once – she went so far as to tease me for being a less energetic lover than her husband – and afterwards she talked animatedly for an hour or so over a quart of California muscatel she'd brought with her.

'Lord, I've been silly lately!' she laughed. 'Mooning and crying around like a schoolgirl!'

'Oh?'

'How in the world could I have taken this business so

seriously? You know what happened to me last night?'

'No.'

'I popped awake at three in the morning – wide awake, like I've been doing every night since this business started. Usually I get the shakes when that happens, and either sit up the rest of the night shivering and sweating or else wake up Joe and go over the whole thing with him again. Well, last night I woke up as usual, and the moon was shining in and I could see Joe lying there asleep – he looks adolescent when he's asleep! – and for some reason or other while I was watching him he started picking his nose in his sleep!' She giggled at the memory and burped slightly from the wine. 'Excuse me.'

'Certainly.'

'Well, that reminded me of that night we peeked in on him through the living-room window, only this time instead of hurting me it just struck me funny! The whole thing struck me funny, and how we were taking it. Joe seemed like a teenager trying to make a tragedy out of nothing, and you just seemed completely ineffectual. Does this make you angry?' She laughed.

'Of course not.'

'And I've been being a runny-nose little girl myself, crying all over the place and letting you two bully me around about such a stupid thing. I felt just like I feel when I let the kids get me down. Lots of times when the kids scream and fight all day I get so worked up at them I end up screaming and crying myself, and I always feel silly afterwards and a little bit ashamed. How can grown people make so much fuss over something so silly? Especially married people with kids?'

'Poor little coitus,' I smiled. In fact, Rennie's high spirits produced a contrary feeling in me: the happier she grew, the more glum I became, and the more she professed to take the matter lightly, the graver it seemed to me.

'Such a completely insignificant thing to take seriously! It's hardly worth thinking about, much less breaking up a marriage over! I could sleep with a hundred different men and not feel any different about Joe!'

'Well, now,' I protested snappishly, 'of course nothing's significant in itself, but anything's serious that you want to take seriously. There's no reason to make fun of another man's seriousnesses.'

'Oh, stop it!' Rennie cried. 'You're as bad as Joe is. I think all our trouble comes from thinking too much and talking too much. We talk ourselves into all kinds of messes that would disappear if everybody just shut up about them.' She drank another glass of wine – her fourth or fifth – while I still nursed my first one. 'You know what I think? I think none of this would have happened if we all didn't have so much time on our hands. I really do. You claim you don't know how you could ever have begun the whole business, but I think you did it because you're bored.'

'Is that so?'

'You don't have any ambitions, you're not very busy or very handsome, you live by yourself. I think of you up here all day long, rocking in your rocking chair, daydreaming and cooking up schemes, just because you're bored. I think the key to your whole character is that you're just bored.'

'I'm not just anything,' I said without conviction. 'Maybe *also* bored, but never *just* bored.' Rennie, it was clear, was practising a little layman's Mythotherapy herself: anybody who starts talking in terms of keys to people's characters is making myths, because the mystery of people is not to be explained by keys. But I was too glum just then to take more than perfunctory note of her playwriting.

'Well, *I* think you're just bored; I don't care what you think. I don't care what you or Joe either one thinks about this mess or about me any more: I've stopped taking it seriously. I've even stopped thinking about it.'

'Good for you.'

'That gets under your skin, though, doesn't it?' she laughed. 'It takes the fun out of it when I stop being hurt. Well, the devil with you! I've stopped being hurt. Look how down in the mouth you are. You look like you've messed your pants or something.' The idea amused her; she giggled vinously. 'That's just how Joe looked this morning – gloomy as a prophet. You're pouting because your game is spoiled. Now cheer up and get drunk with me or else take me home.'

I emptied my glass and refilled it. 'You realize, of course, that I don't believe a word of this. It's brave, but it's not convincing.'

'You don't dare believe it,' Rennie taunted.

'I don't dare to, and you couldn't if your life depended on it.'

'I don't care,' Rennie declared. 'I don't give a damn.'

'I don't believe Joe knows anything about it either.'

'I don't care.'

'He wouldn't get gloomy. He'd walk out.'

'That's what you think. We're tied tighter than that. I don't know why I worried in the first place; no piece of nonsense like this could break Joe and me up. It would take a stronger person than you, Jake. You don't really know anything about Joe and me. Not a damned thing.'

'I said last time you should tell him to go to hell.'

'Maybe I'll tell you both to go to hell.'

'Okay, girl, but watch that left hook of his when you do.'

This remark cancelled the effects of at least three glasses of muscatel.

'I don't think Joe would ever hit me again,' she said seriously.

'Then skip home with that quart of muscatel in you, tweak his nose for him, and tell him you can't think seriously any more about anything as silly as your sex life,' I suggested. 'Tell him the whole trouble is he thinks too much.'

'He wouldn't hit me, Jake. He'd never do that again.'

'He'd fracture your damn jaw for you. Tell him he's acting like a high-school boy! He'll lay you out cold and you know it. Come on, I'll go along with you. If you're right we'll all three chuckle and chortle and snot our noses. We'll shake hands all around and our troubles will be over.'

Rennie was entirely sober now.

'I hate you,' she said. 'You won't let me even try to be halfway happy again for a minute, will you? I can't even pretend to be happy.'

And (*mirabile dictu*) as soon as she assumed my glumness, I was free of it – took up her lost gaiety, in fact, and poured myself another glass of muscatel.

'You feel great, don't you?' Rennie cried.

'Happy human perversity. I'm genuinely sorry, Rennie.'

'You're genuinely cheerful!' she said, whipping her head from side to side.

But such precarious good spirits as these of Rennie's and such unnecessary cruelty as this of mine were rare. Just as the second visit had borne little resemblance to the first, the third (and last in September) was nothing at all like the second. By this time I was involved enough in teaching so that my moods more and more often had their origin in the classroom. On this particular day, the last Friday in September, I felt acute, tuned-up, razor-sharp, simply because in my grammar class that morning I'd explained the rules governing the case forms of English pronouns: it gives a man a great sense of lucidity and wellbeing, if not downright formidability, to be able not only to say, but to understand perfectly, that predicate complements of infinitives of copulative verbs without expressed subjects go into the nominative case, whereas predicate complements of infinitives of copulative verbs *with* expressed subjects go into the objective case. I made this observation to my assemblage of young scholars and concluded triumphantly, 'I was thought to be *he*, but I thought John to be *him*! Questions?'

'Aw, look,' protested a troublesome fellow – in the back of the room, of course – whom I'd early decided to flunk if possible for his impertinence, 'which came first, the language or the grammar books?'

'What's on your mind, Blakesley?' I demanded, refusing to play his game.

'Well, it stands to reason people talked before they wrote grammar books, and all the books did was to tell how people were talking. For instance, when my roommate makes a phone call I ask him, "Who were you talking to?" Everybody in this class would say, "Who were you talking to?" I'll bet ninety-nine per cent of the people of America would say, "Who were you talking to?" Nobody's going to say, "To whom were you just now talking?" I'll bet even you wouldn't say it. It sounds queer, don't it?' The class snickered. 'Now this is supposed to be a democracy, so if nobody but a few profs ever say, "To whom were you just now speaking?", why go on pretending we're all out of step but you? Why not change the rules?'

A Joe Morgan type, this lad: paths should be laid where people walk. I hated his guts.

'Mr Blakesley, I suppose you eat your fried chicken with your fingers?'

'What? Sure I do. Don't you?'

The class tittered, engrossed in the duel, but as of this last rather flat sally they were not so unreservedly allied with him as before.

'And your bacon at breakfast? Fingers or fork, Mr Blakesley?'

'Fingers,' he said defiantly. 'Sure, that's right, fingers were invented before forks, just like English was invented before grammar books.'

'But not *your* fingers, as the saying goes,' I smiled coolly, 'and not your English – God knows!' The class was with me all the way: prescriptive grammar was victorious.

'The point is,' I concluded to the class in general, 'that if we were still savages, Mr Blakesley would be free to eat like a swine without breaking any rules, because there'd be no rules to break, and he could say, "It sounds queer, don't it?" to his heart's content without being recognized as illiterate, because literacy – the grammar rules – wouldn't have been invented. But once a set of rules for etiquette or grammar is established and generally accepted as the norm – meaning the ideal, not the average – then one is free to break them only if he's willing to be generally regarded as a savage or an illiterate. No matter how dogmatic or unreasonable the rules might be, they're the convention. And in the case of language there's still another reason for going along with even the silliest rules. Mr Blakesley, what does the word *horse* refer to?'

Mr Blakesley was sullen, but he replied, 'The animal. Four-legged animal.'

'*Equus caballus*,' I agreed: 'a solid-hoofed, herbivorous mammal. And what does the algebraic symbol x stand for?'

'x? Anything. It's an unknown.'

'Good. Then the symbol x can represent anything we want it to represent, as long as it always represents the same thing in a given equation. But *horse* is just a symbol too – a noise that we make in our throats or some scratches on the blackboard. And theoretically we could make it stand for anything we wanted to also, couldn't we? I mean, if you and I agreed that just between ourselves the word *horse* would mean *grammar book*, then we could say, "Open your horse to Page Twenty," or "Did you bring your horse to class with you today?" And we two would know what we meant, wouldn't we?'

'Sure, I guess so.' With all his heart Mr Blakesley didn't want to agree. He sensed that he was somehow trapped, but there was no way out.

'Of course we would. But nobody else would understand us – that's the whole principle of secret codes. Yet there's ultimately no reason why the symbol *horse* shouldn't always refer to grammar book instead of to *Equus caballus*: the significance of words are arbitrary conventions, mostly; historical accidents. But it was agreed before you and I had any say in the matter that the word *horse* would refer to *Equus caballus*, and so if we want our sentences to be intelligible to very many people, we have to go along with the convention. We have to say *horse* when we mean *Equus caballus*, and *grammar book* when we mean this object here on my desk. You're free to break the rules, but not if you're after intelligibility. If you *do* want intelligibility, then the only way to get "free" of the rules is to master them so thoroughly that they're second nature to you. That's the paradox: in any kind of complicated society a man is usually free only to the extent that he embraces all the rules of that society. Who's more free in America?' I asked finally. 'The man who rebels against all the laws or the man who follows them so automatically that he never even has to think about them?'

This last, to be sure, was a gross equivocation, but I was not out to edify anybody; I was out to rescue prescriptive grammar from the clutches of my impudent Mr Blakesley, and, if possible, to crucify him in the process.

'But, Mr Horner,' said a worried young man – in the front row, of course – 'people are always finding better ways to do things, aren't they? And usually they have to change the rules to make improvements. If nobody rebelled against the rules there'd never be any progress.'

I regarded the young man benignly: he would survive any horse manure of mine.

'That's another paradox,' I said to him. 'Rebels and radicals at all times are people who see that the rules are often arbitrary – always ultimately arbitrary – and who can't abide arbitrary rules. These are the free lovers, the women who smoke cigars, the Greenwich Village characters who don't get haircuts, and all kinds of reformers. But the greatest radical in any society is the man who sees all the arbitrariness of the rules and social conventions, but who has such a great scorn or disregard for the society he lives in that he embraces the whole wagonload of nonsense with a smile. The greatest rebel is the man who wouldn't change society for anything in the world.'

So. This troubled my bright young man no end, I'm sure, and to the rest of the class it was doubtless incomprehensible, but its effect on me was to add to my already-established sense of acumen the delicate spice of slightly smiling paradox. The mood persisted throughout the day: I left school with my head full of the Janusian ambivalence of the universe, and I walked through the world's charming equipoise, its ubiquitous polarity, to my room, where at nine o'clock that evening Rennie found me rocking in my chair, still faintly smiling at my friend Laocoön, whose grimace was his beauty.

She was nervous and quiet. We said hello to each other, and she stood about clumsily for a minute before sitting down. Clearly, some new stage had been reached.

'What now?' I asked her.

She made no answer, but ticked her cheek and gestured vacantly with her right hand.

'How's Joe?'

'The same.'

'Oh. How're you?'

'I don't know. Going crazy.'

'Joe hasn't been giving you a hard time, has he?'

She looked at me for a moment.

'He's God,' she said. 'He's just God.'

'So I understand.'

'All this week he's been wonderful. Not like he was just

after he got back from Washington – that wasn't normal for him. You'd think it was all over and done with.'

'Why shouldn't it be? That's how I felt the day after it happened.'

She sighed. 'So, I just mentioned offhand that I didn't feel like coming up here any more – didn't see any point to it.'

'Good.'

'He didn't say a word. He just gave me a long look that made me wish I was dead. Then tonight he said he'd pretty much come to accept this as a part of me, even though he couldn't understand why it had started, and he'd respect me more if I was consistent than if I repudiated what I'd done. Then he said he didn't see any need to talk about it any more, and that was that.'

'Well, by God, then, the trouble's all over with, isn't it?'

'Except that I don't particularly believe him, and even if I did, I don't recognize myself any more.'

'That's not so awful. I almost never do.'

'But Joe always does. So nothing's solved as long as I can't be as authentic as he is, and see myself in what I do as clearly as I see him in what he does. Joe's always recognizable.'

I smiled. 'Almost always.'

'You mean that time we spied on him? Oh, Jesus!' She shook her head. 'Jake, you know what? I wish I'd been struck blind before I looked in that window. That's what started everything.'

Sweet paradox: 'Or you could say that's what ended everything. But it would start or end anything only for a Morgan. Certainly not for a Horner. In my cosmos everybody is part chimpanzee, especially when he's by himself, and nobody's terribly surprised by anything the other chimpanzees do.'

'Not Joe, though.'

'Maybe the guy who fools himself least is the one who admits that we're all just kidding.'

Sweet, sweet paradox!

'Joe and I have done a Marcel Proust on this thing,' Rennie said sadly. 'We've taken it apart from every point of view we could think of. Sometimes I think I've never understood anything as thoroughly in my life as I do this, and other times – like after I was up here last time, and now – I realize I don't understand any more than I ever did. It's all still a mystery. It tears me up even when I don't see anything to be torn up about.'

'What does Joe think of me lately?'

'I don't know. I don't think he hates you any more. Probably he just doesn't care to deal with you. He thinks your part in it was probably characteristic of you.'

'Which me, for heaven's sake?' I laughed. 'How about you?'

'I still despise you, I think,' Rennie said unemotionally.

'Clear through?'

'As far as I can see.'

This thrilled me from head to foot. I had been not interested in Rennie this night until she said this, but now I was acutely interested in her.

'Has this been just since we slept together?'

'I don't know how much of it is retroactive, Jake; right now I think I've disliked you ever since I've known you, but I guess that's not so. I've had some kind of feeling about you at least since we started the riding lessons, and as far as I can see now it was a kind of dislike. Abhorrence, I guess, is a better word. I don't believe in anything like premonitions, but I swear I've wished ever since August that we'd never met you, even though I couldn't have said why.'

I felt way high on a mountaintop, thinking widely and uncloudedly; hundred-eyed Argus was not more synoptic.

'I'll bet I know one point of view you and Joe didn't try, Rennie.'

'We tried them all,' she said.

I felt like the end of an Ellery Queen novel.

'Not this one. And by the Law of Parsimony it's good, because it accounts for the most facts by the fewest assumptions. It's simple as hell, Rennie: we didn't just copulate; we made love. What you've felt all along and couldn't admit to yourself was that you love me.'

'That's right,' Rennie breathed, looking at me tautly.

'It could be. I'm not being vain. At least I'm not *just* being vain.'

'That's not what I meant,' Rennie said, and she had some difficulty saying it. 'I meant – it's not right that I've never admitted it to myself.'

Now her eyes showed real abhorrence, but it was not clear in them what or whom she abhorred. I grew very excited.

'Well, I'll be damned!'

'That's one of the things that destroys me,' Rennie said. 'The idea that I might have been in love with you all the time occurred to me along with all the rest – along with the idea that I despise you and the idea that I couldn't really feel anything about you because you don't exist. You know what I mean. I don't know which is true.'

'I suppose they're all true, Rennie,' I suggested. 'While we're at it, did you ever consider that maybe Joe's the one who doesn't exist?'

'No.' She whipped her head slowly. 'I don't know.'

'I don't think you have to be afraid of the idea that you feel some kind of love for me. Certainly it doesn't imply anything one way or the other about your feeling for Joe, unless you want to be romantic about it. In fact, I don't see where it implies anything, except that the whole affair is less mysterious than we'd supposed, and maybe less sordid.'

But Rennie clearly accepted none of this.

'Jake, I can't make love to you tonight.'

'All right. I'll take you home.'

In the car I kissed her gently. 'I think this is great. It's funny as the devil.'

'That's about right.'

'Did you tell Joe you suspected this along with the rest?'

'No.' She lowered her eyes. 'And I can't ever tell him. That's the thing, Jake,' she said, looking at me again. 'I still love him more than he or anybody else suspects, but what we had before is just out. This makes it impossible. Even if it's actually not true that I love you, the possibility that I might – the fact that I'm not sure I don't – kills everything. It doesn't solve any problems: it *is* the problem. Can you imagine how it makes me feel when he says he's accepted my relationship with you, and tries to act as if nothing had happened? The whole damned thing's a lie from now on – has been ever since I first admitted to myself that I might love you.'

'Nothing has to be wrecked, Rennie.'

'It's already wrecked, what Joe and I had before, and it was the finest thing any man and woman ever had. There's no room in it for lies or divided affections. I feel like I've been robbed of a million dollars, Jake! If I'd shot him I couldn't feel worse!'

'Do you want me to come inside with you?' I asked.

'No.'

'Aren't you just postponing things?'

'I'm postponing as much as I possibly can,' she said, 'for as long as I possibly can. I'm desperate, and that's the only thing I can think of to do.'

'Joe might have allowed for the same possibility all along,' I offered. 'He's not afraid to look at all the alternatives.'

'It wouldn't make any difference.'

'I just don't see where the situation is desperate. It wouldn't be in my world.'

'I'm not surprised,' Rennie said. I wasn't sure whether she was crying or not, since it was dark in the car. I daresay she was. We sat for some minutes without speaking, and then she opened the door to get out.

'God, Jake, I don't know where all this will lead to.'

'Neither does Joe,' I said lightly. 'Those were his very first words.'

'For Christ's sake try to remember one thing, anyhow: if I love you at all, I don't *just* love you. I swear, along with it I honestly and truly hate your God-damned guts!'

'I'll remember,' I said. 'Good night, Rennie.' She went in without replying, and I drove home to rock a bit and contemplate this new revelation. I was flattered beyond measure – I responded easily and inordinately to any evidence of affection from people whom I admired or respected in any way. But – well, perhaps this is specious, but the connoisseur is by his very nature a hair-splitter. The thing is that even in my current mood I couldn't see much of a paradox in Rennie's feelings, and I was piqued that I could not. The connoisseur – and I had been one since nine-thirty that morning – requires of a paradox, if it is to elicit from him that faint smile which marks him for what he is, that it be more than a simple ambiguity resulting from the vagueness of certain terms in the language; it should, ideally, be a really arresting contradiction of concepts whose actual compatibility becomes perceptible only upon subtle reflection. The apparent ambivalence of Rennie's feelings about me, I'm afraid, like the simultaneous contradictory opinions that I often amused myself by maintaining, was only a pseudo-ambivalence whose source was in the language, not in the concepts symbolized by the language. I'm sure, as a matter of fact, that what Rennie felt was actually neither ambivalent nor even complex; it was both single and simple, like all feelings, but like all feelings it was also completely particular and individual, and so the trouble started only when she attempted to label it with a common noun such as *love* or *abhorrence*. Things can be signified by common nouns only if one ignores the differences between them; but it is precisely these differences, when deeply felt, that make the nouns inadequate and lead the layman (but not the connoisseur) to believe that he has a paradox on his hands, an ambivalence, when actually it is merely a matter of x's being part horse and part grammar book, and completely neither. Assigning names to things is like assigning roles to people: it is necessarily a distortion, but it is a necessary distortion if one would get on with the plot, and to the connoisseur it's good clean fun.

Rennie loved me, then, and hated me as well! Let us say she x-ed me, and knew better than to smile.

During this month I had of course seen Joe any number of times at school, even though our social relationship had ended. If it had been possible I'd have avoided him altogether, not because I felt any less warmth, admiration, or respect for him – on the contrary, I felt more of all these things, and sympathy besides – but because the sight of him invariably filled me with sudden embarrassment and shame, no matter what feelings I had at other times. To feel, as Joe did, no regret for anything one has done in the past requires at least a strong sense of one's personal unity, and such a sense is one of the things I've always lacked. Indeed, the conflict between individual points of view that Joe admitted lay close to the heart of his subjectivism I should carry even further, for subjectivism implies a self, and where one feels a plurality of selves, one is subject to the same conflict on an intensely intramural level, each of one's several selves claiming the same irrefutable validity for its special point of view that, in Joe's system, individuals and institutions may claim. In other words, judging from my clearest picture of myself, the individual is not individual after all, any more than the atom is really atomistic: he can be divided further, and subjectivism doesn't really become intelligible until one finally locates the subject. I shall say that, if this did not seem to me to be the case, I should assent wholeheartedly to the Morgan ethics. As it is, if I say that sometimes I assent to it anyway and sometimes not, I can't really feel that this represents any more of an inconsistency than can be found in the statement 'Some people agree with Morgan and some don't.' In the same way, when upon confronting Joe in the hallways, in the cafeteria, or in my office I felt terribly ashamed of the trouble I'd caused him – when in my mind I not only regretted but actually repudiated my adultery – what I really felt was that *I* would not do what that Jacob Horner had done: I felt no identity with that stupid fellow. But as a point of honor (in which some Horner or other believed) I would not claim this pluralism, for fear Joe would interpret it as a defense.

Only once in September did we have what might be called a conversation. It was very near the end of the month, when, happening to see me alone in my office, he came in to talk for a few minutes. As always, he looked fresh, bright, clean, and sharp.

'Mr MacMahon's complaining that his horses are getting too fat,' he said. 'How come you quit your riding lessons?'

I blushed. 'I thought the course was finished, I guess.'

'You want to pick them up again? It's right much trouble for him to take time to exercise them as much as they need.'

'No, I guess not. I've kind of lost interest, and I don't think Rennie would enjoy it very much.'

'Don't you? Why shouldn't she?'

I should say there was no malice evident in his voice, but I couldn't help thinking I was being embarrassed purposely.

'You know why not, Joe. Why do you even suggest it?' I

was suddenly indignant on Rennie's behalf. 'I feel uncomfortable as hell criticizing you, but I don't see why you're so determined to make her feel worse than she does already.'

He jabbed his spectacles back on his nose.

'Don't worry about Rennie.'

'You mean it's a little late for me to start being thoughtful. I agree. But unless you're out to punish her I don't know why you make her come up to my room and all.'

'I'm not out to punish anybody, Jake; you know that. I'm just out to try to understand her.'

'Well, don't you understand that she's pretty much shot these days? I'm surprised she's held up this long.'

'She's pretty strong,' Joe smiled. 'You probably don't realize that in a way Rennie and I have been happier in the last few weeks than we've been for a long time.'

'How come?'

'For one thing, since this started I've shelved the dissertation for a while, so we've had more time together than usual. We've talked to each other about ourselves more than we ever did before, necessarily, and all that.'

I was appalled. 'You can't say she's been happy.'

'Not in the way you probably mean, I guess. We certainly haven't been *carefree*; but you can be pretty much happy without being carefree. The point is we've been dealing with each other pretty intensely and objectively – exploring each other as deep as we can. That part of it's been fine. And we've been outdoors a lot, because we didn't want to ruin our health over it. We've probably felt a lot closer to each other than ever, whether we've solved anything or not.'

'Do you think you have?'

'Well, we've certainly *learned* some things. For one thing we've found all kinds of ties that we weren't aware of before, so that we probably wouldn't break up even if the thing doesn't straighten itself out. I doubt if I respect her as much as before – how could I? At least not for the same things. But she's been awfully good in this. Pretty damned strong most of the time, and I appreciate that. What do you think of my friend Rennie these days?'

'Me?' I hadn't been especially thinking about what I thought of her, at least since her revelation of two nights earlier. Now I had to think about it quickly. 'Oh, I don't know,' I stalled.

'You must have had a strange picture of us both before. I'd like to know what you think of her now. Are you disgusted with her for not knowing how she feels?'

I leaned back in my chair and regarded the red pencil with which I'd been correcting grammar exercises.

'As a matter of fact,' I said, 'I might be in love with her.'

'Is that right?' he asked quickly, bright with interest.

'I wouldn't be surprised. It was right a couple of days ago, anyhow. I don't feel it very strongly now, but I don't feel that I'm not, either.'

'That's great!' Joe laughed: what he meant, I believe, was *That's interesting*. 'Is that what you felt when you went to bed with her the first time? You could have said so.'

'No. I didn't feel that way then.'

'Does Rennie know about this?'

'No.'

'How does she feel about you?'

'Not long ago she despised me. A week or so ago she said she didn't give a damn.'

'Does she love you?' he asked, smiling.

Now I've said all along that Joe was without guile, but it's almost impossible really to believe that a man is without guile. It is perhaps a great injustice that I couldn't entirely trust that open smile and clear forehead of Joe's, but I confess I did not.

'I'm pretty sure she despises me,' I said.

Joe sighed. He was sitting in the swivel chair next to mine, and now he put his feet on the desk in front of him and clasped his hands behind his head.

'Did you ever consider that maybe I'm to blame for all of this? A lot of things could be explained neatly if you just said that for some perverse reason or other I engineered the whole affair. Just a possibility, along with the rest. What do you think?'

'Perversity? I don't know, Joe. If I see anything perverse it's your sending Rennie up to my place now.'

He laughed. 'I guess you could call all my encouragements of you two perverse now that we know what happened, but if any of it was really perverse it was unconsciously so. But you can't really believe it's perversity that makes me insist on her going up to your place. That business really is a matter of testing her. She's got to decide once and for all what she really feels about you and me and herself, and you know as well as I do that if it weren't for those trips to your place she'd repress that first business as fast as she could.'

'Don't you think you're just keeping the wounds open?'

'I guess so. In fact, that's exactly what I'm doing. But in this case we've got to keep the wound open until we know just what kind of wound it is and how deep it goes.'

'It seems to me that the important thing about wounds is healing them, no matter how.'

'You're getting carried away with the analogy,' Joe smiled. 'This isn't a physical wound. If you ignore it, it might seem to go away, but in a relationship between two people wounds like this aren't healed by ignoring them – they keep coming back again if you do that.' He dropped the subject. 'So you love Rennie?'

'I don't know. I've felt that way once or twice.'

'Would you marry her if she weren't married to me?'

'I don't know. Honestly.'

'How would you take it if it turned out that the best answer to this thing was some kind of a permanent sexual relationship between you and her? I mean a triangle without conflicts or secrecy or jealousy.'

'I don't think that's an answer. I'm the kind of guy who could probably live with that sort of thing, but I don't believe either Rennie or you could.' As a matter of fact, I was interested to notice that at the very mention of marriage and permanent sexual attachments I began to grow tired of the idea of Rennie. Happy human perversity! There was little of the husband in me.

'I don't either. What's the answer, Jake? You tell me.'

I shook my head.

'Shall I shoot you both?' he grinned. 'I already own a Colt forty-five and about a dozen bullets. When Rennie and I first got going on this thing, the time I was out of school for three days or so, I dug the old Colt out of the basement and loaded it and put it on the shelf in the living-room closet, in case either of us wanted to use it on ourselves or anybody else.'

That statement thrilled me. Perhaps it was Joe Morgan, after all, that I loved. He stood up and clapped me amiably on the shoulder.

'No answers, huh?'

I shook my head. 'Damned if I know what to say, Joe.'

'Well,' he said, stretching and walking out the door, 'it's still there in the closet. Maybe we'll use it yet.'

The Colt .45 used as a sidearm by the United States military is a big, heavy, murderous-looking pistol. Its recoil raises the shooter's arm, and the fat lead slug that it fires strikes with an impact great enough to knock a man off his feet. The image of this weapon completely dominated my imagination for the next three or four days after Joe had mentioned it: I thought of it, as Joe and Rennie must have thought of it, waiting huge in their living-room closet all through the days and nights during which they had dissected and examined every minute detail of the adultery – waiting for somebody to reach a conclusion. Little wonder that Rennie's nights were sleepless! So were mine, once that machine had been introduced so casually into the problem. Even in my room it made itself terrifically present as the concrete embodiment of an alternative: the fact of its existence put the game in a different ball park, as it were; flavored all my reflections on the subject with an immediacy which I'm sure the Morgans had felt from the first, but which my isolation, if nothing else, had kept me from feeling.

I dreamed about that pistol, and daydreamed about it. In my imagination I kept seeing it as in a photographic close-up, lying hard and flat in the darkness on the closet shelf, while through the door came the indistinct voices of Joe and Rennie talking through days and nights. Talking, talking, talking. I heard only the tones of their voices – Rennie's calm, desperate, and hysterical by turns; Joe's always quiet and reasonable, hour after hour, until its quiet reasonableness became nightmarish and insane. I'm sure nothing has ever filled my head like the image of that gun. It took on aspects as various as the aspects of Laocoön's smile, but infinitely more compelling and, of course, final. It was its finality that gave the idea of the Colt its persistence. It was with me all the time.

So it was like the realization of a nightmare when, shortly afterwards, I was confronted with the weapon itself in my room, which it had already tenanted in spirit, and that's why I paled and went weak, for I have no abstract fear of pistols. Rennie came in at eight o'clock, after telephoning an hour earlier to say she wanted to see me, and to my surprise Joe came with her, and with Joe came the Colt, in a paper bag. Rennie, I thought, had been crying – her cheeks were white and her eyes swollen – but Joe seemed cheerful enough. The first thing he did after acknowledging my greeting was take the pistol out of the bag and lay it carefully on a little ash-tray stand, which he placed in the center of the room.

'There she is, Jacob,' he laughed. 'Everything we have is yours.'

I admired the gun without touching it, laughed shortly along with Joe at the poor humor of his gesture, and, as I said before, paled. It was a formidable piece of machinery, as large in fact as it had been in my imagination and no less final-looking. Joe watched my face.

'How about a beer?' I asked. The more I resolved not to show my alarm – alarm was the last thing I wanted to suggest was called for – the more plainly I could see it in my voice and manner.

'All right. Rennie? Want one?'

'No thanks,' Rennie said, in a voice something like mine.

She sat in the overstuffed chair by the front window, and Joe on the edge of my monstrous bed, so that when I opened the beer bottles and took the only remaining seat, my rocking chair, we formed most embarrassingly a perfect equilateral triangle, with the gun in the center. Joe observed this at the same instant I did, and though I can't vouch for his grin, my own was not jovial.

'Well, what's up?' I asked him.

Joe pushed his spectacles back on his nose and crossed his legs.

'Rennie's pregnant,' he said calmly.

When a man has been sleeping with a woman, no matter under what circumstances, this news always comes like the kick of a horse. The pistol loomed more conspicuous than ever, and it took me several seconds to collect my wits enough to realize that I had nothing to be concerned about.

'Congratulations!'

Joe kept smiling, not cordially, and Rennie fixed her eyes on the rug. Nobody spoke for a while.

'What's wrong?' I asked, not knowing for certain what to be afraid of.

'Well, we're not sure who to congratulate, I guess,' Joe said.

'Why not?' My face burned. 'You're not afraid *I'm* the father, are you?'

'I'm not particularly afraid of anything,' Joe said. 'But you might be the father.'

'You don't have to worry about that, Joe; believe me.' I looked a little wonderingly at Rennie, who I thought should have known better than to complicate things unnecessarily.

'You mean because you used contraceptives every time. I know that. I even know how many times you had to use them and what brand you use, Jacob.'

'What the hell's the trouble, then?'

'The trouble is that I used them every time too – same brand, as a matter of fact.'

I was stunned. There was the pistol.

'So,' Joe went on, 'if, as my friend Rennie tells me, this triangle was never a rectangle, and if her obstetrician isn't lying when he says rubbers are about eighty per cent efficient, the congratulations should be pretty much mutual. In fact, other things being equal, there's about one chance in four that you actually are the father.'

Neither Joe's voice nor his forehead indicated how he felt about this possibility.

'How sure are you that you're pregnant?' I asked Rennie. To my chagrin my voice was unsteady.

'I'm – I'm pretty late,' Rennie said, clearing her throat two or three times. 'And I've been vomiting a lot for the last two days.'

'Well, you know, you thought you were pregnant once before.'

She shook her head. 'That was wishful thinking.' She had

to wait a second before she said anything else. 'I wanted to be pregnant that time.'

'There's not much doubt,' Joe said. 'No use to hope along those lines. The obstetricians never commit themselves for a month or so, but Rennie knows her symptoms.'

I sighed uncertainly; Joe still gave no hint of his feelings. 'Boy, that complicates things, doesn't it?'

'Well, does it or not? How would you say it complicates things?'

'I guess that depends on how you all feel.'

'Why is that? Look, Horner, you ought to decide what your point of view is going to be. Rennie's the same distance from me as she is from you.'

'We should have allowed for the possibility, I guess,' I suggested carefully.

'Aren't you actually saying that *I* should have allowed for the possibility when I sent Rennie up here? I allowed for all possibilities. That doesn't necessarily mean I like the idea of her being pregnant with your kid. I don't like that possibility a single God-damned bit, if you want to know, and I didn't really look for it to happen. But I did allow for the possibility right from the time I first heard you'd laid her. If you all didn't, you're stupid.'

'It's a possibility I'd never allow for at the time,' I smiled ruefully. 'A bachelor would lead a lonely life if he did.'

'Which heaven forbid.'

I shrugged. I wasn't sure to what extent I was justified in being annoyed by his manner: the thing was too complicated. There was silence for a while. Joe chewed his thumbnail idly, Rennie still stared at the rug, and I tried to keep the gun out of my eyes and thoughts.

'What do you suggest, Joe?'

'Don't say that, now,' he protested. 'It's not all my baby. What do *you* suggest?'

'Well, I can't say anything until I know whether you want to keep the child or put it up for adoption or what. You know I'd pay for the obstetrician and the hospital and all, and the kid's support, if you decide to keep it, or help all I can with an adoption. If I could raise the child myself I'd do it.'

'But you can't vomit for Rennie or split up the labor pains with her.'

'No, I can't do that.'

'You're oversimplifying even when you say *if I decide to keep the kid*. That makes it my responsibility. You say you're willing to take on the expense, but that doesn't mean a thing and you know it. Making it a practical problem, like a money problem, is too easy. I'd be a lot happier if you'd take on your share of responsibility. You don't have to take any shit off of me. That's too easy too.'

'How do I go about taking on responsibility?' I asked. 'I'm willing.'

'Then for Christ's sake take a position and stick to it so we'll know who we're dealing with! Don't throw everything in my lap. What the hell do *you* think I should do? Tell Rennie what you want her to do and what you want me to do, and we'll tell you the same thing. Then we can work on the problem, for God's sake!'

'I don't have opinions, Joe,' I said flatly. Of course the trouble was that I had, as usual, too many opinions. I was on everybody's side.

Joe jumped off the bed, snatched up the pistol, and aimed it at my face.

'If I told you I was going to pull this trigger, would you have any opinions about that?'

I was sick. 'Go ahead and pull it.'

'Horseshit: you'd never have to face up to anything then.' He put the pistol back on the smoking stand. Rennie had watched the scene with tears in her eyes, but she wasn't weeping for either of us.

'What do *you* want to do?' Joe said roughly to her, and when she whipped her head I saw his eyes water also, although his expression didn't change. There was no alliance against me: any who wept, wept for his own sorrows.

'I don't care about anything,' Rennie said. 'Do whatever you want to.'

'I'll be damned!' Joe shouted, with tears on his cheeks. 'I'm not going to do your thinking or his either. Think for yourself, or I don't want anything to do with you! I mean it!'

'I don't want the baby,' Rennie said to him.

'You want to put it up for adoption?'

She shook her head. 'That wouldn't work. If I carried it for nine months I'd love it, and I don't want to love it. I don't want to carry it for nine months.'

'All right; there's the pistol. Shoot yourself.'

Rennie looked at him sadly. 'I will if you want me to, Joe.'

'God *damn* what I want!'

'Did you mean you want an abortion, Rennie?' I asked.

Rennie nodded. 'I want to get rid of this baby, I don't want to carry this baby.'

'Where in hell are you going to find an abortionist around here?' Joe asked disgustedly. 'This isn't New York.'

'I don't know,' Rennie said. 'But I'm not going to carry this baby. I don't want it.'

'Are you going to go to Dr Walsh like last time and let him insult you?' Joe demanded. 'He'd throw you out! I don't believe there's an abortionist in this county.'

'I don't know,' Rennie said. 'I'm going to get an abortion or shoot myself, Joe. I've decided.'

'Well, that sounds brave, Rennie, but think clearly about it: you don't know any abortionists around here, do you?'

'No.'

'And you don't know any in Baltimore or Washington or anywhere else. And you don't know anybody who's ever had an abortion, do you?'

'No.'

'Well, you say you're going to get an abortion or shoot yourself. Suppose you started tomorrow: what are you going to do to find an abortionist?'

'I don't know!' Rennie cried.

'Damn it, if there was ever a time when we've got to think straight, this is it, but you're not thinking straight. You're setting up alternatives that aren't actually open to you.'

Rennie gave a little cry and rushed to the smoking stand, but because I had seen as clearly as Joe that that was what she was being driven to I was ready when she made her move. I dived headlong from my rocker for the gun. I fell short (physical coordination was not my forte), but my fingers closed on the edge of the stand and I pulled stand, gun, and all down on top of me. Rennie, in her rush, struck my head with her shoe, a stunning blow, and fell to her kness. She scrabbled wildly for the pistol, which had landed on my left shoulder blade and slid down beside my armpit. By rolling over on it I kept it from her long enough for me to get my own hands on it, and then fended her off until I was able to get to my feet again. She made no attempt to take it from me, but went back to her chair and buried her face in her hands. Very much shaken, I left the smoking stand where it lay and kept the gun.

'You people are insane!' I said.

Joe hadn't moved, although he too was obviously shaken.

'Explain why, Horner,' he demanded, with considerable emotion.

'The hell I will,' I said. 'Do you want her to blow her damned head off?'

'I want her to think for herself,' Joe said. 'Since you stopped her, you must have some other opinion. Or is it that you just don't want your room messed up? Would you rather we go home and do our shooting?'

'For Christ's sake, Joe, do you love your wife or not?'

'You're begging the question. Do *you* love her? Is that why you stopped her?'

'I don't love anybody right now. I think you're both insane.'

'Stop saying things you can't explain. Would you rather force her to have a baby she doesn't want?'

'I don't give a damn what you all do, but I'm going to hold on to this pistol.'

'You're talking nonsense,' Joe said angrily. 'You refuse to think. You're still talking about *us all*, and you know that's a distortion. You say you don't give a damn what Rennie does, but you take away her ability to choose. You're doing all you can to confuse everything.'

'What the hell do you want?' I shouted.

'I want you to forget about everything except what's to the point and what's beside the point!' Joe said fiercely. 'People act when they're ready whether they've thought clearly or not, and if there's one thing I'd kill you for, Horner, it's for screwing up the issues so that we have to act before we've thought, or taking something as important as this out of the realm of choice. Don't think I'm just talking: I'd kill you for it.'

'What's beside the point, then?'

'Your oversimplifying is beside the point, for one thing: asking me *as the husband* what my position is; referring to Rennie and me together as if this were a conspiracy against you; blocking her actions; talking about perversity and insanity.'

'Damn it, Joe, if I hadn't jumped she'd be *dead* right now! Would you be satisfied with that?'

'We're not playing games, Jake! Forget all the movies you ever saw and all the novels you ever read. Forget everything except this problem. Everything else obscures and confuses it. Stop looking at me as if I'm a monster!' he shouted, losing his temper. 'If you ever knew a guy who's thought straight about these thing's it's me, God damn it! If you're interested, I'll tell you that you and I would probably be dead by this time too, if Rennie had shot herself; but I wouldn't have stopped her. Nobody else you ever met ever loved a female human being, Horner: they just love pictures in their heads. If I didn't love Rennie do you think I could have sat here when she went for the gun? In the name of Christ, Horner, *open your eyes*! Just this one time open your God-damned eyes and try to understand somebody!'

'Do you want me to put this pistol back on the table?'

'*Stop asking me what I want!*'

I was lost.

'Here,' I said, handing Joe the Colt. 'If you're so set on acting by your ideas, you put it back.'

Joe took the gun and unhesitatingly offered it to Rennie.

'Here,' he said gently, gripping the back of her chair for support. 'Do you want it?'

Rennie shook her head without looking at him.

'Maybe she'd like to have you do it for her,' I said, as acidly as possible, but I was so moved I was dizzy.

Joe glanced at me. 'Do you want me to shoot you, Rennie?' he asked sarcastically. She shook her head again. Joe picked up the smoking stand, replaced the pistol on it, and went to his seat on the bed.

'So Jake, you've decided we'll have the baby. Do you have any more opinions?'

I couldn't speak. Like Rennie, I shook my head. It is a demoralizing thing to deal with a man who will see, face up to, and unhesitatingly act upon the extremest limits of his ideas.

'Apparently you don't,' Joe said contemptuously. He rose and began putting on his topcoat. 'Do you want to come home now?' he asked Rennie.

Rennie rose and put on her coat. At the last minute Joe slipped the Colt into his pocket. He was extremely upset.

'Look, Joe,' I called out as they left. 'If Rennie *could* find an abortionist, what would you say?'

'What do you mean? What difference would it make what I said?'

'I mean how would you feel about the idea of her going through with an abortion?'

'I don't like it,' Joe said flatly. 'If it was a really competent abortion done in a good hospital by a good obstetrician it wouldn't matter, but it couldn't possibly be that. Rennie's in perfect health, and the only abortion she could get even in the city would be a half-ass job by some half-ass doctor who could mess her up for the rest of her life.' He turned to go.

'I'll see if I can find somebody to do it,' I said, 'and if I can find somebody decent I'll pay for it.'

'Horseshit,' Joe said.

Chapter Eleven
The next morning, early, my eyes opened suddenly

The next morning, early, my eyes opened suddenly, and I leaped in a sweat from my bed with a terrible feeling that Rennie was dead. I called the Morgans at once, and could scarcely believe it when Rennie herself answered the telephone.

'I'm sorry I woke you up, Rennie. God, I was afraid you'd shot yourself already.'

'No.'

'Listen,' I begged. 'Promise me you'll wait awhile, will you?'

'I can't promise anything, Jake.'

'You've got to, damn it!'

'Why?'

'Well, if for no other reason, because I love you.' This, I fear, was not true, at least in the sense that any meaningless proposition is not true, if not false either. I'm not sure whether I knew what I was saying when I told Joe I loved Rennie, but at any rate I couldn't see any meaning in the statement now.

'So does Joe,' Rennie said pointedly.

'Yes, all right, let's say he loves you more than I could ever love anybody. He loves you so much he's willing to let you shoot yourself, and I love you so little that I'm not.'

Rennie hung up. I dialed her number again. This time Joe answered.

'Rennie doesn't want to talk to you,' he said. 'That was a stupid thing you said a minute ago – stupid or malicious.'

'I'm sorry. Listen, Joe, do you think she'll commit suicide?'

'How the hell do I know?'

'Will you stay home with her today and see that she doesn't? Just today?'

'Of course not. For one thing, I can't think of anything more likely to make her do it tomorrow.'

'Then you *don't* want her to, do you?'

'That's beside the point.'

'Just today, Joe! Look, I might be able to get hold of somebody for her if you won't let her do anything today.'

'Do you know an abortionist? Why didn't you say so last night?'

'I'm not sure. I don't know any myself, but I know several people in Baltimore who might know of one. I'm going to call them now. Make her promise to sit still till I see.'

'Rennie doesn't take orders from me.'

'She will, and you know it. Tell her I know a doctor but I've got to call him to make arrangements.'

'We don't operate that way.'

'Just today, Joe!'

'Hold on,' he said. 'Rennie?' I heard him call to her. 'Did you intend to kill yourself today?'

I heard Rennie ask why I wanted to know.

'Horner says some of his Baltimore friends might know of an abortionist,' Joe said. I was furious that he told her the truth. 'He's going to call them and see.'

Rennie said something that I couldn't make out.

'She says she doesn't want to talk about anything,' Joe said.

'Look, Joe, I'll call around. Maybe it won't even be necessary to have an abortion. I'll try to get hold of some Ergotrate. That ought to do it. Tell Rennie I'll stop out there today or tonight and either bring the Ergotrate with me or else have something definite arranged.'

'Yeah, I'll tell her,' Joe said, and hung up.

Now it wasn't quite true – in fact it wasn't at all true – that I had friends in Baltimore who might know abortionists, for I had no friends in Baltimore or anywhere else. What I did next was telephone every doctor in Wicomico, in alphabetical order. To the first one I said, 'Hello. My name is Henry Dempsey. We're new in town and we don't have any regular doctor. Say, listen, my wife's in a terrible predicament: we have two kids already, and she thinks she's pregnant again. She's not a healthy girl – physically okay, you know, but not *psychologically* healthy. In fact she's under psychiatric care right now. I frankly don't think she could stand the strain of another pregnancy.'

'Really?' said the doctor. 'Who's her psychiatrist?'

'You might not know him,' I said. 'He's in White Plains, New York, where we used to live. Banks. Dr Joseph Banks.'

'Does your wife commute to White Plains for treatment?' the doctor asked innocently.

'We just moved, sir, as I said, and we haven't been able to find another psychiatrist yet.'

'Well, that's out of my line.'

'I know, sir; I didn't mean that. I'm afraid my wife might commit suicide over this pregnancy, before I can get her to another psychiatrist. She's in a terrible state. Frankly, I was wondering if you wouldn't prescribe Ergotrate or something for her. I know it's out of line, but this is a desperate case. In a year, two years, she could very well be adjusted enough to have all the kids we want – we don't want a *large* family, but we'd like to have three or four. A pregnancy now will mess her up completely.'

'I'm sorry, Mr Dempsey,' the doctor said coldly. 'I can't do that.'

'Please, Doctor! I'm not asking you to go outside the law. I'll get a sworn affidavit from Dr Banks in White Plains. Will that be okay? He'll take all the responsibility.'

'No, Mr Dempsey. I appreciate your dilemma, but my hands are tied.'

'Doesn't the law allow you to take measures when the woman's life is in danger?'

'It's not what the law says, I'm afraid: it's what the people in town *think* the law says, and frankly the people around here are as opposed to abortions as I am, whether they're done by drugs or surgery. Besides, if your wife's trouble is mental, it's not that clearly a matter of life or death.'

'It is! Dr Banks will tell you so!'

'I'm sorry, Mr Dempsey. Good-by.'

I tried the same story on the other doctors whom I found listed in the telephone book – those who would speak to me at all – only I located my mythical psychiatrist in Philadelphia instead of White Plains, in case I had to drive up there to get the proper postmark on a fake letter. Also, after consulting the Philadelphia directory in the lobby of the Peninsula Hotel, I changed the psychiatrist's name from Joseph C. Banks to Harry L. Siegrist, the name of a bona fide psychiatric practitioner whom I picked at random from the book. But all the doctors turned me down. My nerve began to flag: so predisposed was I to obeying laws, and so much did I fear, as a rule, the bad opinion even of people whom I neither knew nor cared about, it was all I could do to tell my elaborate fiction just once, and with each refusal it became harder to repeat. The effort was demoralizing.

Doctor No. 7, to my inexpressible relief, seemed not quite so unreceptive to my story. His name was Morton Welleck, and he sounded like a younger man than his colleagues.

'Now, Mr Dempsey,' he said, when I'd finished my piece, 'you realize that any doctor who agrees to help your wife is assuming considerable responsibility, don't you?'

'Indeed I do, Dr Welleck. If there's any way for me to legally assume all the responsibility, I'll do it gladly.'

'But unhappily there isn't. I sympathize with your problem, though, and the law does provide that where there's clear danger to the patient's life, certain measures can be taken at the physician's discretion. You admit that Mrs Dempsey is in good physical condition, so the question is whether her psychological condition is as serious as you believe it is. That would be a difficult thing to prove if anybody wanted to make an issue out of it, and I may as well tell you that certain of my older colleagues in Wicomico would jump at the chance to make an issue out of a thing like this. Frankly, I'm not the martyr type.'

But I saw the shadow of a chance in Dr Welleck's tone.

'Wouldn't a sworn affidavit from Dr Siegrist do the trick?' I pleaded. 'He'd be glad to provide one.'

'It might,' Dr Welleck admitted. 'Of course, I'd have to examine Mrs Dempsey myself, if only to make sure she's pregnant!' We both laughed, I more tightly than he. 'And I'd want to ask her a few questions, you know, even though I'm not a psychiatrist.'

'Certainly. I'll have her come right down to your office.' I hoped fervently that Dr Welleck was new in town.

'Do that,' he said, 'and have Dr Siegrist call me from

Philadelphia, would you? We can decide whether it's advisable to get the affidavit or not, and he can explain Mrs Dempsey's problem in more detail.'

The prospect of driving to Philadelphia at once and impersonating a psychiatrist appalled me, but it seemed my only hope.

'All right,' I agreed, 'I'll telephone him as soon as I can and have him call you.'

'That will be fine,' Dr Welleck said. He paused a moment. 'You realize, Mr Dempsey, that I can't promise anything. Like a lot of small towns, Wicomico is dead set against frustrating Mother Nature. Mainly, I'll admit, it's the older doctors here who are responsible: I doubt there's been a legal abortion here for years and years. Professional ethics aside, they're a collection of old sticks-in-the-mud. If they and some of the religious groups in town got wind of anything like this they'd crucify the poor fellow who did it. We can't always be as liberal as some of us might like to be.'

'I understand perfectly, Doctor, but this really is a matter of life or death.'

'Well. We'll see what we can do.'

Dr Welleck's manner gave me some confidence that he could be swindled. For one thing, he talked too much: three of the doctors I'd called had refused to discuss anything at all over the telephone, and none of the others had been anything like so garrulous as young Dr Welleck. Also, from the nature of the conversation I gathered that he was finding it difficult to compete with the older practitioners, perhaps because he was new in town. Any professional man who would criticize his colleagues to a perfect stranger on the telephone was, I guessed, a man with whom arrangements could be made.

But Philadelphia! To fake a letter was one thing – I could be anybody in a letter – but I found it almost insuperably difficult to be even Henry Dempsey on the telephone: how could I be Dr Harry L. Siegrist? There was no time to waste; already it was ten o'clock, and Philadelphia is two and a half hours from Wicomico. Luckily it was Saturday – I had no classes to teach, but the college library was open. I drove out there at once, borrowed the first textbook on abnormal

156

psychology that I could find, and set out for Philadelphia without delay. I'd gone no more than ten miles before I realized that if an affidavit had to be mailed from Philadelphia, it would certainly have to be a typewritten document, and I'd never be able to find a typewriter in a strange city. Back home I went, breaking the speed limits, and rushed up to my room. It was after eleven when I got there.

To whom it may concern, *I wrote, scratching desperately for sentences*: Susan Bates Dempsey, age twenty-eight, wife of Henry J. Dempsey of Wicomico, Maryland, was a patient of mine between August 3, 1951, and June 17, 1953, shortly after which time Mr and Mrs Dempsey left Philadelphia to live in Wicomico. Mrs Dempsey became my patient on the advice of her husband and her physician, Dr Edward R. Rice of this city, after suffering frequent periods of acute despondency. During two of these periods she threatened to take her own life, and once even slashed her wrists with a kitchen knife. Examination indicated that Mrs Dempsey had pronounced manic-depressive tendencies, the more dangerous because during her most acute depressions her two young sons often became the objects of her hostility, although at other times she was a competent, even a superior, mother. Mrs Dempsey suffered markedly from the fear that she might lose her husband's affections: in her depressive states she was inclined to believe that the birth of her sons had detracted from her beauty, and this belief tended to focus her resentment upon her children. However, because she felt only hostility and not persecution, and because her periods of despondency alternated with periods of intense exuberance, even jubilation, my diagnosis was subacute manic-depressive psychosis rather than paranoia.

During the period of her treatment, the amplitude of Mrs Dempsey's manic-depressive cycle showed an appreciable decrease, and at no time after becoming my patient did she threaten to take her life or the lives of her children. She responds satisfactorily to competent psychotherapy, and with continued treatment I believe her condition can be stabilized. When the Dempseys left Philadelphia I recommended that her treatment be continued if possible, but suggested to Mr Dempsey that immediate resumption was not urgent. However, I also recommended that Mrs Dempsey avoid pregnancy until completely cured, since her former pregnancies had been largely responsible for her condition.

I believe that an accidental pregnancy at this time may produce a critical recurrence of her despondency; that she may again threaten to take her life, rather than carry the fetus; and that she may very well carry out her threat even if psychiatric treatment were resumed at once. I unhesitatingly recommend, even urge, that for the protection of her other children and herself, Mrs Dempsey's pregnancy be aborted at the earliest possible moment.

I signed the letter, '*Harry L. Siegrist, M.D.*', put it into an envelope, and hurried back to my car. I stopped along the road to eat lunch and bone up on the manic-depressive psychosis, and by shortly after three o'clock I was in a telephone booth in a Penn-Whelan drugstore on Walnut Street in Philadelphia, placing a long-distance call to Dr Welleck in Wicomico. My hands shook; I sweated. When I heard Dr Welleck's receptionist answer, and the operator asked me to deposit sixty cents, I dropped a quarter on the floor: my courage barely sufficed to retrieve it and ask for Dr Welleck.

'I'm sorry, Dr Siegrist,' the receptionist said after I'd introduced myself. 'Dr Welleck is at the hospital just now.'

'Oh, that's too bad!' I exclaimed in gruff disappointment. 'I don't suppose you could reach him?'

'I'm afraid not, sir; he's in surgery this afternoon.'

'What a bother!' I was immensely relieved, almost joyous, that I wouldn't have to speak to him, but at the same time I feared for my plan.

'I'll have him call you as soon as he comes in, if you like.'

'Oh, now, I'm afraid that won't do,' I said peevishly. 'My vacation started today, and Mrs Siegrist and I will be in Bermuda all through October. Mr Dempsey reached me just as we were closing up the house – thank heaven! Another hour and we'd have been gone. You know, this is something of an emergency, but my plane leaves two hours from now and I couldn't say where I'll be between now and then. Dr Welleck *will* administer Ergotrate, won't he? This could turn into a nasty thing.'

'He wanted to talk to you, Dr Siegrist.'

'I know, I know. Well, see here, I'll have my secretary type up an affidavit before I leave – this is quite a routine thing, you know – and I'll have it notarized and sent special delivery and all that. What a nuisance that I can't talk to Dr Welleck personally!' I said with some heat. 'I can't emphasize too much the seriousness of this sort of thing with a manic-depressive like Mrs Dempsey. She could behave perfectly normally one moment and shoot herself the next, if she hasn't already. Really, Dr Welleck should give her the Ergotrate at the earliest possible moment. Tonight if possible; tomorrow at the very latest. I've already arranged with Mr Dempsey to place his wife under the care of one of my colleagues until I get back, but this thing really must be taken care of first.'

'I'll tell Dr Welleck at once,' the receptionist said, clearly impressed.

'Please do, and he'll get the affidavit tomorrow morning.'

'Could you give me your Bermuda address, sir, in case Dr Welleck wants to get in touch with you?'

Great heavens! 'Mrs Siegrist and I will be stopping at the Prince George Hotel,' I said, hoping there was such a place.

'The Prince George. Thank you, sir.'

'And please, tell Dr Welleck to get that Ergotrate into Mrs Dempsey as soon as he can. I'd hate to lose a patient over something as silly as this. I don't blame the man for being cautious, but I must say that if it were I, she'd be aborted by this time. A layman could tell she's manic-depressive, and her suicidal tendencies stick out all over. Good-by, now.'

I hung up, and very nearly fainted. A big obstacle was behind me, but there was a still bigger one ahead. I found a notary public in a loan office two blocks down Walnut Street (which I prayed Dr Siegrist didn't happen to patronize) and went in quickly before my nerve failed. It is my lot to look older than my years, but I could scarcely believe anyone would seriously take me for a certified psychiatrist. Besides, it is even more difficult to act out a fiction face to face with the man you're lying to than it is to do it on the telephone. Finally, I wasn't at all sure that notaries didn't demand identification before administering the oath and seal. Assuming the most worldly manner I could muster, I asked a clerk where the notary public was, and he directed me to the assistant manager's desk across the room.

'Howdy do,' smiled the assistant manager, a squat, bald-headed, cigar-chewing little man with steel-rimmed glasses.

'My name's Siegrist,' I said genially: 'Harry Siegrist. I've a paper here somewhere to be notarized, if I haven't left it at the office.' I smiled and made a leisurely search of my pockets. 'Oh yes, here you are, you little rascal.' I fetched the letter from my inside coat pocket, opened it, and casually scanned it. 'Mmm-*hmm*. There you go, sir.'

The assistant manager read the document carelessly.

'Boy oh boy,' he said. 'She's a real bat, isn't she, Doc?'

'Not as bad as some we get,' I chuckled.

'Ha!' said the notary. 'You ought to see some of the boobies we get in here. You could make a fortune.'

I waited to be asked for my credentials.

'I swear,' the notary mused absently, 'I think it's all in their heads. Well – ' He began fumbling in his desk drawer. 'Raise your right hand a little bit, will you, Doc?'

I did, and he likewise.

'Now, then, d'you swear before God that the blah blah blah blah and all that?' he asked, still digging around in his desk with the other hand.

'I do.'

'Won't make no difference whether you do or not if I can't find my seal,' he said cheerfully. My head reeled – after my good luck in finding a notary as cynical as he was credulous, could my scheme hang on such a mischance?

'Ah, there she blows,' he said, fishing out the seal. He clamped the official impression on my letter and signed it. Then he called two nearby clerks over to sign as witnesses. 'Don't mind reading it,' he told them. 'Just put your John Hancock where it says.' They did. 'All right, Doctor: buck and a half.'

I paid him with a bill from my wallet, holding my identity card from view, and left with my letter, which I dropped into the first deposit box I encountered. So much for Philadelphia – it was four o'clock, and I had to get home fast. In general I was amazed at the success of my plan, but four distressing things were on my mind. First, I had no idea whether Dr Welleck would be convinced by my completely non-technical affidavit, which for all I knew any M.D. might be able to recognize as spurious at first glance; at any rate, it was entirely possible that if any doubt remained in his mind the coincidence of Dr Siegrist's taking so immediate a vacation might turn that doubt into skepticism: should Welleck at any time be dubious enough to call the office of the real Dr Siegrist, the jig was up. Second, I had deliberately not left a telephone number with Welleck, and of course there was no Henry Dempsey in the Wicomico directory; despite the fact that there are human beings without telephones, Welleck's inability to reach me, should he try before I got home and called him, could add to his suspicion. The third unknown was even more worrisome: even if everything else worked out perfectly and Welleck consented to administer the Ergotrate, it was quite possible that he was not new in town at all and might know Rennie. Finally, even if he didn't, there was one more danger: so innocent was I of the business of abortion that, for all I knew, Welleck might require that Rennie go to the hospital for something or other, since the thing was going to be legal, and even if Welleck himself didn't know her, someone at the hospital surely would.

As soon as I reached my room again I called Welleck at his house.

'Oh, Mr Dempsey,' he said, a little coldly. 'I've been trying to telephone you.'

'I'm sorry, Doctor. We haven't had a phone put in yet, and I have to use my landlord's. I'd have called you earlier, but I've been driving my wife around in the country today, to sort of keep her mind off things.'

'Well, Dr Siegrist called from Philadelphia.'

'Did he? Good! I barely caught him before he left on his vacation. Did you get anything straightened out?'

'I didn't talk to him. I was in surgery. He talked to my receptionist, and he's sending down an affidavit. My understanding is that he strongly recommends the abortion.'

'Whew!' I laughed. 'You don't know how relieved I am.'

'Yes. Now he said something to my receptionist about giving the Ergotrate tonight, but I'm afraid I can't do it until I have the affidavit in my hands. If he mailed it special delivery this afternoon, I should get it at least by Monday morning.'

'That's wonderful.'

'You give me your landlord's number and I'll let you know when the affidavit comes so you can bring Mrs Dempsey in to the office.'

'Well, now, my landlord's right touchy about receiving calls for me, and frankly this is none of his business. I'd rather he knew nothing about it, because he's a terrible gossip. Couldn't I call you?'

'Perhaps that would be better. Despite the fact that this won't be illegal, we'd just as well keep it quiet. Call me around noon on Monday, and if I have the affidavit I'll give you an appointment for after lunch.'

'That's fine.'

'Oh, one more thing. I have a standard authorization form that I use for sterilizations, abortions, and the like. Both you and your wife will have to sign it, and you'll have to get it notarized. You could do that Monday morning if you like. Just pick up the form from my receptionist.'

'Okay. Swell. Good night, Doctor.'

Another document, another notary, another hurdle to clear – but by this time I was past caring. I drove in weary triumph out to the Morgans' house to announce my success. On their doorstep I got the cold shudders: I'd been out of town most of the day – what if I was already too late? Joe answered the door.

'Oh, hello, Jake. You look sick.'

'Is Rennie okay?'

'She's still with us, if that's what you mean. Come on in.'

Rennie was waxing the kitchen floor. She scarcely acknowledged my presence.

'Well, I think it's all set,' I said, feigning tranquillity. 'If you want an abortion, Rennie, you can get a shot of Ergotrate Monday afternoon.'

Joe showed no reaction to the news. Rennie came to the kitchen doorway, waxing rag in hand, and leaned against the doorframe.

'All right. Where do I have to go? Baltimore?'

'Nope. Right here in town. Just don't tell me you know Dr Morton Welleck.'

'Dr Welleck. No, I don't know him. Do you, Joe?'

'I know of him. He's been here about two years. You mean the damned fool's an abortionist?'

'Nope,' I said, not a little proudly. 'He's a completely legitimate doctor, and a pretty good one, so I hear. And everything's going to be completely legal. You don't have to feel guilty or afraid of going to him at all.'

'How come?' Joe asked.

'As a matter of fact, I told him pretty much the truth. I said you had two kids already and wanted more later, but you were so despondent about getting pregnant just now that I was afraid you were on the verge of suicide. Of course it was a little more elaborate than that.'

'How was it more elaborate, Jake?' Rennie asked wonderingly.

'Well, I had to jazz it up a little. You're my wife these days, for one thing: Mrs Henry J. Dempsey, of the Philadelphia Dempseys.'

'What?'

I warmed to the story then, exhilarated by my day's adventures, and told them in detail about the telephone calls, the trip to Philadelphia, the letter, the impersonations of Dr Siegrist, and the assistant manager of the loan office. They listened in astonishment.

'So, all Mr and Mrs Dempsey have to do now is sign an authorization Monday morning and get it notarized, and we're set. You don't have to act crazy or anything, and once you've had the shot you can forget the whole business.'

Joe watched Rennie with interest.

'That's absurd,' she said at once.

'Isn't it fantastic?' I grinned, not wanting to believe she meant what I feared she meant.

'It's horrible!'

'You'll do it, won't you?'

'Of course not. It's out of the question.'

'Out of the question! Good Christ, Rennie, I've run my ass off today getting it set up, and you say it's out of the question. Nothing will happen, I swear!'

'That isn't the point, Jake. I'm through lying. Even if I didn't have to sign anything or say anything it would still be lying. You should've known I wouldn't want anything to do with it.'

The whole edifice came down. Joe's expression didn't change, but I felt a great unanimity of spirit between him and Rennie. I was out of it.

'Shoot yourself then, damn it!' I cried. 'I don't know why I bothered to sweat my tail off for you today anyhow, if you don't really want an abortion. Obviously you were just being melodramatic last night.'

Rennie smiled. 'I *am* going to shoot myself, Jake, as soon as it's clear that you can't arrange an abortion. I wasn't just being dramatic. I don't care who does the job or where it's done or under what circumstances, but I won't tell lies or assent to lies, and I won't pretend to be anybody but myself. I don't know anybody and Joe doesn't either. If you hadn't said you thought you did, I wouldn't have waited this long.' She rubbed her hand once across her stomach. 'I don't want this baby, Jake. It might be yours.'

She was clearly sincere. I looked desperately to Joe for support, but he was noncommittal. Again I felt their unanimity. It occurred to me to accuse them of romanticism; to make fun of their queer honor – God knows it needed poking fun at, and a great part of me longed to do the job wholeheartedly – but I no longer trusted this strategy: it might only confirm what was already evidently a pretty fixed resolve.

'Don't do it yet, Rennie,' I said wearily. 'I'll think of something else.'

'What will you think of, Jake? If you had any real ideas you wouldn't have started with something as fantastic as this business today. If you think I'll change my mind if you stall long enough, you're wrong.'

'What about the boys? Have you given them a thought, or are you going to plug them too?'

'You're asking questions you don't have to ask,' Joe said.

'Don't play games, Jake,' Rennie said. 'Do you have anything on your mind or not?'

'Yes, I do,' I said. 'I know a woman in town who's had a couple of abortions. I'd have thought of her before if I hadn't been so excited. I'll see her tomorrow and find out where she had them done.'

'I don't believe you,' Rennie said.

'It's the truth, I swear it.'

'What's her name, then? Don't make up one.'

'Peggy Rankin. She teaches English at the high school.'

Rennie went to the telephone at once and looked for the name in the directory.

'8401,' she said. 'I'll call her and ask her.'

'Don't be silly! She's not married. Would she admit something like that to a stranger?'

'You call her, then. Right now. You must not be a stranger if you know that about her.'

'You're making it impossible. Women don't work that way – other women, anyhow. I'll see her tomorrow and let you know tomorrow night.'

'I think you're stalling, Jake.'

'Well, think it, damn it! Are you so trigger-happy you can't wait twenty-four hours?' I felt as though I'd explode any instant from sheer desperation, but still Joe watched us impassively. There were books and notebooks open beside the telephone on the writing table: he'd been working on his dissertation! Rennie thought a moment.

'I'll wait till tomorrow night,' she said, and went back to waxing the floor.

Rennie had stated the matter exactly when she accused me of stalling in hopes that she'd change her mind, but I could no longer entertain such hopes. Certainly I hadn't the slightest idea whether Peggy Rankin had ever had an abortion, and I had no reason to expect that she'd help me even if she could, for I'd not seen her since the time early in September. She had telephoned me – first hopefully, then angrily, and at last pleadingly – a number of times in the past few weeks, but I'd received her calls without encouragement. The next morning, Sunday, I telephoned her.

'Jake Horner, Peggy. I have to see you about something important.'

'Well, I don't want to see you,' she said.

'This is something awfully serious, Peggy, believe me.'

'Yes. It has been about a month, hasn't it?'

'Listen, it doesn't have anything to do with that. I'm trying to help somebody who needs help very badly.'

'You're a real humanitarian.'

'Peggy, for God's sake! I won't pretend I've been very thoughtful of you, but this is a pretty desperate thing. I realize there's no reason why you should do me any favors.'

'That's right.'

'Look, you've got me over a barrel. You might not be able

to help these friends of mine even if you wanted to, but they're in such a spot that I'd do absolutely anything to help them out. Name your own conditions.'

'What do you want me to do?'

'All I want you to do is let me talk to you for a few minutes. As I said, you might not be able to help at all, but there's just a chance that you might.'

'Who are the friends?'

'I can't talk over the phone. Can I see you today?'

'Jake, if this is another line I'll kill you.'

'It's no line!' I said vehemently. 'This doesn't have anything to do with me. When can I see you? The sooner the better.'

'Well. All right, then. Come on over now. But God, Jake, be straight this time.'

'This is straight.'

I drove over to her place immediately, and she received me with great suspicion, as though she expected to be assaulted at any moment.

'I don't even like to have you in here,' she said nervously. 'What is it?'

'The wife of one of the guys at school is pregnant, Peggy, and she's going to kill herself if she can't get an abortion.'

Peggy's face went hard. 'What a monster you are! And you come to me for help!'

'You don't understand yet. They're both good friends of mine, and they don't know where to get the abortion.'

'Am I supposed to know? Why doesn't she have the kid, if she's married?' This last with some bitterness.

'She's got two already, and frankly there's some question about who's the father of this one. That's why she's desperate. Her husband knows all about it. She just made one slip.'

'Jake, are you the one?'

This I took to be a crucial question: her willingness to help might hinge on my answer, and I had no idea which answer she wanted to hear.

'That's right, Peggy.' I looked her straight in the eye, putting all my money on honesty. 'It was the stupidest thing I ever did in my life, and now she's going to shoot herself. I've messed them up completely. All I can do now is try to clean up as much of the mess as I can.'

'When did you start cleaning up your messes?'

'Two days ago. If I can't find a way to help them by tonight, it'll be too late. That's all the time I've got.'

'She won't kill herself,' Peggy said contemptuously. 'If women killed themselves out of remorse I'd have been dead at least since July.'

'She will, Peggy. She'd be dead now if I hadn't stopped her, and she'll be dead tomorrow if I can't help her.'

'What do you care?'

I still looked her straight in the eye. 'I said I'm trying to clean up my messes.'

'You mean *this* mess.'

'I mean all my messes.'

'Some of them it's too late to clean up.'

'Maybe. But I'm going to do my best.'

'What's that?'

'I don't know, Peggy. I'm new at this. Right now I'm doing whatever people want me to do. I said you could name your conditions.'

Peggy stared at me awhile.

'Who's this girl?'

'Rennie Morgan. Her husband teaches history at the college.'

But obviously Peggy was more concerned about herself.

'Do you think I've had abortions before? I guess you'd assume that, though, wouldn't you?'

'I'm not assuming anything. I hoped maybe you'd know somebody who has had one, or that maybe you'd have heard of an abortionist.'

'Suppose I did know of one?'

'I said already there's no reason why you should help me, and I take it you don't feel one way or the other about Rennie Morgan – or maybe you dislike her, I don't know. All I can say is that this is my last chance to keep her from committing suicide, and I'll do absolutely anything to get your help.'

'You must love her a lot.'

'If I do I don't know it. Do you know of an abortionist, Peggy?'

After a while she said, 'Yes, I do. I had to find one myself, two years ago.'

'Who was it?'

'I haven't decided yet that I'm going to help you, Jake.'

'Look,' I said, in the straightest tone I could manage, 'you don't have to assert your position; I'm aware of your position. You don't have to hold out for anything; I've already told you to write your own ticket.'

'I could help you,' Peggy said: 'this man's still around, and he'd do the job. His price is two hundred dollars.'

I thought it would be effective if I stood close in front of her, laid my hands on her shoulders, and leaned down to look into her eyes. And so I did.

'What's yours?' I asked, with appropriate calm.

'Oh, Jake, I could name a high price! You've been desperate for a day or two, but I've been desperate for fifteen years!'

'Name it.'

'Why? Once she'd had the operation, you'd leave me.'

'You want me to marry you, Peggy?'

'That would be my price,' she said.

'I'll do it.'

'You probably would. Then which would you do afterwards? Leave me flat, or torture me for the rest of my life?'

'Neither one of those sounds like a good way to clean up messes,' I grinned.

'You couldn't possibly do anything but hate me. No man ever loved a woman he was coerced into marrying.'

'Try me.'

Peggy was extremely nervous, excited by the position she had me in, a little afraid of her temerity.

'How can I believe you, Jake? You haven't done one single thing to make me believe you can be trusted.'

'I know it.'

'And yet you say you're being sincere this time?'

'That's right.'

'You don't love me.'

'I don't love anybody. But I've been a bachelor a good

while, and even without this abortion thing I owe you enough to last a right long time.'

Peggy shook off my hands and whipped her head in a manner quite like Rennie's.

'What is it about you? Even when you're being kind you put me in a false position – a humiliating position.'

'Well, you be quiet, then. Let me propose to you. I've decided that I want to marry you. If I ever said an honest thing in my life, that's it.'

'You never did say an honest thing to me, did you?'

'I just said one. I'd marry you today if we could get the lisence on Sunday. We'll get it tomorrow and get married on Wednesday.'

'You said she had to know tonight.'

'That's right. All you have to do is tell her you know a guy. You can call her right now. I think that'll do it. Tell her that for personal reasons or something you can't give his name until Wednesday. If she agrees to wait, I'm satisfied.'

'But if she doesn't, that's that?'

Another crucial question, but the proper answer was obvious.

'If she doesn't, there's nothing else I can do for her, but I don't see where that would change my obligation to you. You'd have done all I asked, and I'd do everything I promised.'

Now Peggy began to cry, squirming with indecision.

'I'll marry you and love you as much as I can ever love anybody, for the rest of my life,' I swore.

She wept for a while without replying, until I began to grow apprehensive. Something else had to be done, immediately. I considered embracing her: would that turn the trick, or spoil everything? I was aware that every move was critical now; any word or action – or any silence or inaction – could convince her suddenly of my sincerity or insincerity. Peggy Rankin! I was cursed with an imagination too fertile to be of any use in predicting my fellow human beings: no matter how intimate my knowledge of them, I was always able to imagine and justify contradictory reactions from them to almost anything. A kiss now: would she regard it as evidence that I was overplaying my hand, or as evidence that I was too sincere to care whether she thought me insincere? If I made no move, would she think my inaction proof that I couldn't carry the fraud further, that I was so sure she was hooked that no further move was necessary, or that in my profound sincerity I was afraid to move for fear she'd think my proposal a mere stratagem after all?

I took her head in my hands and turned her face up to me. She hesitated for a moment and then accepted a long kiss.

'Thank God you believed me, Peggy,' I said quietly.

'I don't.'

'*What?*'

'I don't believe a single lying word you've said since you walked in here. I should have hung up on you when you called. Please get out.'

'Good Christ, Peggy! You've got to believe me!'

'If you don't get out I'm going to scream. I mean it.'

'Don't you believe Rennie Morgan's going to shoot herself?' I shouted.

She let out a yell, and I had to clap my hand over her mouth to stop her. She kicked and pummeled me, and tried to bite my hand. I forced her back into her chair, sat on her lap to keep her legs still, and clamped my other hand around her throat. She was fairly strong, and it was all I could do to hold her – with Rennie it would not have been possible at all.

'I'm more desperate than you think, damn it! I meant it when I said I'd marry you, and I mean it when I say I'm going to throttle you right this minute if you don't help me.'

Her eyes got round, I took my hand off her mouth, and as soon as she tried to holler again I squeezed her windpipe hard – really hard, digging my thumb and forefinger into the sides of her neck.

'Stop it!' she squeaked. I let up, afraid I'd really damaged her. The breath rushed into her lungs with a great croak.

'Who's the abortionist?' I demanded.

'There isn't any,' she said, clutching her throat. 'I don't know any! I was just trying to –'

I slammed her as hard as I could and ran out of the place.

There was nothing else to do: whether I had been sincere

or not, whether she had been lying or not, made no difference now. I went home and sat in the rocking chair. It was already eleven-thirty in the morning. I was out of straws to clutch at, and out of energy, beaten clear down the line. I tried to force my imagination to dream up another long shot, but all I could think of was Rennie, eight or ten hours from that moment, going to the living-room closet without a word. Joe, perhaps, would be bent over a notebook on the writing table. He might hear Rennie put down – her newspaper? – and go to the closet. I could imagine him then either continuing to stare at the notebook, but no longer seeing the words he'd written, or maybe turning his head to watch her open the closet door. The boys would be asleep in their room. I didn't believe Rennie would come back into the living room to do it. There in the closet, where the half-open door would stand between her and Joe, she'd reach the Colt down from the shelf, move the safety catch off, put the muzzle to her temple, and pull the trigger at once, before the feel of the barrel against her head made her vomit. I believed she might sit down on the closet floor to do it.

That was as far as I could imagine with any clarity, for I'd never seen a bloody corpse. For perhaps two hours – that is, until about one-thirty – this sequence of actions repeated itself over and over in my imagination, up to the moment of the explosion. Drastic courses: I could go out there and – try to rush for the gun? But what would I do with it? They'd simply look at me, and Rennie would use something else later. Grab Rennie and hold her, if possible. Forever? Call the police and tell them – that a woman was about to commit suicide. What could they do? She'd be sitting home reading the paper, Joe working at the writing table. Tell her I've arranged an abortion – with whom? For when? Tell her – what?

My rocking slowed to a nearly imperceptible movement. Except for the idea of the gun against Rennie's temple, the idea of the lead slug waiting deep in the chamber – which was not an image but a tenseness, a kind of drone in my head – my imagination no longer pictured anything. My bladder was full; I needed to go to the bathroom, but I didn't go. After a while the urgency passed. I decided to try to say

Pepsi-Cola hits the spot, but after the first couplet I forgot to say the rest. The urge to urinate returned, more sharply than before. I couldn't decide to get up.

Someone downstairs turned a radio on loud, and I jumped to my feet. It was three o'clock: the half-minute that I thought I'd spent not getting up to go to the bathroom had been an hour and a quarter! A moment later I hurried downstairs to the car; I drove out past the Morgans' at sixty miles an hour, out in the country to Vineland, and to the Remobilization Farm. I found Mrs Dockey in the entrance hall, tying up large corrugated boxes with rope.

'Where's the Doctor? I have to see him right away.'

She jerked her head toward the back of the house. As I went through the reception room I noticed rolled carpets, disarranged furniture, and more paper boxes.

'You're upset,' the Doctor observed as soon as he saw me. Dressed in a black wool suit, he was reading the Sunday paper on the back porch, which in cold weather was converted into a sun parlor. He was, fortunately, alone: most of the patients were either taking the air out front or lounging in the reception room. 'Sit down.'

'I had a touch of my trouble this afternoon,' I said.

'Immobility?' He put down his paper and looked at me more carefully. 'Then you haven't been applying the therapies.'

'No, I'll confess I haven't. I've been awfully busy lately.'

It was cool outside, even chilly, but the sun shone brightly, and out over a marshy creek behind the farmhouse a big gray fish hawk hung motionless against the wind. I didn't know where to start.

'If that's so,' the Doctor said critically, 'I don't understand why you were immobilized.'

'I think I can explain it. What I've been doing is trying to straighten out some problems that have come up.'

'Well. This time I'm afraid I'll have to know the problem, since it developed after you started therapy. Maybe we'd better go into the Progress and Advice Room.'

'I can tell you right here. It won't take long.'

'No. Let's go into the Progress and Advice Room. You go

on in – tell Mrs Dockey so she'll know where we are – and I'll be there in a minute.'

I did as he said, and a little while later he came in and took his position facing me. He'd changed into a white medical jacket.

'Now, what is it?'

With my knees straight in front of me and my arms folded across my chest, I told him the story of my brief affair with Rennie, and its consequences. To my surprise it came rather easily, so long as I stuck to the actual events and made no attempt to explain anybody's motives. The most difficult thing was to handle my eyes during the telling: the Doctor, as usual, leaned forward, rolling his unlit cigar around in his mouth, and watched my face the whole time; I focused first on his left eye, then on his right, then on his forehead, the bridge of his nose, his cigar – and it became disconcerting that I couldn't hold my eyes still for more than a few moments. I told him all the details of my search for an abortionist, and even my interview with Peggy Rankin. It was enormously refreshing to articulate it all.

'There's no question at all about Rennie's resolve,' I said at last. 'She'll commit suicide tonight if I can't tell her something definite, and I ran out of possibilities at eleven-thirty this morning. It was after that that the paralysis set in, and it lasted until an hour or so ago, when somebody downstairs from me turned a radio on. She'll shoot herself five or six hours from now.'

'Is this your idea of a tranquil existence?' the Doctor demanded irritably. 'I told you to avoid complications! I told you specifically not to become involved with women! Did you think your therapies were just silly games? Were you just playing along with me to amuse yourself?'

'I don't know, sir.'

'Of course you do. For a long time you've considered me some kind of charlatan, or quack, or worse. That's been clear enough, and I allowed you to go on thinking so, as long as you did what I told you, because in your case that sort of attitude can be therapeutic itself. But when you begin to disregard my advice, then that attitude is very dangerous, as I trust you see now.'

'Yes, sir.'

'Do you understand that if you'd kept up with your treatment you wouldn't be here right now? If you'd studied your *World Almanac* every day, and thought of nothing but your grammar students, and practiced Sinistrality, Antecedence, and Alphabetical Priority – particularly if you thought them absurd but practiced them anyway – nothing that happened would have been a problem for you.'

'Frankly, Doctor, I've been more concerned about the Morgans lately than about myself.'

'And you see what's happened! I didn't tell you to make friends! You should have been thinking of nothing but your immobility.'

It was time to tell him why I had come out to see him, but he went on talking.

'Now clearly this paralysis you just had is a different sort from what you had before. In Penn Station it was inability to choose that immobilized you. That's the case I'm interested in, and that's the case I've been treating. But this was a simple matter of running yourself into a blind alley – a vulgar, stupid condition, not even a dilemma, and yet it undoes all I'd accomplished.'

'Doctor, excuse me – that girl's going to shoot herself!'

'It would serve you right if the husband shot you. Mythotherapy – Mythotherapy would have kept you out of any involvement, if you'd practiced it assiduously the whole time. Actually you did practice it, but like a ninny you gave yourself the wrong part. Even the villain's role would have been all right, if you'd been an out-and-out villain with no regrets! But you've made yourself a penitent when it's too late to repent, and that's the best role I can think of to immobilize you. Well!' he exclaimed, really disturbed. 'Your case was the most interesting I've treated for years, and you've all but ruined it!'

For a full two minutes he chewed his cigar in angry silence. I was terribly conscious of time slipping by.

'Can't you –'

'Be quiet!' he said impatiently. After a while he said, 'The girl's suicide will be entirely anti-therapeutic. Even disastrous. For one thing, the husband might shoot you, or you might even shoot yourself, you've relapsed so badly. These two eventualities I could prevent by keeping you here on the farm, but he might get the police to hunt for you when he finds out you're gone, and I don't want them out here. You've completely botched things! You've spoiled two years of my work with this silly affair.'

'Can't you give her a shot of Ergotrate, Doctor?' I asked quickly.

The Doctor removed the cigar from his mouth for a moment in order to look at me the more caustically. 'My dear fellow, for what earthly reason would I have Ergotrate here? Do you think these ladies and gentlemen conceive children?'

I blushed. 'Well – could you write a prescription?'

'Don't be any more naïve than you have to. You could just as well write one yourself.'

'God. I don't know what to do.'

'Horner, stop being innocent. You came out here to ask me to abort the fetus, not to talk about your immobility.'

'Will you do it?' I begged him. 'I'll pay anything you want to charge.'

'An empty statement. Suppose I wanted to charge seven thousand dollars? What you mean is that you'll pay up to maybe five hundred dollars. And since you'd renege on payments after the thing was done, the possible price couldn't be more than one or two hundred. Unless I'm greatly mistaken you haven't more than that on hand.'

'I've got about two seventy-five, Doctor. I'll give it to you gladly.'

'Horner, I'm not an abortionist. I've aborted perhaps ten fetuses in my career, and that was years ago. If I performed an abortion now I'd jeopardize this whole establishment, the future welfare of my patients, and my own freedom. Is two hundred and seventy-five dollars enough for that? Or five thousand, for that matter?'

'I can't offer you anything else.'

'Yes, you can, and if you do I'll abort the girl's fetus.'

'I'll agree to anything.'

'Certainly. But whether you keep your agreement is another matter. I'm preparing to relocate the farm – no doubt you noticed the things in the entrance hall and the reception room. For a change, we're moving because we want to and not because we have to; I've found a better location, in Pennsylvania, and we're leaving Wednesday. Mrs Dockey would have contacted you tomorrow if you hadn't come out here today. Now, then, if it weren't for this, the abortion would be out of the question; since we're moving anyway, I'll perform it tonight.'

The shock brought tears to my eyes, and I laughed sharply.

'What I'd like to do is simply give you a catheter for the girl. If she walked around with that in her for a day or two it would induce labor and abort the fetus. She'd hemorrhage a lot, but the hospital would have to accept her as an emergency case. This would be better because she wouldn't have to come out here at all, but it takes too long; she might not even start labor until Wednesday, and she'd be so miserable with the catheter in her uterus that she'd probably kill herself anyway. Bring her out here tonight, and I'll scrape the uterus and get it over with.'

'I will! Lord, that's wonderful!'

'It's not. It's sordid and disgusting, but I'll do it as a last resort to save your case. What you have to do in return is not only give me all the money you've got to help move the farm to Pennsylvania, but quit your job and come with us. I require this for two reasons: first, and most important, I want you on hand twenty-four hours a day so I can establish you on your schedule of therapies again; second, I'll need a young man to do a great deal of manual labor while the new farm is being set up. That will be your first therapy. Perhaps my fee is too high?'

I remembered the old men in the dormitory.

'Don't dawdle, Horner,' the Doctor said sternly, 'or I'll refuse. Your case is a hobby with me, but it's not an obsession, and you annoy me as often as you entertain me.'

'I'll do it,' I said.

'Very well. Tonight I'll do the abortion. You'll have to bring a check for the money, since it's Sunday. Tomorrow you let the college know you're quitting, and Wednesday morning be at the Greyhound terminal in Wicomico at eight-thirty. You'll meet Mrs Dockey and some of the patients there and go up with them on the bus.'

'All right.'

'Do you want me to explain all the things I can do to make sure you keep your promise, or at least make you awfully sorry you broke it?'

'You don't have to, Doctor,' I said. 'I'm exhausted. I'll keep it.'

'I'm sure you will,' he smiled, 'whether you are or not. All right, that's all.' He stood up. 'The patients go to bed at nine. Bring the girl out at nine-thirty. Don't shine your headlights on the house, and don't make noise; you'll alarm everybody upstairs. And bring your check and your bankbook, so I'll know the check's as large as possible. Good-by.'

As I went out, I found Mrs Dockey still stolidly tying up boxes in the entrance hall.

'The Doctor told me about moving,' I said to her. 'It looks like I'll be going along with you, for a while, anyhow.'

'Okay,' she growled, without looking at me. 'Be there at eight-thirty sharp. Bus leaves at eight-forty.'

'I will,' I said, and half ran to the car. It was then close to five o'clock.

Chapter Twelve
I stood in the Morgans' living room with my coat still on, for it was not suggested that I stay

I stood in the Morgans' living room with my coat still on, for it was not suggested that I stay for dinner or anything else. Both Joe and Rennie were in the kitchen, leisurely preparing supper for the boys. They seemed in good humor, and had apparently been joking about something.

'Where have you been this time?' Rennie asked.

'Everything's settled,' I said.

'All you have to do is catch the next plane to Vatican City,' Joe told her, mocking the weariness and relief of my voice, 'and tell the man you're the Pope's concubine.'

'I said once and for all I won't lie,' Rennie laughed.

'I'll pick you up at nine o'clock,' I said. 'The appointment's for nine-thirty. It won't be Ergotrate.'

Rennie's smile faded; she paled a little.

'Have you really found somebody?'

'Yes. He's a retired specialist who runs a convalescent home out near Vineland.'

'What's his name?' Joe asked unsmilingly.

'He wants to stay anonymous. That's understandable enough. But he's a good doctor. I've known him for several years, before I came here. In fact, I took this teaching job at his suggestion.'

They showed some surprise.

'I've never heard of a convalescent home out that way,' Rennie said doubtfully.

'That's because he keeps the place private, for his patients' benefit, and because he's a Negro doctor with an all-white clientele. Not many people know about him.'

'Is he safe?' Joe asked, a little suspiciously. They were both standing in the kitchen doorway by this time.

'That doesn't matter,' Rennie said quickly, and went back to the stove.

'Will you be ready at nine?' I asked her.

'I'll be ready.'

'You'll want to come too, won't you?' I asked Joe.

'I don't know,' he said dully. 'I'll decide later.'

It was as though I'd spoiled something.

Back in my room, the pressure off, I experienced a reaction not only against the excitement of the days just past but against my whole commitment. It was not difficult to feel relieved at having finally prevented Rennie's suicide, but it was extremely difficult to feel chastened, as I wanted to feel chastened. I wanted the adventure to teach me this about myself: that regardless of what shifting opinions I held about ethical matters in the abstract, I was not so consistently the same person (not so sufficiently 'real', to use Rennie's term) that I could involve myself seriously in the lives of others without doing damage all around, not least to my own tranquillity; that my irrational flashes of conscience and cruelty, of compassion and cynicism – in short, my inability to play the same role long enough – could give me as well as others pain, and that the same inconsistency rendered it improbable that I could remain peacefully in painful positions for very long, as Joe, for example, could remain. I didn't consistently need or want friends, but it was clear (this too I wanted to learn) that, given my own special kind of integrity, if I was to have them at all I must remain uninvolved – I must leave them alone.

A simple lesson, but I couldn't properly be chastened. My feelings were mixed: relief, ridiculousness, embarrassment, anger, injured pride, maudlin affection for the Morgans, disgust with them and myself, and a host of other things, including indifference to the whole business.

Also, I was not a little tired of myself, and of my knowledge of my selves, and of my personal little mystery. Although I had, in fact, no intention of keeping my pledge to go to Pennsylvania with the Doctor, I composed a brief note to Dr Schott, informing him of my resignation: my play for responsibility had indeed exhausted me, and I was ready to leave Wicomico and the Morgans. In a new town, with new friends, even under a new name – perhaps one could *pretend* enough unity to be a person and live in the world; perhaps, if one were a sufficiently practiced actor . . . Maybe I would marry Peggy Rankin; take her surname; father a child on her. I smiled.

At a few minutes before nine o'clock I went to get Rennie, and found her and Joe just finishing a late dinner by candle-light.

'Big occasion,' Joe said dryly. He flicked on the light at once and blew out the candles, and I saw that they'd been eating hot dogs and sauerkraut. Allowing Rennie to put her coat on by herself he started carrying dishes to the sink.

'How long does this take?' he asked me.

'I don't know, Joe,' I said, acutely uncomfortable. 'I shouldn't think it would take very long.'

'I'm ready,' Rennie said. She looked bad: white and shaky. Joe kissed her lightly and turned the sink faucet on to wash the dishes.

'You're not coming?' I asked him.

'No.'

'Well –' I said. Rennie was already headed for the door. 'See you after a while.'

We went outside. Rennie bounded gracelessly ahead of me down the sidewalk, and opened the car door before I could do it for her. She sniffed a little, but held back the tears. I drove out the highway toward Vineland.

'This really turned into a mess, didn't it?' I said sympathetically. She stared out the window without answering. 'I'm terribly sorry that any of it happened.'

She gave no clue to her feelings. The thing that I was sharply conscious of was her loneliness in what had happened and what was about to happen – the fundamental, last-analysis loneliness of all human beings in critical situations. It is never entirely true, but it's more apparent at some times than at others, and just then I was very much aware of her as apart from Joe, myself, values, motives, the world, or history – a solitary animal in a tight spot. And Joe, home, washing the dishes. Lonely animals! Into no cause, resolve, or philosophy can we cram so much of ourselves that there is no part of us left over to wonder and be lonely.

'This fellow's really a fine doctor,' I said a minute later.

Rennie looked at me uncomprehendingly, as if I'd spoken in a foreign language.

'Rennie, do you want me to take you home?'

'If you do I'll shoot myself,' she said hoarsely.

When we came to the end of the driveway leading to the farmhouse, I cut out the headlights and drove quietly into the yard. I explained to Rennie that the Doctor didn't want me to disturb his patients, but I'm afraid the theatricality of it did her nerves no good. As I ushered her into the farmhouse I felt her trembling. Mrs Dockey and the Doctor were waiting for us in the reception room. They both scrutinized Rennie frankly, and some contempt was evident in Mrs Dockey's expression.

'How do you do, Mrs Morgan,' the Doctor said. 'We can begin right away. Mrs Dockey will take you to the Treatment Room.

Wordlessly Mrs Dockey walked toward the Treatment Room, and Rennie, after a second's uncertainty, jumped to follow that formidable woman. My eyes watered. I didn't know how to go about distinguishing compassion from love: perhaps it was only compassion I felt for her.

'Did you bring the check and the bankbook?' demanded the Doctor.

'Yes.' I handed them to him. On the next-to-last check stub the balance read two hundred eighty-seven dollars and thirty-two cents, and the next check was made out to that amount and signed. 'I didn't know who to pay it to.'

'I'll write that in. Very well, come along. I want you to watch this, for your own good.'

'No, I'll wait out here.'

'If you want the abortion done,' the Doctor said, 'then come along and watch it.'

I went, most unwillingly. The Doctor donned his white jacket, and we went into the Treatment Room. Rennie was already on the examination table with a sheet up to her neck. I was afraid she'd object to my presence, but she gave no sign of approval or disapproval. Mrs Dockey stood by impassively. The Doctor washed his hands and drew up the sheet from Rennie's abdomen.

'Well, let's see if you're pregnant, first.'

When his fingers touched her to begin the examination, she jumped involuntarily. A minute or so later, when the Doctor slipped his hands into rubber gloves, greased the fingers, and began the internal examination, she started sobbing.

'Now stop that,' the Doctor said irritably. 'You've had children before.' After a while he asked, 'How old do you think the fetus is?' Rennie made no answer, and he didn't ask her anything else.

'All right, we may as well get to work. Hand me a dilator and a curette, please,' he said to Mrs Dockey, and she went to the sterilizer nearby to get them. The surgical instruments clinked in the sterilizer, and Rennie's sobbing became looser and louder. She twisted a little on the examination table and even began to raise herself.

'Lie down and be quiet!' the Doctor ordered sharply. 'You'll wake everybody up.'

Rennie lay back again and closed her eyes. I began to be sick as soon as the Doctor accepted the bright curette from Mrs Dockey; I resolved to keep my eyes on Rennie's face instead of the operation.

'Fasten the straps,' the Doctor said to Mrs Dockey. 'You should have done that before.' A wide leather strap was secured across Rennie's diaphragm. 'Now, then, hold her right leg, and Horner, you hold the other one. Since we don't go in much for obstetrics here I didn't bother to buy a table with stirrups on it.'

Rennie's legs were drawn up and spread wide in the lithotomy position. Mrs Dockey gripped one, pressing the calf against the thigh, and I, very reluctantly, held the other.

'I'm sorry, Rennie,' I said.

Rennie whipped her head and moaned. A few moments later – I would guess that the Doctor had applied his curette, but I wasn't looking to find out – she began screaming, and tried to kick free.

'Hold those legs!' the Doctor snapped. 'She's cutting herself to pieces! Shut her up, Horner!'

'Rennie – ' But I couldn't say anything else. She was terrified; I think she no longer recognized me. Her face swam through my tears. For an instant she relaxed, fighting

for control, but almost at once – another scrape of the curette?
– she screamed again, and struggled to raise herself.

'Okay,' the Doctor said disgustedly to Mrs Dockey. 'The
curette's out. Let go of her leg and shut her up.'

Mrs Dockey pushed Rennie's head down and clamped a
hand over her mouth. Rennie kicked wildly with her free leg;
the Doctor jumped clear, upsetting his stool, and cursed. I
inadvertently glanced away and saw blood on the sheet under
Rennie's abdomen, blood on her upper thighs, blood on the
Doctor's gloves. The vomitus rushed to my mouth, and I was
barely able to swallow it down.

'She's already hemorrhaging,' the Doctor said to Mrs
Dockey. 'Keep her quiet for a minute, and I'll get an
anesthetic.'

I began to catch Rennie's fear. She lay quiet again for a
moment, and her eyes pleaded with me.

'Take your hand off,' I told Mrs Dockey. 'She won't
holler.' Mrs Dockey removed her hand warily, ready to clap
it back at once.

'Jake, I'm scared,' Rennie cried softly, trembling all over.
'He's hurting me. I don't like being scared, but I can't help
it.'

'Are you sure it's too late to quit, Doctor?' I called across
the room, where he was fitting a rubber hose to two tanks of
gas on a dolly.

'No use to now,' he said. 'I'd be finished by this time if
she'd cut out her foolishness.'

'Do you want to go home, Rennie?'

'Yes,' she wept. 'But let him finish. I want to hold still, but
I can't.'

'We'll take care of that,' the Doctor said, no longer annoyed. He wheeled the gas tanks over to the head of the table.
'The way you were jumping around I could very well have
punctured your uterus. Relax, now.'

Rennie closed her eyes. The Doctor handed the mask to
Mrs Dockey, who with some relish held it down over Rennie's
nose and mouth. The Doctor immediately opened valves,
and the gases made a soft rush into the mask.

'Breathe deeply,' the Doctor said, watching the pressure
gauges.

Rennie inhaled deeply two, three, five times, as though anxious to lose consciousness. Her trembling subsided, and her legs began to go limp.

'Check the pulse,' the Doctor told Mrs Dockey.

But as she reached for Rennie's wrist with her free hand, Rennie's stomach jerked inwards, and she vomited explosively into the mask. A second later a horrible sucking sound came from her throat, and another. Her eyes half opened briefly.

'Bronchoscope!' the Doctor said sharply, jerking the mask away. Rennie's face was blue: the sucking noise stopped. 'Take the strap off, Horner! Quick!'

I tore at the strap with my fingers; couldn't see it clearly for the water in my eyes. Another gurgling explosion came from Rennie's chest.

'*Bronchoscope!*' the Doctor shouted.

Mrs Dockey ran back to the table with a long tubelike instrument, which the Doctor snatched from her hands and began to insert into Rennie's mouth. The vomitus was all over her face, and a small puddle of it lay under her head, in her hair. Her face darkened further; her eyes opened, and the pupils rolled senselessly. My head reeled.

'Get oxygen ready!' ordered the Doctor. 'Horner, take the pulse!'

I grabbed Rennie's wrist. Maybe I felt one beat – anyway, no more after that.

'I don't feel any!' I cried.

'No,' he said, less excitedly. He withdrew the bronchoscope from her windpipe and laid it aside. 'Never mind the oxygen, Mrs Dockey.' Mrs Dockey came over unhurriedly to look.

And so this is the picture I have to carry with me: the Treatment Room dark except for the one ceiling floodlight that illuminated the table; Rennie dead there now, face mottled, eyes wide, mouth agape; the vomitus running from a pool in her mouth to a pool under her head; the great black belt lying finally unbuckled across the sheet over her chest and stomach; the lower part of her body nude and bloody, her legs trailing limply and clumsily off the end of the examination table.

'So,' the Doctor sighed.

'How'd it happen?' Mrs Dockey asked.

'She must have eaten a big meal before she came out here,' he said. 'She should've known better. Vomited it up from the ether and then aspirated it into her lungs. What a mess this is!'

I was stunned past weeping. Shock set in at once, and I was forced to find a chair before I fell.

'Straighten up, Horner; this won't do.'

I couldn't reply. I was fighting nausea and faintness.

'Go lie down on a couch in the reception room,' he ordered, 'and prop your feet up. It'll pass. We'll clean her up, and then you'll have to take her out of here.'

'Where?' I cried. 'What am I going to do?'

'Why, take her back home. Don't you think her husband wants the body?'

I lurched for the door, but fell flat before reaching it. When I revived I was lying in the reception room, and the Doctor was standing nearby.

'Swallow these,' he said, giving me two pills and a glass of water.

'Now, then, pay attention. This is serious, but it'll be all right if you keep hold of yourself. We took her out to your car. Don't do anything silly like trying to dispose of her secretly. I've called the husband and explained that she'd be awhile coming out of anesthesia. The best thing for you to do is take her right to her house and tell the husband she's dead. Be in a panic. Tell him she seemed all right until you got halfway home, and then she started vomiting and got strangled – the autopsy will pretty much bear that out. He'll call the hospital ambulance, and they'll discover the abortion, but that's okay. You'll be asked questions; that's okay too. Don't tell them where it was done until tomorrow; after that it won't matter. I'm leaving tonight with a few of the patients in the station wagon, and Mrs Dockey will stay here to handle things. The house and phone are in her name, and she'll say she's one of my patients who set up the home. You don't know my name, and she'll give them the wrong one and plead ignorance of the whole business. They can't hold you or her either, and they won't be able to find me. Here, take this.' He gave me an envelope. 'That's your bus fare and enough money to last you until Wednesday. Our plans are the same. Meet Mrs Dockey and the other patients Wednesday morning at the Greyhound station, and she'll tell you then if there has to be any change in our plans. Do you feel able to drive now?'

I couldn't answer: all my grief had returned in a rush with consciousness.

'You look all right,' he said curtly. 'This thing was everybody's fault, Horner. Let it be everybody's lesson. Go on, now; get it over with.'

The pills must have worked: when I stood up this time I didn't feel faint. I went out to the car and got in. Rennie was lying curled on the back seat, dressed, washed, her eyes closed. It was too big a thing to know what to think about it, to know how to feel. I drove mechanically back to the Morgans' house.

It was about eleven when I got there. The grounds and most of the house were dark, and there was no traffic on the highway. I rang the doorbell, and when Joe answered I said, 'She's dead, Joe.'

He winced and shoved his glasses back on his nose. Tears sprang into his eyes and ran at once down both cheeks.

'Where is she?'

'Out in the car. She vomited from the ether and strangled to death on it.'

He walked past me out to the car. With difficulty he took her out of the back seat and carried her into the house, where he laid her gently on the daybed. Tears poured down his face, but he neither sobbed nor made any kind of noise. I stood by helplessly.

'What's the name of that doctor?'

'I don't know, Joe. I swear to Christ I'm not protecting him. I've been going to him, but he never told me his name. I'll explain it to you when you want to hear it.'

'Where does he operate?'

'Out past Vineland. I'll tell the police – '

'You get out fast.'

'All right,' I said, and left at once.

I sat up through the rest of the night waiting to hear from either Joe or the police, but no one called. I wanted terribly to call the police, to call the hospital, to call Joe – but there was no reason to call anyone. What Joe was doing I had no idea; for all I knew he might have done nothing yet – might still be regarding her on the daybed, making up his mind. But I decided to let him take whatever action he wanted to – even killing me – without my interference, since he hadn't wanted my help. Unless he requested differently, I intended to answer everybody's questions truthfully, and I hoped the Doctor had been mistaken: I hoped with all my heart that there was some way in which I could be held legally responsible. I craved responsibility.

But no one called. I was presented in the morning with the problem of deciding whether to go to school or not, and I decided to go. I couldn't telephone Joe; perhaps someone at school would have heard some news.

When I reached the college I went directly to Dr Schott's office on the pretext of looking for mail. Dr Schott was in the outer office, along with Shirley and Dr Carter, and it was apparent from their expressions that they'd heard of Rennie's death.

'Good morning,' I said, uncertain how I'd be received.

'Good morning, Mr Horner,' Dr Schott said distractedly. 'We've just heard a terrible thing! Joe Morgan's wife died very suddenly last night!'

'What?' I said, automatically feigning surprise and shock. So, it seemed that they didn't suspect my part in her death: my feigned surprise was proper until I found out what was on Joe's mind.

'Terrible thing!' Dr Schott repeated. 'A young girl like that, and two little children!'

'How did it happen, sir?'

He blushed. 'I'm not in a position to say, Mr Horner. Joe naturally wasn't too coherent on the phone just now . . . A shock, you know – terrible shock to him! I believe she died under anesthesia last night in the hospital. Some kind of emergency operation she was having.'

'That's awful, isn't it?' I said, shaking my head.

'Terrible thing!'

'Shall I call the hospital?' Shirley asked him. 'Maybe they'd have some information.'

'No, no,' Dr Schott said at once. 'We musn't pry. I'll telephone Joe later and ask if there's anything I can do. I can't believe it! Mrs Morgan was such a fine, healthy young thing!'

It was evident to me that he knew more than he was telling, but whatever Joe told him must not have involved me. Dr Carter noticed my eyes watering and clapped me on the shoulder. It was known that I was some kind of friend of the Morgans.

'You never know,' he sighed. 'The good die young, and maybe it's best.'

'What'll he do about the children?' I asked.

'Lord knows! It's tragic!' It was not certain what exactly he referred to.

'Well, let's don't say any more about it than we have to,' Dr Carter advised, 'until we hear more details. It's a terrible shock to all of us.'

I guessed that Dr Schott had confided to him whatever information he had.

So on Monday and Tuesday I taught my classes as usual, though in a great emptiness of anxiety. Tuesday afternoon Rennie was buried, but because the college could not declare a holiday on that account Dr Schott was the only representative of the faculty at the funeral. A collection was taken by Miss Banning for a wreath from all of us: I gave a dollar from what little money the Doctor had given me. At the moment when Rennie was lowered into the earth, I believe I was explaining semicolons to my students.

It was given out at the college that Mrs Morgan had not died from anesthesia after all, but had strangled when a morsel of food lodged in her throat, and had succumbed en route to the hospital. This is what appeared in Tuesday's newspaper as well – Dr Schott must have been a power in the community. Moreover, it was rumored that Mr Morgan had submitted his resignation; everyone agreed that the shock of his wife's death was responsible – that Joe very understandably wanted a change of scenery for a while. The boys were being cared for by Mr and Mrs MacMahon, Rennie's parents.

But later Tuesday afternoon I heard the truth of the matter from Dr Carter, who accosted me as I was leaving school for the last time.

'I know you were a friend of Morgan's,' he said confidentially, steering me away from a group of students nearby, 'so you might as well know the truth about this business. I'm sure it'll go no further.'

'Of course not,' I assured him. 'What is it?'

'Dr Schott and I were terribly shocked, Horner,' he said. 'It seems that Mrs Morgan really died from the effects of an illegal abortion someplace out in the country near here.'

'No!'

'I'm afraid so. When he took her to the hospital they found out she'd strangled under anesthesia, and there were obvious signs of the abortion.'

'That's a terrible shame!'

'Isn't it? Dr Schott managed to keep everybody quiet, and the police are investigating secretly, but so far they haven't had any luck. Morgan claims he doesn't know who the doctor was that did it or where the thing was done. Says his wife arranged it on her own and he wasn't there when it happened. I don't know whether he's lying or not; there's no way to tell.'

'Good Lord! Can they punish him for anything?'

'Not a thing. But here's the unfortunate part: even though Schott's kept everything hushed up, he decided he can't in good conscience keep Morgan on the staff. It's a bad thing in itself, and it would be worse if the students got wind of it. You know, a small college in a little town like Wicomico. It could lead to a great deal of unpleasantness. Frankly, he asked for Morgan's resignation.'

'Oh, the poor bastard!'

'Yes, it's a pity. You won't say anything, will you?'

I shook my head. 'I won't tell a soul.'

I was going to be denied, then, the chance to take public responsibility. Rennie was buried. I was still employed, my reputation was untouched, and Joe was out of a job.

Lord, the raggedness of it; the incompleteness! I paced my room; sucked in my breath; groaned aloud. I could imagine confessing publicly – but would this not be a further, final injury to Joe, who clearly wanted to deprive me of my responsibility, or at any rate wanted to hold his grief free from any further dealing with me? I could imagine carrying the ragged burden secretly, either in or out of Wicomico, married to Peggy Rankin or not, under my real name or another – but was this not cheating my society of its due, or covertly avoiding public embarrassment? For that matter, I couldn't decide whether marrying Peggy would be merciful or cruel; whether setting police on the Doctor would be right or wrong. I could not even decide what I should *feel*: all I found in me was anguish, abstract and without focus.

I was frantic. Half a dozen letters I started – to Joe, to the police, to Peggy, to Joe again – and could finish none. It was no use: I could not remain sufficiently simple-minded long enough to lay blame – on the Doctor, myself, or anyone – or to decide what was the right course of action. I threw the notes away and sat still and anguished in my rocking chair. The terrific incompleteness made me volatile; my muscles screamed to act; but my limbs were bound like Laocoön's – by the serpents Knowledge and Imagination, which, grown great in the fullness of time, no longer tempt but annihilate.

Presently I undressed and lay on the bed in the dark, though sleep was unthinkable, and commenced a silent colloquy with my friend.

'We've come too far,' I said to Laocoön. 'Who can live any longer in the world?'

There was no reply.

Sometime during the night the telephone rang. I was naked, and since the window curtains were open I answered the phone in the dark. Joe's voice came strong, clear, quiet, and close over the wire.

'Jake?'

'Yes, Joe.' I tingled in every nerve, thinking, among other things, of the big pistol in his closet.

'Are you up to date on everything?'

'Yes. I think so.'

There was a pause.

'Well. What are your plans? Anything special?'

'I don't know, Joe. I guess not. I was going to follow your lead, whatever it turned out to be.'

Another pause.

'I might leave town too,' I said.

'Oh yes? Why?'

No alteration in his voice, no hint of his attitude at all.

'I don't know. How about you, Joe? What'll you do now?'

He ignored the question.

'Well, what's on your mind, Jake? What do you think about things?'

I hesitated, entirely nonplused. 'God, Joe – I don't know where to start or what to do!'

'What?'

His voice remained clear, bright, and close in my ear. Tears ran in a cold flood down my face and neck, onto my chest, and I shook all over with violent chills.

'*I said I don't know what to do.*'

'Oh.'

Another pause, a long one; then he hung up and I was left with a dead instrument in the dark.

Next morning I shaved, dressed, packed my bags, and called a taxi. While I waited for it to come, I rocked in my chair and smoked a cigarette. I was without weather. A few minutes later the cabby blew his horn for me; I picked up my two suitcases and went out, leaving the bust of Laocoön where it stood on the mantelpiece. My car, too, since I saw no further use for it, I left where it was, at the curb, and climbed into the taxi.

'Terminal.'